G000126111

Duke of Thorns

AN HEIRESS GAMES NOVEL

Sara Ramsey

Duke of Thorns is a work of fiction. Names, characters, places and incidences are the products of the author's imagination or are used fictitiously. Any resemblance to actual events, locales, or persons, living or dead, is entirely coincidental. The Publisher does not have any control over and does not assume responsibility for author or third-party websites or their content.

Copyright © 2014 Sara Wampler
All Rights Reserved.
Cover Design by Patricia Schmitt (Pickyme)
Cover Photography by Jenn LeBlanc

ISBN (epub): 978-1-938312-08-3
ISBN (paperback): 978-1-938312-09-0

For Katie, my favorite grasshopper

Disturb us, Lord, when we are too well pleased with ourselves,
When our dreams have come true
Because we have dreamed too little,
When we arrived safely
Because we sailed too close to the shore.

Disturb us, Lord, when
With the abundance of things we possess
We have lost our thirst
For the waters of life;
Having fallen in love with life,
We have ceased to dream of eternity
And in our efforts to build a new earth,
We have allowed our vision
Of the new Heaven to dim.

Disturb us, Lord, to dare more boldly,
To venture on wider seas
Where storms will show your mastery;
Where losing sight of land,
We shall find the stars.

- Sir Francis Drake, 1577

PROLOGUE

She was going to die.

And when Callista Briarley found her watery grave, as her father had six years earlier, she would deserve it.

The rasp of blade against bone drew her attention as soon as she entered the officers' dining room, new and horrifying enough to bring it to the fore over the firing of twenty-four pounders and hoarse, shouted orders from the deck above. Callie swallowed.

Briarleys always died pursuing something stupid. Callie should have known this voyage would kill her.

Captain Jacobs had assured her it would be an easy victory, a matter of minutes. The merchant ship they were trying to capture was outmanned and outgunned. But he hadn't anticipated the appearance of a British warship. That's when he had ordered her below, sending his cognac with her — as though she was cargo, and not the ship's owner.

It was her fault the injured man was here. It was her fault they were all here. If she survived the battle, she would have to fix it.

She waited until the surgeon had finished, not wanting to distract him with her presence. Callie's maid, Mrs. Jennings, and two

1

cabin boys held the injured sailor down in case he awoke before the butchering ended. She swallowed again as the saw slid through the last bit of flesh. The surgeon grunted as he caught the arm, then handed it to the cook's mate, casually, like it was a shank of lamb instead of a man's limb.

She took a breath and joined her maid at the head of the table. "How can I help?" she asked.

"You shouldn't see this, miss," Mrs. Jennings said.

"No one should. But since I am here, I may as well do something."

The surgeon ran a knife through the flame of the lamp, heating it until it was red hot. She forced herself to watch as he pressed it against the stump of the man's arm. She didn't bring a handkerchief to her nose as the smell of burning flesh overwhelmed her. The sailor stayed blessedly unconscious, but Callie watched it all, bearing witness.

She had agreed to let her men become privateers. Captain Jacobs' persuasive nature, so like her father's, had convinced her.

But this...

The sizzling stopped. The cannon fire continued.

The surgeon ordered one of the cabin boys to swab and sand the floor in preparation for more patients. The cook's mate and the other cabin boy carried the sailor off to a berth. Callie waited until they were gone, then started to pace again.

"Don't even think of going above, Callista Briarley," Mrs. Jennings warned.

Her lady's maid, who had been her nursemaid as a child, knew her too well. "I want to do something," Callie said.

"You have to learn someday that you cannot fix everything," Mrs. Jennings said. "This is something you cannot fix."

Callie stared at her for a moment. Mrs. Jennings somehow looked serene, even with blood splattered over the apron she'd quite sensibly donned before assisting the surgeon. Her hair had greyed a bit since she'd left England with the Briarleys nearly twenty years earlier, and she'd added at least two stone of weight to her short, formerly slender frame. But she was just as imperturbable as always.

Callie, by contrast, was perturbed. *Very* perturbed. And she was sure she looked wild enough to give her emotions away.

"I will fix it," Callie said. "I will fix all of it."

"You can't very well fix that poor man's arm," Mrs. Jennings said gently. "Nor can you decide whether we drown. You'd do much better for yourself if you had a bit of whisky and waited for this to be over."

Sometimes Callie hated how well Mrs. Jennings knew her.

"Captain Jacobs gave me cognac," she said, trying to lighten the mood. "I don't think I have the stomach for cognac and whisky both."

"I'm sure you would if you tried. You can stomach more than a lady should."

"Are you encouraging my hoydenish ways now?" Callie asked. "If I'd known a sea battle was all it took, I would have done this years ago."

"Hoydens are more useful in sea battles than ladies are," Mrs. Jennings said frankly. "Drink your cognac, and we can discuss your manners in the morning."

Callie smiled. But she didn't take her maid's advice. She paced instead, waiting.

It felt like an eternity, but it must have been only another five or ten minutes before she heard a most welcome sound. The shouting above turned, in an instant, from battle cries to celebration. And Callie realized the guns had stopped.

She rushed out of the cabin and scrambled up the ladder-like stairs before Mrs. Jennings could remind her to behave herself. The deck teemed with men — most of whom appeared to be whole — and was partially shrouded with fallen sails. She looked instinctively to the mast. Her colors still flew.

She whooped — a scream of vicious, victorious joy that a woman wasn't supposed to feel, let alone give voice to. If she were gentler, more ladylike, she would have immediately thought of the loss of life and limb, of the brutality of men and their warlike ways. She probably should have fainted, or at least pretended to.

But despite all her misgivings, she still liked to win. And the fact that her men had won — and against the British in the bargain — gave her swift, sharp delight. If she'd remembered her hat, she would have tossed it in the air.

Captain Jacobs was too observant to miss the moment when her voice joined the din. "Ahoy, Miss Briarley," he shouted from his post near the wheel. "I give you His Majesty's *Adamant*."

He gestured grandly toward the ship next to them. It had suffered more than her own *Nero*, which was a rather stunning fact. *Nero* was a sloop, designed more for speed than direct assault, and had been refitted for battle only a few months earlier. *Adamant* had been purpose-built for combat, but had somehow been outgunned despite its superior strength.

Some of her men had boarded *Adamant* and were herding the British sailors below decks. She watched the proceedings for a few moments, her pleasure slowly cooling. By taking a British frigate in his first engagement of the cruise, Captain Jacobs would be more convinced than ever that privateering was their destiny.

She picked her way over the ropes and rigging to join him near the wheel. "You must be pleased with yourself, Captain Jacobs," she said as soon as she could talk without shouting.

The captain laughed. "Cognac settled your nerves, did it? Always knew you'd come around. I told you this would be over within minutes. *Nero* can prevail against all but the worst enemies."

Even though he had just won a great victory, Callie privately doubted that *Nero* was as good as he boasted. *Nero* had started as a merchantman, part of the fleet her father, Lord Tiberius Briarley, had won at a card table in Jamaica in '05. The man he'd won it from had shot himself as soon as he'd sobered up and realized what he'd lost. Lord Tiberius had relocated with alacrity to Baltimore, taking Callie but leaving her mother's grave behind.

She'd never quite forgiven him for that. Not that it mattered. Tiberius did what Tiberius wished to do.

And when he had wished to seek out a new fortune in the Orient in '07, Callie had stayed in Baltimore. She'd left enough homes behind. At seventeen, she was more interested in refurnishing the Baltimore house than she was in smuggling opium.

At eighteen, when she got word that he'd gone down with his ship, her desire for a home only grew.

But homes required money. And the only money she had was tied up in Tiberius Shipping. In the last five years, Callie had grown it into a thriving business, with Captain Jacobs ostensibly at its head. His wife had chaperoned her, rather ineffectually, and they had both let her have her way with the enterprise. Between Callie's business sense and the captain's knowledge of the ships under their command, Tiberius Shipping had become a significant part of Baltimore's maritime economy.

The war, though, had changed everything. And with the embargoes against American commerce in Europe and the British blockade descending around Baltimore, there was more money to be made from privateering than from commerce.

Provided, of course, that one didn't think too closely about the danger of such endeavors.

She wished Jacobs had confined himself to their agreement, looking only for easy targets. "It's a shame you had to shift your efforts to the frigate instead of taking the merchant prize," Callie said.

Captain Jacobs grinned. He was in his early forties and had spent nearly his whole life at sea, adding deep grooves to the corners of his eyes and a dark tan that Callie might match if she kept forgetting her hat. But for all the discipline and difficulty of life on the water, the captain still had a sense of humor.

"I didn't say I failed to take it," Jacobs said. "I merely forgot to present it to you."

He gestured starboard. At a distance of nearly half a league, the merchantman should have been able to escape them while they dealt with *Adamant*. But she had been completely unmasted and now floated, helpless, waiting for capture.

Callie held out her hand for Jacobs' eyeglass. She brought the ship into focus and saw men standing, rather glumly, along the rails, watching *Nero* for their next maneuver.

"How did you take them both?" she asked.

"That ship, *Crescendo*, must have the worst luck. She could have escaped when *Adamant* arrived — we'd only exchanged two or three volleys, suffering no injuries ourselves, but we had to turn all our efforts to *Adamant*. But *Adamant*, in one of the worst displays of gunnery I've ever had the privilege to witness, overshot us completely with their first round and took *Crescendo*'s mast clean off. If the captain isn't court-martialed for it, the British have gone soft."

"And where is the captain of *Adamant*?" Callie asked.

"Surrendering his sword to my first mate, if he knows what's good for him," Jacobs said. "My first mate will take *Adamant* to Havana for the prize court to distribute, if it's not too damaged to sail. And we'll continue there as well, either towing *Crescendo* or sinking it if we need to set a faster pace. Once we're all safely arrived there, you can buy passage on to England as you planned."

They were still a week out from Havana, with any number of hostile British ships between them and their destination. Callie looked across to *Adamant* again, using Jacobs' eyeglass this time. As he'd said, the

British captain was surrendering his sword, looking deeply chagrined. He had a smudge of soot across his cheek that looked utterly out of place with his crisp blue coat and sharp, patrician features. Whatever he was saying to the first mate looked like it was meant to be a threat, but the first mate just laughed it off and tucked the sword under his arm before gesturing the captain toward the hold.

Adamant's captain looked over at *Nero*. Callie dropped the eyeglass. Seeing the man's face in such close relief didn't bring her pleasure. But at thirty yards, the set of his shoulders made his anger obvious. He shaded his eyes to look at Captain Jacobs, as though memorizing whatever he could of the man who had beat him. Then his gaze swept over her, contemptuous. He'd already dismissed her.

She handed the eyeglass back to Captain Jacobs. "You've made yourself an enemy there," she said as the British captain went down into the hold of the ship he'd lost. "I'm sure he expected to be given his sword back after the surrender ritual."

"Cowards don't deserve their swords," Jacobs said. There was no humor in his voice as he said it. "He disabled *Crescendo* and struck his own colors well before they were at the point of going under. He won't be on the seas enough to trouble me if that's the best he can offer."

"I'm beginning to reconsider our arrangement," she said. "I didn't expect you to court such dangers."

Jacobs laughed. "If you want to tell the crew they're to stop earning prizes when they've just succeeded, you'll need more than me at your back. And I won't be there — I'll be leading the mutiny against you."

He still sounded jovial. Nothing would prick his mood that day. But there was steel in his voice.

And she couldn't do anything about it. Not when the men would listen to their captain instead of their owner.

He continued as though he hadn't threatened her. "You should go below again, Miss Briarley. You'll grow cold up here once the excitement wears away. No need for your talents until we assess the value of *Crescendo*'s cargo, and that will have to wait until we set ourselves to rights. We'll find you a pretty bauble in their hold. You'll feel better about all of this when you see your share of the prize."

She didn't obey immediately. But he didn't expect her to. He just left her standing where she was, rooted to the deck.

The unfairness of it all held her pinned. She nibbled on her thumbnail, a habit she returned to when she forgot her gloves. Capturing merchant ships and recovering the revenues the British blockade had cost her seemed like a decent enough plan. The American government was willing to grant privateering licenses to supplement its inadequate navy, and it felt like half the ship owners in Baltimore had become privateers since the war had begun. Jacobs was happier than she'd ever seen him, putting his old battle skills from the British Navy into better use. He'd never been much for business. He'd been content enough letting her manage the sales and manifests while he sailed his own ship and acted as a figurehead.

But when she'd agreed to his plan to turn her ships into privateers — naïvely, she could now admit — she had thought they would only take commercial vessels. She hadn't expected to go up against the very British Navy that her captain and half her crew had deserted from over the years. Not that she had any pity for the Navy — if they insisted on mistreating their sailors so dramatically, they deserved to lose them.

The Navy wouldn't see it that way, though. If they captured her British-born sailors, they would immediately press them back into service. They needed warm bodies to fight Napoleon, and their brutal discipline would force obedience. They would imprison the Americans, letting them languish in horrid conditions while waiting for a prisoner exchange.

And, she supposed, there was a possibility she could be imprisoned as well. Even more unlikely, since no one in the Navy would believe a woman capable of running a privateering enterprise. And she was technically British, not American. But that wouldn't make it easier for her to sleep at night.

Callie sighed. She went below, reluctantly. It felt cruelly unfair to leave the victory to the men while she hid in the shadows, pursuing a more clandestine strategy. But she would follow through with her plan.

When she reached her cabin, Mrs. Jennings was there. "Did you fix everything?" her maid asked.

"You are not setting a good example for my tongue," Callie said. "Don't you always say sarcasm is unbecoming?"

Mrs. Jennings smiled. "You may pretend it wasn't sarcasm if you'd like to answer the question."

"Then, as a matter of fact, I *did* fix everything. Not the poor man's arm, of course. But Captain Jacobs took two ships. We aren't in danger of drowning. And I've decided to wear my hat and gloves for the rest of the voyage."

Her maid looked more shocked by the last statement than the first. "Have you taken ill, Miss Briarley?"

"No," Callie said. She smoothed a finger over her ragged thumbnail. "But I have the Briarley name to think of."

"You have never cared for the Briarley name."

"Of course I haven't. But if I'm to become the Briarley heiress, I must maintain appearances."

Mrs. Jennings' mouth dropped open. "I thought you weren't going to accept. You said we were going to England to wait out the war."

Callie had refused every offer to return to England after her father had drowned on his final, quixotic voyage. Lord Tiberius Briarley had been a conniving charlatan — but he had also been the youngest son of the Earl of Maidenstone. Her grandfather had insisted, repeatedly, that she move to England, but she had declined. Her father often lied, but his hatred of his father had seemed genuine.

She should have refused the most recent invitation as well. The old man was dead now, leaving terms that seemed designed to make her and her only remaining female cousins fight over Maidenstone Abbey and the rest of the estate. The man her grandfather had left in charge of settling this farce — Ferguson, the Duke of Rothwell and her closest male relation on her grandmother's side — had invited her to a summer house party at Maidenstone.

It wasn't a party, though. It was a matchmaking opportunity, with a single goal in mind — whichever girl made the best match, according to Ferguson's judgment, would inherit the estate.

It was ludicrous.

She had very nearly turned it down. She didn't want a husband. From what she'd seen, husbands were only good for kissing and making babies. If she married, the man would want her to keep his house and follow his lead until he buried her.

She'd far rather run a shipping company and sacrifice the kissing, if it meant she could follow her own lead.

But with the war escalating, she'd felt she had no other choice. She wasn't wanted in Baltimore, either. Her father had never bothered to become an American, and some factions in the republic's government wanted to see British citizens like her removed from major ports like Baltimore, no matter her allegiances.

Callie saw the writing on the wall. Captain Jacobs wouldn't bow to her command, not when he had bloodlust and prizes dancing through his dreams. The American government could order her removed from the coast at any moment, costing her the comfortable, if lonely, life she'd built in Baltimore. She thought she could bribe the authorities to let her stay, but if she could not, the alternative was untenable.

She had nowhere to go.

Callie didn't give a fig for the Briarley legacy, or for Maidenstone Abbey. But the idea of winning it, of having something permanent...

She liked the sound of that. Even if it meant marrying someone she didn't particularly care for. This business with Captain Jacobs had reminded her, cruelly, of her place. She couldn't rely on a friendly business agreement to control her company, or her life. She needed a husband, preferably one who could be trained — one who would let her use his name for her own ends. If she became a widow, even better.

She was already a privateer. She may as well become a mercenary. It was a good plan, if she ignored the morality of it — and what marriage to an unloved stranger might mean.

Callie pulled on her gloves like they were gauntlets. "Find me a hat, Mrs. Jennings. I must find the most easily managed husband in England. And I must look the part of a lady if I'm to do it."

CHAPTER ONE

Salcombe, near the Devonshire coast - six months later

"I trust you've guessed why I have assembled you in a backwater such as this."

Gavin Emmerson-Fairhurst, better known to the world as the Duke of Thorington, drawled the words. He ran his gaze over each sibling in turn, gauging their moods.

None of them were frightened yet. "I've no idea," Portia said, yawning. "You've kept us in this horrid inn for three weeks. Must you have rolled us out of our beds before breakfast to tell us your intentions?"

It was already eleven in the morning, but Thorington didn't comment on the time. He caught Anthony, the youngest, rolling his eyes.

"You know our dear guardian," Anthony said in a carrying whisper. "Our schedules are of little concern to him."

Thorington tapped his fingers on the table and refrained from commenting on the 'schedules' he had impacted. He would grant that three weeks in the small village of Salcombe had bored all of them to death. But they lived on his largesse — their schedules had always been set at his whim.

Portia and Anthony, the youngest at twenty and nineteen, tended to unite forces whenever Thorington called the family together. The others, though, were more unpredictable in their allegiances. Serena, twenty-two, was as likely to spar with Portia as she was to support her. But today Serena had chosen to share a settee with her sister rather than aligning herself with Rafe — the one member of the family she usually idolized.

Thorington would have made the same choice. Rafe had been awake until dawn, pursuing whatever meager entertainments could be found in a village of Salcombe's size, and he reeked of whisky and tobacco smoke. He sprawled now in the chair farthest from Thorington, one arm draped over his eyes as though even the thought of light was enough to make the demons scream in his head. Pamela and Cynthia, born between Rafe and Serena, weren't present. They had their own husbands and families, and so they were spared from Thorington's machinations. And their father's bastards — more numerous than their mother's — never figured into Thorington's calculations, save for the annuities he owed them.

Thorington stood and adjusted the drapes until every window down the long wall of the pub's private dining room streamed sunlight. Rafe groaned and burrowed deeper into the chair. "Can we not delay whatever it is you want until tonight, Gav? I need a bed, not a lecture."

Rafe was the only one who still called him Gav. The rest may well have forgotten that they'd ever had a brother named Gavin. To the youngest three, Gavin had raised them for the entirety of their living memory. Even before their parents had died, he was the one who had kept them fed, sheltered, and safe. By the time he'd become the Duke of Thorington at twenty-four, they were already accustomed to his caretaking.

Caretaking he could suddenly no longer provide them.

"It's not a bed you need, Rafe," Thorington said as he returned to the table he'd claimed as his desk. "Nor can I afford to give you one."

Rafe lifted his arm enough to look at Thorington with one bleary eye. Whatever he saw forced him upright.

"Don't say your luck's run out?" he asked quietly.

Thorington nodded, once.

Rafe exhaled. "I thought it might have when you started losing at cards."

Portia sniffed. "You'll recover your gambling debts. You always do. May I be excused now?"

Serena stared at him, then put a quelling hand on her sister's knee. "Mayhap we should hear the rest of this."

What could he say? They didn't particularly like him. But he had given them every comfort, every bit of security he could provide.

Portia, for once, was silent. Even Anthony sat up. They all looked to him. They always looked, ultimately, to him. When their house had gone unheated, they came to him. When the creditors had threatened and the greengrocer stopped delivering and even the most devoted retainers muttered about missing wages, they came to him. Their father had left them in a tremendous bind.

And he had fixed it all. Made it all safe and secure again, safe enough for them to forget their wounds and mutter instead about how he was too controlling, too cold, too devilish.

He couldn't fix it anymore. Not without a massive, unimaginable influx of funds. And there was no sense in delaying the inevitable.

He scrubbed his hand over his jaw. "It is past time that all of you married. I want to see it done within a month."

Rafe put his arm over his eyes again. Serena and Portia gaped at him with identical expressions of confusion. Only Anthony didn't react — which was a reaction of its own, given how voluble the boy usually was.

"I am glad none of you object," Thorington said drily.

Portia's confusion turned to a potent glare. "I could have married any number of times if you'd only allowed me to."

Serena couldn't let that go without comment. "He would have allowed it if you weren't so fond of impoverished cavalry officers."

"Better cavalry officers than dancing masters," Portia shot back. "None of your paramours found favor with Thorington either."

Thorington sighed. "I will arrange everything. All you must do is accustom yourself to the notion and choose your dresses. Something you already have would be preferred. Your husbands can pay the next modiste's bill."

"Anthony and I haven't a thing to wear," Rafe complained. "All my dresses are shockingly out of season."

"You can shift for yourself," Thorington said. "I'll take care of Anthony."

Anthony was still quiet. At nineteen, he was everything Thorington might have been then — alternating between cocksure confidence and moments of boyish doubt, simmering rebellion and childish clinging to safety.

Thorington had seen every tantrum, heard every sullen recrimination. But he'd also played spillikins with him, told stories to him, given him dreams of princesses and castles rather than the reality of what a younger son faced. He should have bought Anthony a military commission or found him a clergy position as soon as he had left Eton. But the memory of Anthony, a squalling newborn in his arms, as their father threw their mother out of the house...

That memory sometimes made him soft.

He forced his face into something distant, something unassailable, and waited to speak until he knew his façade was back in place. "If you've wondered why I've dragged you all into Devon for the summer rather than going to our family seat, the Maidenstone estate is two miles from here. We will go there this afternoon."

Anthony's face turned pale, nearly matching his perfectly starched cravat. He always dressed immaculately when Thorington called them on the carpet, even if he claimed not to care. "You can't be serious," he said. "Ferguson would never invite you."

That was true. The party's organizer — Ferguson, the Duke of Rothwell — had no love for Thorington. But Thorington had secured an invitation through other channels. This wasn't an opportunity he could afford to lose.

"Maidenstone?" Rafe asked. He sounded entirely sober now. "I knew it was close, but I didn't think you'd have any interest there. You don't mean to go after one of the Briarley heiresses, do you?"

Thorington snorted. "I'm far too old for any of those chits. And I've already married for a large dowry once. It's time for Anthony to earn his keep."

The reference to his dead, mostly unlamented wife further soured the mood. "I would think you, of all people, would refuse to condone another arranged marriage after what Ariana did to you," Anthony said bitterly.

"It wasn't arranged — it was forced."

They all knew it was. She'd trapped him most effectively, in one of those situations where he had to do the gentlemanly thing and marry her despite having no love at all for her. But then, giving her the title she wanted for the dowry he needed had saved his whole family from disaster.

Anthony, with his romantic notions and no memory of their former poverty, wouldn't see it that way. "Making me marry one of the Briarley heiresses wouldn't be forced?" he retorted.

Thorington shrugged. "You can choose whichever of them you prefer. That's a better option than I had."

Anthony scowled. "It isn't my fault you lost at cards. And I shan't pay your debts with my heart."

It was a brave, bold phrase, one he tried to back up with a puffed-up chest and dramatic inhale. But Thorington's arched brow was sharp enough to puncture his resolve.

"You aren't paying my debts," Thorington said. "This is for your benefit, not mine. If you prefer not to marry an heiress, I can use my influence to make you a private secretary to a richer man than I. Is that what you prefer?"

Anthony's pale face was the ghost of a memory. He had been so sickly as a child, so likely to slip away from a mere cough or infected cut. It sometimes felt like a miracle that Anthony had survived, when Thorington could only see the fevered child rather than the healthy adult.

"I want to have a choice," Anthony said.

Thorington almost relented then. What if the Briarley heiresses were like Ariana — conniving social climbers who would always demand more? Could he condemn Anthony — *Anthony* — to that?

"Choice is a luxury, not a right," Thorington said. Anthony flinched, but this wasn't the time for mercy. "We can't afford that luxury at the moment. I've ordered your valet to pack your things. We will make our grand entrance at Maidenstone this afternoon. Our residence in Salcombe has been of long enough duration that you can get a marriage license from the bishop at Exeter as soon as you offer for one of them — no need to wait for banns."

The seriousness of the situation, and how much he had planned for it, seemed to strike all of them. The girls turned pale. Anthony, with his blond hair and fair cheeks, was always pale, but a flush slowly spread over his skin. "You can't force me to marry any of them," he said.

"I won't have to," Thorington replied. "You can choose between the security of an heiress and the peril of being disowned. I don't have to be a prophet to know what you'll decide."

"You aren't my brother," Anthony said.

There was an awful moment of silence. The girls both looked at their feet. Rafe dropped his arm over his eyes again. But Anthony didn't back down this time — he met Thorington's coldest look without flinching.

Thorington couldn't make his life better, though. If Anthony didn't marry someone, preferably someone wealthy, before the direness of Thorington's situation came to light, he might never get another chance. Third sons with no wealth were not in high demand.

And Thorington would rather see them all settled well, even if they hated him, than risk ruining their lives because of his debts.

"You are welcome to say whatever you wish about our relationship," Thorington said. "But I remain your guardian. And I will see you in the carriage this afternoon even if I must order the servants to drag you there. I trust you know better than to cause such a scene in the neighborhood where you may someday be the master of the estate."

Anthony stared at him for another long moment. Then he left, not asking to be excused. Portia cast Thorington a reproachful glare before rushing after her favorite sibling. Her voice, calling after their brother, scoured him. Every footstep rushing up the stairs was a body blow; the slam of a faraway door was a shot to his stomach.

Then, silence.

He looked at Rafe. "Nothing to say?" he asked.

Rafe dropped his arm, along with all pretense of nonchalance. "Serena, be a dear and excuse us?"

Serena ignored him. "What happened? Why are you so put out by a few losses at the gaming hells?"

"Don't concern yourself," Thorington said. "There's enough left for your dowry."

Only if she married before the middle of September, when the quarterly bills came due. But he didn't clarify, and she didn't care anyway. "My dowry doesn't matter," she said. "And you've only lost five or ten thousand in recent months, according to the *Gazette*. That's hardly enough to signify."

His losses had been reported in the gossip sheets, unprecedented as it was for him to come out the loser. Thorington shrugged. "You shouldn't discuss gambling debts with a gentleman."

"But…"

"Serena," Rafe said gently.

Serena glared at Rafe, then turned her focus back to Thorington. "What if I want to worry? I've precious little else to do with my time. Why won't you let me help you?"

"I'm not your responsibility," he said. "If you want to worry, do so — I can't stop you. But you can't help me, save by marrying someone appropriate."

Serena's mutinous scowl was answer enough. But she followed it with, "I wish you would find someone who can cut you down. Heaven knows you need it. Then the rest of us mortals may have a chance to help you."

It would have made him laugh if it didn't sound like a curse. Thorington knew something of curses. It was the reason he was in his current predicament. He didn't want to learn anything more about them.

He gestured to the door. "Pack your things."

Serena scowled again, but she didn't fight him. She flounced out of the room, slamming the door behind her. No one came to investigate all the noise — but then, with the extravagant sum he had paid to rent every room in the small establishment for the last three weeks, he could tear the entire building down from the rafters to the floorboards and the owner would probably offer to build him another one.

Thorington examined his cuffs. "Do you wish to follow her?" he asked Rafe, not looking up.

"Of course," Rafe said. "I'd be a fool to stay when you're in your 'savior of the family' mood."

"It hasn't bothered any of you to be saved. Or if it has, you've never spurned my money."

Rafe moved to a chair directly across from Thorington's. The shift in position brought him uncomfortably close — made the grim light in his eyes more apparent, more direct. "You've never given a damn for what bothered us. How bad is it?"

"What is the opposite of whatever luck I've had in the last decade?"

Rafe whistled. "I would pour you a drink if the thought of another round didn't make me ill. Surely it isn't…"

"It is," Thorington said flatly. "Everything I could have lost is lost."

"I know you've been losing at cards, but surely the rest is safe," Rafe said.

"You should disabuse yourself of the notion that you know my affairs better than I do," Thorington said.

That skin-flaying voice usually won the day, but Rafe was immune to Thorington's charms. "Your money is in land, shipping, and industry," Rafe said. "Serena's right — ten thousand pounds lost in a gaming hell is nothing to you. That isn't reason enough to sell Anthony into marriage. And you are incapable of staying broke for long."

Thorington drummed his fingers on the table again. "That's no longer true."

Rafe led himself to the obvious conclusion. "So your curse is truly broken? Allow me to say I'm disappointed."

If it were anyone else, Thorington would have laughed and called it a bit of superstitious nonsense. But Rafe was the only person in his family who knew exactly where their unlimited funds had come from over the past decade. And it wasn't just luck. Nor was it from Thorington's own efforts — he had no illusions about his business acumen. Dukes were bred to rule countries, not count shillings. It made them singularly ill-equipped for modern life.

All the luck he'd had over the past decade could be attributed, solely and completely, to an ancient curse. He'd thought it was a joke at first. How could it not be a joke? He had been so sure that he and his friend Alex, the Earl of Salford, were having a lark when they had found that ancient Egyptian dagger, cut their palms, and made their wishes.

Thorington had wished for wealth, as any man would who faced inheriting a bankrupted estate. And his wish had come true. Sure, his father had died immediately, which had stopped the old duke from draining the last of his coffers. And Ariana had tricked him into marriage — not the bride he would have wished for, but she brought with her a fortune as the heiress of a City merchant. Those consequences were bad enough that he'd never been happy about his wealth, even as it had made life easier for his siblings.

The curse had a dark sense of humor. He never forgot it; never let himself be lulled into a false sense of security, since it could kill anyone who threatened his finances too completely. But the money had flowed. His family had been beautifully clothed and sumptuously fed while idling around his house.

Until Alex, his former friend, had broken the curse three months earlier. And as quickly as Thorington's wealth had arrived, it abandoned him.

"I am disappointed as well," Thorington said. "Much as I'm relieved that the curse won't find another bored, unhappy heiress for me, I can't say I'm pleased that the books won't balance anymore."

Rafe steepled his fingers together and rested his chin on them. "The duchy is in better financial shape than it's been at any time in the past two centuries. Don't gamble or do anything particularly stupid, and you should be fine for years. There's more than enough time to retrench and plan for an estate that isn't held up by this curse of yours."

When Rafe was sober, his mind was sharper than anyone's. But he didn't know the extent of Thorington's woes. "I would assume the same, if I didn't know how fast everything is slipping away."

If the curse had had a dark sense of humor during its existence, it was positively diabolical in its absence. Every investment, every business venture — all of it had failed, or was sliding over the precipice.

Rafe couldn't believe him. "You have thousands of acres of farms and forests," he said. "That's never going to change."

"The land is poor," Thorington said. "The rents cover the cost of improving the ground and staffing the manor house, but not much else. Why do you think no previous duke was as rich as our peers?"

"Our forbearers were all idiots," Rafe said. "No surprise they couldn't manage anything beyond drinking and wenching."

Thorington laughed. "You're descended from the same stock, unless you'd rather claim bastardy."

Rafe shrugged. "Wouldn't mind it if Mother had gotten me from someone with a bit more soul than Father."

Of all their mother's children, Rafe and Gavin were the only ones whose parentage had never been questioned. "You're out of luck there," Thorington said.

Rafe sighed, as though that knowledge was worse than anything else Thorington had told him. "The old man left you with a damnable mess. But you have the coal mines, even if you don't have arable land."

Coal had been miraculously discovered near Fairhurst, his country estate, a few weeks after the curse had begun. He shrugged. "They ran into a wall of solid granite the day after the curse ended. I doubt they'll find coal there again, even though they're blasting for it."

Rafe frowned. "Factories, then. You have a host of them making supplies for the war…"

"They've all decided to strike," Thorington said.

"At the same time?"

"Indeed. My agents are trying to find strikebreakers, but it is proving difficult."

Rafe's frown deepened. "What about your ships? They can't strike — the sailors would be whipped for it."

"I've had word that the whole of the Caribbean fleet was captured by American privateers."

"All five of them?" Rafe asked. "Those damned Americans have grown bold."

"Quite bold. *Crescendo* almost made it to Jamaica, but some incompetent Navy captain cost me her as well. The rest are no doubt being sold or scrapped as we speak."

"You still have your Asian fleet."

Thorington shrugged. "They're weeks overdue. I wouldn't pin my faith on their return."

He ticked off his misfortunes as though they were a list of minor nuisances, not major losses with hundreds of lives attached to each. Rafe whistled. "I'll grant this doesn't sound promising, Gav."

Thorington snorted. "Any other piercing observations from that intellect of yours?"

"Only that I'm glad you never got into the whisky trade, or we might be facing a shortage. I may need that drink after all."

Thorington gestured at the bottle he'd bought from the innkeeper. "Be my guest."

"As always," Rafe said, reaching for the whisky. "I suppose I must find some other means of supporting myself if you can't keep me."

"You can stay at Thorington House. It will be incommodious when the creditors strip its furnishings, but no worse than what you lived through on the Peninsula."

Rafe shuddered, an exaggerated motion that Thorington might have found amusing if it weren't for the brief, haunted look in his eyes. "The back gardens will make a suitable pasture for goats — I got quite handy at roasting them during the war. Promise you won't infest the place with lice, though."

"You can fumigate it as often as you wish. Once Anthony and the girls are safely settled, you will have it to yourself."

Rafe had finished pouring his drink, but with that comment, he tipped the bottle again and added another finger of whisky to his glass. "And where are you going? The Duke of Thorington belongs at Thorington House."

Thorington shrugged. "Europe, most likely. I'd planned to go to Egypt after Ariana died, but I don't have the funds now. And I won't have people laughing over my changed fortunes. Thorington House can rot. It would have rotted already, were it not for the money brought in by the curse. We were always doomed."

Rafe sipped his whisky. Some of the tightness around his mouth relaxed, then disappeared. Thorington averted his gaze. Rafe was a problem he couldn't fix.

"If you think you're doomed, you likely are," Rafe said. "You, of all people, should know that prophecies come true."

Thorington retrieved the bottle. It was expensive stuff — more than he should have spent when there was nothing left, but he had to keep up appearances. The extravagance of renting the entire inn less than five miles from their destination was part of his plan. If Anthony seemed to come from riches, he'd be seen as a better candidate for a lady's hand.

Perhaps he was doomed. Perhaps he was destined to be the last in a sad, sorry line of idiots and miscreants. But his siblings wouldn't — couldn't — be punished for his failings.

He took a swig straight from the bottle, welcoming the burn.

Rafe raised an eyebrow. "That looks like something only an ill-mannered wretch such as I would do."

"I should practice desperation," Thorington said. "Wouldn't want to look out of place on the Continent."

His brother's smile wasn't comforting. "You aren't good at desperation, much as I'd like to see you desperate for something."

"Unkind," Thorington said. "You know I will not enjoy being impoverished again."

"It isn't poverty that I wish for you. I just…think it would be good for you to care for something."

"I thank you for the judgment, Saint Rafael. As though you care for anything."

Rafe shrugged. "No judgment. No sainthood." He sipped his drink again. "No caring, either. But *you* should try caring, at least once, before you give up the notion."

"I'll find an Italian shepherdess to keep me warm," Thorington said.

"Such a romantic. That plan will never work."

"My plans always work."

"Be sure to save enough money to post a letter detailing your escapades. I'd wager your Italian shepherdess will toss you out to pasture as soon as she realizes you'd rather arrange her life than lift her skirts."

Thorington gestured rudely, then pushed the bottle away and stood up. "Don't get too foxed. I'm going out, but we will make our entrance at Maidenstone by mid-afternoon."

Rafe gave him a mock salute before pouring more whisky into his glass. "Yes, Mother. I'll have the nursemaid wash behind my ears as well."

Thorington waited until he'd left the room before he let himself grin. Rafe would find a way to provide for himself. Whether he would live another decade was uncertain, but he would go his own path without ever asking Thorington for help. The others, though, were too young and too sheltered to make their own fates.

His trunks were already packed. He ordered the servants to finish making his family ready. Then he set out on the road from Salcombe to Maidenstone Abbey, veering off into the forest before he reached the house. He didn't want to listen to his siblings' mutinous rumblings, not when he needed to stay focused on the task at hand.

There was nothing left to reconnoiter between Salcombe and Maidenstone — he had seen it all in the last three weeks as he rambled over the countryside and considered his options. He had stopped walking in London years earlier, traveling as a duke should with glossy carriages and priceless horseflesh. But Gavin, the man he had once been, enjoyed walking. And he'd enjoyed walking again over the past three weeks, even if the beauty of Maidenstone Wood and the dramatic sea cliffs beyond it was marred by his endlessly churning thoughts.

He'd delayed as long as possible. But there was nothing for it.

He would find an heiress for Anthony. It was the only option that would keep the boy safe. If he could find husbands for his sisters at the same time, even better.

And once they were settled, he would leave for Europe and let his siblings curse what he had done to them. Better for them to hate him in safety than to miss their only chance at security.

CHAPTER TWO

Callie refused to believe in omens. But she could admit that it was a trifle…discomforting when her stolen mare stopped at the very edge of the circular glade Callie had spent half an hour looking for and refused to take another step.

"Go on, you stupid thing," Callie muttered. She tapped her booted heels against the horse's sides, glad that her divided traveling skirts were suitable for riding astride.

She would have rather taken a bath than a ride. She had spent several long days in a carriage with Mrs. Jennings, who seemed to grow more cheerful even as Callie turned surly. They had spent the previous night dozing upright against the walls of their hired coach. The journey from Baltimore to Havana to London had taken so long that she was in danger of missing the start of the party. Callie had planned to have at least two months in London to refresh herself, buy a new wardrobe, and learn how British society behaved.

Instead, her ship from Havana had been captured twice — first by Americans, then by the British. They'd nearly gone down in a storm near the Azores. She was sure the coachman had gone out of his way so he could charge them extra. And so a journey that should have taken three months had cost her almost six.

Mrs. Jennings hadn't spoken to her for nearly a week after the storm. They'd been reduced to eating moldy bread and drinking watered rum. Callie hadn't starved, drowned, or come down with scurvy. But she was feeling distinctly bedraggled and bedeviled.

She should have stopped somewhere the night before and rested. But she had been impatient. And in her impatience, she had miscalculated. Maidenstone Abbey's butler had sniffed as though she had dragged herself out of a gutter. Her cousin Lucretia had looked down her aquiline Briarley nose and stated, flatly, that Callie should have sent warning.

The way she said it made it sound like Callie shouldn't have come at all.

There wasn't a warm welcome for her at Maidenstone Abbey. She hadn't expected one, although she hadn't realized how much she had hoped for one until she realized that it would not be forthcoming. Her father had hated his brothers as much as he'd hated his father, and it seemed that the animosity was both mutual and generational.

Still, she wasn't going to sit in a back parlor and wait meekly for a room. She was a potential heiress, not a beggar — even if she smelled like one. And one of the only worthwhile lessons her father had taught her was to brazen out a bad situation as though she was still in control.

So she had turned on her heel, gone to the stables, and stolen Lucretia's horse.

Her father had left a map of the estate, and she'd studied it often enough to memorize it. She'd ridden straight for the last remnants of Maidenstone Wood, now little more than a charming forest separating Maidenstone Abbey from the small village of Salcombe. The abbey had been built two miles from the sea cliffs, far enough back to stay hidden from the seafaring raiders who once plagued the coast. That hadn't stopped the raids, but the abbey had survived them all.

Until one of Callie's ancestors had used Henry VIII's persecution of the monasteries to steal the abbey and turn it into his private estate.

The fact that his own brother had been the abbot hadn't been enough to stop the slaying.

But when she finally found the clearing where that bloodshed had happened — a place that had been protected by a flag of truce before becoming an ambush — it wasn't as impressive as she had expected. And it shouldn't have scared the horse. The mare stayed still, right at the edge of the clearing, tense but not yet attempting to bolt. The horse hadn't balked when entering the woods, and it hadn't shied when rabbits and birds had crossed their path.

It was a relief that Callie wasn't superstitious. All of the stories her father had told her of the Maidenstone — both the stone itself and the grand Maidenstone Abbey that had been named after it — had involved omens, curses, or worse. If his horse had balked at this point, he would have turned around and never returned.

Instead, she slid off the horse and looped the reins loosely around a nearby tree. Then she stepped into the clearing.

She held her breath as she did so. But lightning didn't strike. Phantoms didn't descend upon her. She took another step. If she had let herself be ruled by the same superstitions that ruled her father, she would have sold all their ships after he'd gone down in one of them.

And besides, the illogical part of her that took her horse's balking as an omen likely *wanted* it to be an omen.

You should turn back, it whispered, seductively. *You should return to Baltimore, where you belong.*

But that voice wasn't a dark spirit or ancient ghost. It was her own heart. And her heart had no place making decisions.

She took a step, then another. The clearing was as perfectly manicured as Maidenstone's vast lawn. Lucretia must have ordered a gardener to tend it regularly. It took twenty paces to cross to the center. She stopped in front of the ancient granite pillar — the original Maidenstone. Her father had kept a drawing of it in his study in Baltimore, but the artist's pencil hadn't captured the encroaching moss or the weathered, pock-marked texture. It was taller than she was, perhaps six feet in height. But it was its shape that compelled attention. It curved in, then out, like an hourglass — or the curve of a woman's waist.

There was no face and nothing else to suggest humanity. Still, she understood the superstition now. The legend was that a girl had fallen in love with the devil there. But when he had come to take her away forever, she had repented at the last moment, and God — or whatever pagan idol the original inhabitants had worshipped — had turned her to stone to save her. The Briarleys had built upon that legend, believing that whichever one of them deserved the favor would see their sins washed clean there.

She removed her glove and reached out, tracing three fingers over the ancient symbols carved into the stone.

It was just a rock, but in the perfect stillness of the clearing, she suddenly felt sad. She hadn't expected to feel anything at all. Despite her father's stories, she had developed no special love for the place. All she cared was that her grandfather had treated her father poorly — a family tradition, it seemed. As a child, that knowledge had been enough.

But seeing Maidenstone Abbey for the first time that morning — standing now in the place her ancestors had thought was the center of all their good and bad fortune — gave her a twinge of possessiveness.

The Briarleys were on the verge of dying out. Centuries of murder, treason, debauched living, and poor decisions had nearly wiped them from the earth. There would never be another Earl of Maidenstone. The title had gone extinct with her grandfather's death. Either she, Octavia, or Lucretia would inherit the house — through making the best marriage, this time, unless one of them turned to the old Briarley ways and killed the others.

Callie was more interested in finding a willing pawn to make her husband than she was in winning the estate. But seeing Lucretia's condescending smile, hearing her slow her speech as though Callie was a blithering idiot instead of an American...

Callie was enough of a Briarley to find pleasure in the idea of stealing Maidenstone from Lucretia.

And anyway, she would need it if she was tossed out of Baltimore by whoever won after the war. If she won it, she would have it forever. Maidenstone Abbey had survived Viking raids, wars, fires, and any number of other calamities. Unlike all the other houses she'd lived in, it was solid. And it would remain solid.

Her fingers ran over the only row of symbols she understood. Some ancestor, leaving his mark, had carved the family motto into the stone.

"*Briarley contra mundum*," she whispered.

Briarley against the world. It would have been more accurate to say they were against each other, but she understood the logic of it.

A crack sounded in the undergrowth behind her. A flurry of wings destroyed the stillness. She dropped her hand and twisted, expecting to see her mare bolting — and instead found a man watching her.

"Impressive, isn't it?" he said, gesturing toward the pillar with his walking stick. "Or impressive for Devon, at least. I find Stonehenge at Salisbury far more intriguing."

His voice seemed condescending, not threatening. Still, Callie didn't care to discover what his intentions might be. She walked toward her horse, conscious that it would bring her closer to him than she was comfortable with. But the mare was her only means of escape.

"You startled me, sirrah," she said, feigning confidence. "I thought these woods were quite safe."

"'Sirrah'?" he repeated. "Did you learn your English from a book, or are you one of the ghosts Maidenstone is known for?"

Callie flushed. He had stopped a couple of yards from her horse, choosing to lean against a tree at the edge of the clearing rather than continuing his advance. She supposed it was meant to put her at ease. But alone, in unfamiliar terrain, she couldn't take any comfort from the gesture.

She didn't want to show any fear, so she chose to banter instead. "I have better manners than to converse with a stranger in the woods," she said. "Particularly one who would give me insult."

She reached the mare, putting on her glove before unwinding the reins. But she couldn't mount without a step, and the only promising rock was on the edge of the clearing. She tugged the reins. The beast moved four steps, but not toward the rock; instead, it chose to sidle away and return to grazing.

"A ghost would be similarly unable to guide a horse," the man observed. "But your accent tells me my theory about books is more likely."

Callie stiffened her spine. "I am neither a ghost nor a simpleton. And I am a competent rider when given the proper mount."

"Then I would like to see you properly mounted."

She *wasn't* a simpleton — but even a simpleton wouldn't miss that intended joke. There was a hint of something in his voice…surely it wasn't heat? He sounded too cutting for something like a flirtation.

She looked at him more fully. He was tall, his height further extended by a hat that even she knew must have been frightfully expensive. His dark hair curled just a bit beneath it, brushing against an expertly tied cravat. His attire was meant for the City, not the woods. The gleam of his boots was too sharp for a peasant.

But a gentleman wouldn't have said something like that to her.

"You are not welcome to continue conversing with me if you cannot show more respect," she said.

He shrugged. The roll of his shoulders was elegant, like the soft swell of the sea. "If you want to find someone proper, turn yourself around and return to whatever backwater you've washed up from. I assure you that Maidenstone is full of only the worst sorts of fortune-hunters and miscreants."

Callie mostly didn't hear anything after the word 'backwater.' The roaring in her ears made it too difficult to parse out single words from the overall feeling of being slapped. Every person she'd met in England so far, from the overbearing captain of the ship that had brought her from Havana to London, to the driver she'd hired to bring her to Maidenstone, to her odious cousin, had made her feel like she didn't belong. But hearing such a sentiment from a strange man in the woods was really too much.

"I am from Baltimore, not a backwater," she said through gritted teeth. "And if you are an example of what awaits in that house, then I thank you for warning me away."

She tried one more time to guide the mare into the clearing. She would leave the mare behind if she couldn't drag it with her.

The horse refused to take another step.

She eyed the stranger again. The man didn't move, other than to raise an eyebrow. But she was conscious of the danger she had strayed into — and it took more willpower than usual to think that the mare's behavior hadn't been an omen. On horseback she would have had a chance of escaping him.

She couldn't outrun him if he gave chase on foot.

"You would be better off selling that horse for meat," he observed.

She tugged at the horse's bridle. The stupid animal shook its head and ignored her.

"Would you care to buy it?" she asked. "I will give you a fair price."

The man smiled. "You are pretty enough to sway me, my dear. But I only make bargains that are useful to me. Willfulness is not a trait I cherish in horses or women."

Callie stared at him. He had called her pretty enough. But had he really just said…?

She dropped the reins. "I'll give her to you as a gift."

"Why would you do that?"

She smiled as sweetly as possible. "If you're at Maidenstone, you must be one of the fortune-hunters. Sell the mare with my compliments and buy yourself a ticket on the next stage to London, if the country air makes you so ill-tempered."

His stare gave her a chance to see his eyes. When surprise widened them, they were a startling emerald green — eyes that seemed capable of every seduction.

The pleasure of surprising him, combined with those brilliant eyes, provided a sharp thrill she hadn't expected to find with their conversation. But his slow, unexpected smile tipped the balance entirely in his favor. It made the corners of his eyes crinkle, made the arch of his dark brows seem conspiratorial rather than judgmental.

It made all the thoughts leave her head.

He was beautiful. He might have preferred the word handsome, but that wasn't strong enough. His was a harsh, masculine beauty, but it was beauty nonetheless. He was perhaps thirty-five, although his attitude made him seem older and his smile made him younger. But the experience carved into his skin somehow enhanced his appeal.

Callie was dazzled.

It was a singularly unpleasant realization. She hadn't come to Devon to be dazzled. And this man, whoever he was, was not husband material.

But she wasn't so dazzled as to miss the moment when his smile turned from genuine amusement to calculation. "Baltimore, you say?"

"Did I say that?" she asked.

"You will learn that I have an excellent memory," he said.

"It seems unlikely that I would learn such a fact, since I've no wish to continue our acquaintance."

He shrugged again. "At least you admit we are acquainted. Although it would be in your best interests to pretend you've never seen me when we meet again."

"Why are you so sure we'll meet again? You do not know my business in the neighborhood."

"You must be the Baltimore heiress, Miss Briarley. I had begun to wonder if you would arrive in time. I suspected you were dead, incompetent, flighty, or some combination of the three. No woman with an ounce of sense would miss this opportunity."

"The opportunity to converse with a gaggle of idle aristocrats?"

The man smiled. "You are charming, Miss Briarley. You'll need extensive lessons, of course, but that can be arranged."

"I do not need lessons," Callie said. "I've been out of the schoolroom for years."

"Yes, I'm aware of your advanced age. But it was a Baltimore schoolroom. I doubt you learned anything useful for the life you shall have here."

Really, the insults. She wasn't sure whether to be more offended at the comment about her age — as though twenty-three had any comparison to his own age — or her schooling. She drew herself up. "I speak French, read Latin, can calculate a row of sums faster than my father's business manager, and have mastered all the ancient histories. That's a far sight better than what I've heard your spoiled English misses can do."

"My sisters might take offense at that," the man said mildly. "Probably not, though. Too well-bred to care what an American thinks of their skills. But while I find your education…interesting, it's hardly useful. I will arrange for lessons."

She gaped at him. He looked her over — a slow, roving gaze that made her blush. His eyes tracked down, lingering on her chest, then tracing over her waist to take in her divided skirt and booted feet. She was still dusty from her interminable journey on the road from London. Her riding skirt was the only clean garment left in her trunks after months at sea, save for her evening dresses. She wished, fervently, that she had worn something else — something more flattering.

Then she told herself to stop being stupid. The man was awful. Did it matter what he thought of her?

"Perhaps a modiste as well," he murmured, almost to himself. "I shall consider whether one from Bath will do, or whether to wait the extra days for a better one from London. Tell me you have a maid capable of dressing your hair and she just forgot to use her skills."

Her hand curled into a fist. Her father had taught her how to hold it so that she wouldn't break her thumb — perhaps the most worthwhile lesson he'd given her — and she was tempted to give the stranger a demonstration. "You will arrange no such things, sirrah. I do not know you, and I sincerely hope I shan't see you again."

"Willfulness," he said, sighing. "Still better than your cousins, I suppose. I've heard no redeeming virtues for either of them."

"What is your name?" she demanded.

He tsked. "We haven't been introduced."

She would have to murder him. It wouldn't be the first blood spilled in the clearing. She counted to ten in her head, trying to calm herself. Finally, she said, "We've broken enough rules in this conversation to fill a broadside. Surely telling me your name won't hurt."

He unfolded himself from his chosen tree and strolled toward her. He gripped his walking stick, carrying it like a weapon. There was a devilish gleam in his eyes and a new smile playing on his lips, one she hadn't seen yet.

One that seemed anticipatory.

She backed up until she brushed against her horse. The mare

didn't move. And the man's brilliant green eyes held her pinned.

He took her fist, pulling it away from her side as though she'd offered it to him. He bowed over it, grazing a kiss across her knuckles. But his eyes never broke contact with hers.

"Miss Briarley, a pleasure," he murmured.

Her heart fluttered. She would have cursed it, but any air she had for words had already left her.

He straightened and let her hand slip from his grasp. She realized that her lips were slightly parted, that she probably looked as shocked as if he'd bashed her in the head with a rock. But she couldn't find her composure.

Then he tipped his hat to her. "I bid you good day, Miss Briarley."

He turned away from her. He took three steps, then five…then it became clear that he was really leaving.

"But you didn't tell me your name," she said.

She was still stunned enough that it was almost a whisper. He looked back over his shoulder. "In good time, my dear. It would really be for the best if no one knew we had met here. That would certainly ruin you. And I assure you that you would not like to be forced into wedlock with me."

The part of her that was still dazzled by him disagreed. But the part that needed a husband who would serve as a mere figurehead, who would let her rule herself…

That part thought she should run from this man and never look back.

"I think my simple American tongue can refrain from betraying our acquaintance," she said.

He grinned, a fleeting little bit of amusement that dazzled her again. "I knew you were trainable. Practice your curtsey, if you never used it in the colonies. I look forward to seeing it when we meet."

He walked away, not waiting for a response. Which was just as well, really — Callie didn't think her slackjawed stare would have won her any points in their verbal battle.

She waited until he was gone. The forest fell back into its usual rhythm. Without a predator lurking, the birds sang again. Sunlight filtered through the branches. She turned back to the Maidenstone. It was serene, bathed in sunlight — no sign that the devil had ever crossed its path.

Callie shivered. The stranger was a man, not the devil.

And he was best forgotten. Even if the idea of marrying a weak-willed, uninteresting man suddenly held less appeal than it had before.

CHAPTER THREE

An hour later, Callie had given her stolen horse back to the stables and returned to Maidenstone Abbey's main entrance. But the staff's welcome was still frosty. "How can you not have a room prepared for me?" Callie asked.

The butler, a man of middling age and middling features, looked down his nose at her. She had given him nearly two hours, between her search for the Maidenstone and the time she had spent attempting to understand — or forget — the man she'd met there. But her ride had only made her dustier, especially since she'd led the mare nearly halfway back to the house before the horse would let her remount. She was sure more hair had escaped her pins than remained confined within them. And if she had smelled of sea and sweat before, she now smelled of horse as well.

She probably looked every bit as wild as the British expected Americans to be. But she didn't show her discomfort. She stared at the butler until he was forced to answer. "My mistress received no acceptance of your invitation," he said. "You must understand that this party is one of the most important events in England this summer. We will have two dukes and an assortment of lords and ladies, not even counting all of the other guests."

He sounded as proud as if he had invited them himself. "I'm

sure you're all agog at the thought of bowing and scraping to such illustrious individuals," Callie said drily. "But I assure you I am easier to maintain. I only need a room and a bath."

The butler sniffed. "Shall I show you to the conservatory, Miss Briarley? You may wait there while I consult with my lady."

He looked at her divided skirt as he said it — or, more likely, at the dirt flaking off her boots onto the tiled floor. The front entrance hall was a grand, overwhelming space that spanned the height of two stories. It was part of the wing that had been built most recently, in the style of the last three decades. Her father hadn't seen it completed. But the wings beyond it — Jacobean, Tudor, and even remnants of the Gothic Maidenstone Abbey itself — might still be as he had described them to her.

If she ever moved beyond the foyer.

The curiosity that had driven her into the forest now demanded to see the rest of the house. And her pride required that she change her dress — particularly if that infuriating man she'd met in the woods was, as she suspected, another houseguest.

Callie knew she didn't have the most feminine outlook. But she still liked to feel pretty. And it was difficult to feel pretty when she hadn't had a proper bath in months — even if the man in the clearing had looked at her as though he didn't mind.

She shoved the stranger from her mind again and gave the butler all the hauteur she usually used on arrogant sea captains. "I won't risk missing dinner because you cannot find a way to accommodate me. Now, if you please, arrange for a room immediately, or I shall find one. I assume your lady would prefer that I not embarrass her by knocking on doors."

The butler looked as though he hated her. But before either of them could do something regrettable, her cousin Lucretia rushed into the foyer, with a young blonde woman following close behind her.

"The duke's entourage is driving up. Call the footmen to attention."

The butler clapped his hands. Callie looked over her shoulder and saw four footmen who had been waiting in the anteroom next to the great front door pour out and arrange themselves on either side of it, with one of them ready to open the door as soon as steps sounded outside. The butler examined them, found everything to his liking, and turned back to his mistress. "And Miss Callista?" he asked. "Where shall I put her?"

Lucretia glanced at her as though she was a street urchin begging for scraps. "The Tudor wing, I suppose. Have a scullery maid take her up. The upstairs maids are too busy, and we'll need all the footmen for the duke's baggage."

The butler reached out a hand to take her elbow. Callie wrenched her arm away. "This isn't a very warm welcome, cousin," she said, trying for a pleasant tone rather than an angry or wounded one. "Did you not intend to invite me?"

Lucretia laughed. Her face was startlingly similar to Callie's own, with dark eyes and a straight, aquiline Briarley nose. But laughter didn't seem to come naturally to her. There was something too pained about it to think she found any joy in the sound.

"You were invited, not that I had any say in the matter," Lucretia said. "But this is still my house."

The blonde girl, whom Callie had nearly forgotten, took a step forward. She couldn't have been more than twenty, but the look in her eyes seemed older. She put a hand on Lucretia's shoulder, as though to restrain her, and smiled at Callie. "What Lucretia meant to say, Miss Briarley, is that you must be in want of refreshment after your journey. Shall I take you to find your maid so that you may rest a bit before dinner?"

Callie hesitated. She didn't want to give in. She knew the Tudor wing was the least appealing of all of them, and Lucretia must have meant it as an insult. But this girl seemed nicer than Lucretia — nice enough that Callie wanted to accommodate her. And Callie *did* want a bath. Six months of seawater ablutions were enough to swear off ships forever.

She had waited too long, though. The great doors swung open behind her, so well oiled as to be almost silent. A breeze teased its way through her wayward hair. Lucretia plastered a smile on her face that was too guarded to ever be sincere.

"Your grace," Lucretia said, stepping around Callie. "Lady Maidenstone and I are delighted you have joined us."

Lady Maidenstone? Callie glanced sharply at the blonde. She had heard that her grandfather had remarried before the end, but this girl…

And then she heard a voice she could already recognize anywhere.

"Miss Briarley," the stranger from the woods said. "The pleasure is mine."

*   *   *

Thorington had wanted to put on a show such as Maidenstone had never seen. He, of all people, should have known better than to make such a wish.

Callista Briarley hadn't seen him enter. Her back was to the door, facing Lucretia. Her stance was militant. It appeared that Callista had only just arrived herself. And however she had occupied herself in the previous hour, it had not been with the attentions of a lady's maid.

He wouldn't let his eyes linger on the view of her from behind — a view he'd seen, all too briefly, at the Maidenstone clearing before she had turned to find him watching her. The divided skirt covered all it should. Dusty, it should have had no appeal at all. But the flare of her hips beneath the riding jacket, the way she stood ready to seize the world...

He lingered too long, despite his intentions. Lucretia Briarley was greeting him, with the same wary, frightened smile he usually earned from polite women — the kind of women who couldn't help but be polite, even to someone who might hurt them. And so he returned her greeting, with the drawl that always heightened others' nerves, and watched his intended quarry.

Callista flinched.

Thorington smiled.

Lucretia, trying hard to pretend that she wasn't entirely overwhelmed by him, offered him her hand and curtsied as he kissed it. "May I present Lady Maidenstone?" she asked, gesturing to the blonde chit behind her.

Thorington bowed. He'd heard of Lady Maidenstone, but never met her. She wore lavender, the last stage of mourning. Her blue eyes seemed to take up the entirety of her face.

She'd barely been more than a child when the earl had married her. "My condolences that you must still wear mourning for the old goat," he said to her.

Lucretia flushed. Lady Maidenstone was startled into giving him a real smile before she curtsied. When she came up from it, she had forced the corners of her mouth into submission. "It is only for another month, your grace. But I thank you for your sympathy."

She would have been a sensation in London if she had come out there. She'd never had the chance, though. If the rumors were true — and, seeing this girl, Thorington knew them to be — the old Earl of Maidenstone had, in all but deed, bought her from her impoverished family for the chance of getting a son after his last heir had died.

If life was fair, the girl should have inherited everything — she would have deserved it, even if she'd only been tied to the man for two years. But she hadn't succeeded in producing a child. And Lord

Maidenstone hadn't seen fit to give her anything for her troubles. She would get whatever portion he'd settled on her at marriage, and nothing else.

Life was not fair. There was no use in feeling sorry for her, even if he wished to. And so he dismissed her as useless to him. No matter what her charms were, her loveliness would go to a man who could afford to do without a dowry.

He returned his gaze to Callista. She turned, finally, as though confronting her own death.

Her hair was wilder, her skirts dirtier, her hands clenched as though ready to do him violence. She was taller than the other women in the room, perhaps five feet and eight inches — but the two inches she had over Lucretia seemed like more when her rage added stiffness to her backbone. She had gotten just enough sun under the brim of her slightly-skewed hat to warm her skin.

And she had breasts to match those hips. She was proportioned like an Amazonian conqueror, not a coquette.

He smiled again. When he finally brought his eyes back to her face, she was flushed — and it wasn't with pleasure.

Lucretia made no move to introduce her. "Present your guest to me, Miss Briarley," he commanded. "She hasn't had the honor of meeting me."

It was a subtle warning. He hoped Callista remembered that she wasn't supposed to know him.

"You've a funny definition of honor, sirrah," Callista said.

Lucretia gasped. Behind him, Rafe laughed. Thorington merely raised an eyebrow. "You must be the American cousin," he said, in his exaggerated drawl. "Am I your first duke?"

For once he hadn't meant an innuendo to it, but she blushed as though he had. She tilted her chin up, though, and stared him down. "I had a thoroughbred named Duke once. But I found he didn't match the promise of his bloodlines."

"Charming," Thorington murmured. "But we still haven't been properly introduced."

There was a brief, dark pause, as though no one wanted to interrupt whatever it was they had between them. Then Lady Maidenstone stepped forward. "May I present to you Miss Callista Briarley? Miss Briarley, his grace the Duke of Thorington."

He grabbed Callista's hand before she had properly offered it to him. "A delight," he said as he brushed his lips over her hand.

When he had done it before, little more than an hour earlier, her fingers had curled lightly in his — a momentary, and no doubt unintentional, surrender. Now, when his lips caressed over her knuckles, he had the vague premonition that she would rather hit him than let him touch her.

But she had just enough sense not to hit a duke in a public setting. She did not, however, have the sense to curtsey to him. He felt her sway into the very beginning of one — but then she stopped herself.

"An honor to meet you, of course." She stayed standing straight, no sign of deference. And she didn't call him 'your grace,' as any other woman would have.

He didn't want to drop her hand. There was a spark in her eyes that he had never seen before — a challenge he found nearly irresistible.

But he remembered his plans. He tucked her arm neatly into the crook of his own and guided her toward his siblings, ignoring her protests. "Lord Rafael, Lord Anthony, Lady Serena, Lady Portia," he said, gesturing to each of them in turn. "All as honored to meet you as you are to meet them."

Given the daggers his sisters were shooting at her, and the way she was trying to escape him, the statement was accurate. None were honored, and none were subtle about it.

Anthony looked her over and frowned. But he reserved his glare for Thorington.

Only Rafe was civil. "Miss Briarley," he exclaimed, as though he'd waited ages to meet her. "Have you only just arrived from America? You must tell me how you are finding Devonshire."

Trust Rafe to seem vastly intrigued — he could charm anyone when he was in the mood for it. Callista stopped struggling for just a moment and nodded at him. "Baltimore to Havana to London took six months of travel, with no time to rest before arriving this morning. I've no opinion of Devonshire other than to hope there aren't maggots in the meat."

Lucretia gasped again. "Your grandfather would be appalled at the thought, Miss Briarley," she said in quelling tones as she stepped up to their group.

Callista shrugged. "If he would have kept me waiting for a room like you have, he probably wasn't too particular about his housekeeping."

Rafe made a soothing sound, trying to play peacemaker. "These house parties are so difficult to arrange, aren't they? Particularly this one. Half the fortune-hunters in Britain will be trying to win you both."

He included Lucretia in his assessment — charitably, to Thorington's mind. But Lucretia unbent just a little. "Indeed, Lord Rafael. But I'm sure Lady Maidenstone and I have looked forward to your family's arrival. We are honored that you've chosen to attend."

She said it politely, but there was a question in her voice. And with good reason. Thorington had taken the highly unusual — some would say unacceptable — step of writing to Lady Maidenstone and demanding an invitation. Even for him, it was a bold approach. But he never would have been invited on his own merits.

Thorington didn't react to her question, beyond a slightly dangerous smile. Lucretia's gaze flickered over to him, but when she saw that smile, she immediately returned her attention to Rafe.

Callista, who was still trapped next to him, would have said something cutting if she'd seen Thorington's smile. Lucretia, though, did what was expected of her. She was pretty enough, but she was smaller than Callista, as though she had been made for pouring tea instead of fighting battles. And her face had the same Briarley nose, framed by the same glossy brown hair — but her face was too closed off, her hair too perfect.

Lucretia was almost certainly the safer choice. But Callista…

"And where is the third member of your Briarley triumvirate?" Rafe asked.

"Octavia will arrive whenever she wishes to arrive, I'm sure," Lucretia said. "She always does."

There was an awkward silence after that, but Rafe filled it gracefully enough with a question about the weather. Rafe's sole skill was putting others at ease. His charm was so effortless, his smile so steady, that no one would have guessed that demons haunted him. And it gave Thorington a moment to consider his plans.

It would have been unnatural if he hadn't considered keeping Callista for himself. He didn't particularly want a wife — being vowless, after ten years with Ariana, was still pleasing enough that he wasn't ready to take on a new obligation.

But he wasn't opposed, either. He knew how to keep a wife. It was mostly a matter of writing cheques for her wardrobe. Or occasionally taking her to the opera, with the expectation that she would let him into her bed after. Easy business, transacted coolly, with an eye toward the balance on his ledgers rather than the needs of his heart.

However, if his lack of luck held, he would run through whatever money a bride brought him in less than a year. It was a better plan to leave the heiress for his brother, who could make use of her economic assets even if he wasn't in love with her.

He assessed the situation with the coldness of a mercenary. Callista had given up trying to retrieve her hand. But she ignored all of them, choosing instead to stare off into the middle distance like a martyr awaiting the fire.

Anthony, younger than her, had less composure. He still stood in the doorway, unwilling to cross the threshold, blocking the footman who looked perturbed over holding the door open. He looked from Callista to Lucretia and back again as though Thorington had asked him to choose a circle of Hell to dwell in. Then he pressed a hand to his mouth as though he might be sick.

Thorington, for once, took pity on him. He dropped Callista's hand. "How thoughtless of me, to keep you conversing with us when you no doubt wish to rest," he said. "I am sure your room is ready now."

He said this with a sharp look at Lucretia, who nodded automatically. No one would gainsay a duke. "One of the footmen will take you to the Tudor wing, Miss Briarley," she said, sounding faint.

"That will do for now," Callista said. "Send my maid to me as well."

"And a bath, I think," Thorington said.

The silence was absolute as color bloomed on Callista's cheeks. She finally nodded, all bravado, as though she'd suggested it. "And a bath. And tell my maid to fetch my pistol from my trunks."

She turned on her heel and walked away, leaving the footman Lucretia frantically gestured at to trail in her wake. She let him catch her at the other end of the hall, no doubt because she needed directions and didn't want to ask for them.

She was magnificent.

Lucretia coughed delicately as Callista disappeared. "I apologize for her, your grace. She is newly from America and isn't yet familiar with our ways. I assure you that you will find better company during your stay here."

For once, he didn't say what he wanted to — that he would rather talk to Callista than anyone else. Instead, he murmured his thanks. Then the butler escorted his family to their rooms — spacious chambers in the newest section of the house, two floors up from the entryway, where only the best guests would be housed. They would have two hours to rest before assembling in the drawing room at four o'clock for drinks before dinner.

Thorington would need all of that time to consider his plans. But Anthony didn't wait above fifteen minutes before knocking on his door.

"I cannot do this," Anthony said.

His cravat was askew and his blond hair was mussed. His right boot was scuffed. Anthony had broken himself of the habit of digging his shoe into the floor after discovering the pleasure of a perfectly polished pair of Hessians, but in moments of extreme emotion he sometimes forgot his vanity.

Thorington, already stripped down to his shirt and breeches, glanced at his valet. "Give us a moment," he said.

As soon as the door closed, Anthony repeated himself. "I cannot do this. I cannot marry either of them."

"It's early days, Anthony," Thorington said. "You'll feel better once you've accustomed yourself to the idea."

"*No.*" Anthony paced to the window, looking out over Maidenstone's carefully kept lawn. "I don't intend to marry for ages — and even if I did, it wouldn't be either of the Briarleys. Lucretia is provincial and Callista is entirely improper. Can you imagine either of them hosting parties in London? Even for this," he said, gesturing toward the estate beyond the glass. "Even for this, it's too high a price to pay."

Those were the words of someone who didn't remember the days when Thorington House had leaked like a sieve. Anthony had never wanted for anything. He'd never wondered how to pay for something — he'd always signed his vowels and sent the bill to Thorington. He'd never heard their parents screaming over the modiste's bill, over their mother's trips to Bath, over the annuity for their father's latest cast-off mistress.

"It's a low price, actually," Thorington said. "You don't have to love your wife. You just have to give her your name."

"You say it as though it's nothing," Anthony said.

Thorington shrugged. "It's a small price for having a roof over your head."

"But they're both so…"

He shuddered. Thorington loosened his cravat and tossed it onto the bed. "I'll grant Lucretia might not appeal. But Callista would make you a fine wife."

"*Callista?*" Anthony's voice was as scandalized as if Thorington had told him he must marry a prostitute. "She looks like she was raised trapping furs and distilling liquor. She will never get vouchers to Almack's if she cannot be bothered to curtsey to a duke. Can you imagine how the patronesses would react to such a snub?"

Thorington snorted. He had no trouble recalling her image, but what he remembered was different from Anthony's interpretation. True, with her strong, supple limbs and fearless stance, she could have claimed she had trapped her way up and down the Hudson and he would have believed her.

And, oddly, he wouldn't have minded it.

He should have found her entirely unappealing. He liked his women like he liked his beds — soft, snug, and easily abandoned in the morning for more worthwhile pursuits. Callista Briarley wasn't soft. And she would not be easily abandoned.

But he needed security for his siblings, not another problem. So he ignored the memory of her, of how she'd drawn the first real laugh out of him in ages. Anthony would discover her humor. Anthony would see beyond the wild hair and overly exuberant smile to find the remarkable woman she could become. *Anthony* would love her as she deserved.

"You can choose Lucretia instead, if you wish," Thorington said. "Or perhaps you'll take a liking to Octavia when you meet her. But I am confident that Callista is the most appealing of the three. She may be a barbarian, but barbarians can be civilized. Lucretia would be harder to entertain. And everyone in England knows Octavia is too much trouble after the scandal she caused in London a few years ago."

Anthony frowned. "My needs aren't so extravagant that I must marry an heiress. I can reduce my expenditures if you ask me to."

Thorington snorted again.

"I can," Anthony insisted.

"Give up your curricle?"

Anthony nodded.

"And the blood bays? You'll find it difficult to gain entrance to the Four Horse Club without horseflesh."

Anthony swallowed. "I can find other entertainments."

"Your tailor? Membership at White's? The next term at Cambridge? Your Grand Tour?"

His brother fell silent. He had been flushed earlier, but now his face was entirely drained of color.

Thorington could have left it there, but he needed Anthony to see the problem at hand. "You think your needs aren't extravagant because I pay for your housing and entertainments. Father left you nothing in his will. Your continued survival is solely due to my largesse. And my largesse is coming to an end."

Anthony looked out the window again. Thorington never mentioned his younger siblings' disputed parentage — the reference to the will was as close as he ever got to the subject. And he already regretted it. But Anthony had to understand what was at stake.

"I don't need an heiress," Anthony said, in a smaller voice. "I would be content with a small cottage and room for a garden."

"An heiress could pay for someone to maintain that garden for you. And you would miss London if you could not keep a house there."

"I shall stay with friends when I visit the city," Anthony said, turning back to Thorington with bravado in his voice.

His breezy confidence broke Thorington's heart. But it also made him angry. "You haven't any idea what your life would be if I didn't take care of you. Now, you will marry one of the Briarley heiresses. If you want me to arrange it so you don't have to choose between them, I shall. But there will be no more discussion of the matter."

Anthony gave Thorington a speaking glare, but he knew when there was no point in continuing an argument. After a long moment, he left. But he didn't slam the door as Thorington expected him to. He shut it softly — as though Thorington wasn't worth his anger anymore.

Thorington sighed. He turned back to the washstand, stripped off his shirt, and splashed cool water on his face.

It wasn't enough. He dunked his head in the basin instead. He held his breath until the pressure in his lungs overwhelmed the scream of frustration waiting there.

Then he pulled his face out of the water, gasping. He should have told Anthony before today. Should have given him time to adjust to the idea of marriage. But the last three weeks in Devonshire, rambling over the woods and fields, had very nearly felt like a gift. Anthony had gone with him some days. It was the first time that Anthony had begun to feel like his brother, not his responsibility. The boy had even cracked a few jests. It was little wonder Anthony seemed so popular with his friends, even though Thorington rarely saw that side of him — he had a wicked sense of humor when he forgot that Thorington controlled his purse strings.

They hadn't discussed anything of importance. But at least their silences had been easy.

They might never be easy again.

He shoved his wet hair out of his eyes and looked out the window at the view Anthony had spurned. It was good land, with a solid house and productive tenants. Anthony needed that. He would be a good man someday — the seeds of it were already there, even though he was too young for such a responsibility. But Thorington had been even younger when he had begun to raise his siblings. Anthony would grow into it.

Thorington would see to it that he had the chance to be more than just a rumored bastard with no income. Even if Anthony hated him for it.

His valet returned then. Thorington dressed for dinner as though preparing for battle. Anthony might not want Maidenstone Abbey, but Thorington would hand it to him on a platter if he had to.

And if Callista Briarley was the key to the kingdom, he'd hand her to him as well.

CHAPTER FOUR

At a quarter past four, Thorington stood outside one of Maidenstone's drawing rooms and willed himself to focus. The mantle he wore in public — his identity as the Duke of Thorington — was something he could slip into effortlessly. There had been a time, years earlier, when he had just been Gavin. Now, he knew how to command a room, how to fill it with his presence until others were dazzled by the show he gave them.

He would dazzle everyone. They would only see the Duke of Thorington, as cool and imperturbable as always. None of them knew about the small stack of letters awaiting him when he'd arrived — the first tentative requests for payment from his many and varied creditors, forwarded by his business manager with a rather worried note. None of them knew that he had very nearly shouted at his valet when the man had ruined a jacket Thorington couldn't afford to replace.

Thorington, for all his faults, didn't shout at servants.

He strode through the doors. The rest of the room fell away. The other suitors knew better than to get in his way.

He was the Duke of Thorington, and he would take what he sought.

He took in the scene like a predator looking for the most delicious prey. Rafe stood near the empty fireplace, surveying the room just as

Thorington did, although he was probably looking for liquor rather than heiresses. Anthony and the girls were just visible through the doors to the connecting drawing room, talking to a circle of Anthony's friends. Anthony wouldn't lack for company here, since half the families in the ton would have sent their sons in an attempt to win Maidenstone.

No sign of Callista, though. If he weren't so well-schooled, he would have grinned. Whenever she arrived, he suspected she would make an entrance.

But while he waited, he may as well pursue his agenda. He found his first quarry almost immediately. Lucretia sat near the opposite wall with Lady Maidenstone, under a portrait of Lord Maidenstone. It was a bad likeness. Thorington had seen the old earl in the House of Lords on numerous occasions, before his final series of illnesses over the last three years had confined him to Maidenstone. The painting had captured his hauteur, but not his charm.

The granddaughter beneath the painting had all the hauteur as well. Thorington hoped she had some of the charm. If Anthony didn't care for Callista, Lucretia was the next best option — Octavia, by all accounts, was far too scandalous. Anthony already had expensive tastes. A woman with a similarly destructive bent would ruin him.

He walked up to Lucretia, his pace leisurely, as though he knew she'd wait for him to say whatever he wished to say. "Lady Maidenstone, Miss Briarley," he said, giving them the honor of a small bow. "Maidenstone Abbey is exquisite. If you keep it, by some miracle, I hope to be invited to visit again."

Callista might have punched him for being unapologetically rude, but Lucretia was more reserved. "Thank you, your grace," she said, even as two spots of color bloomed on her cheeks. "I hope the party shall show it to its best advantage."

The girl positively reeked of pride. He might even smell it if he stepped closer, but he kept his distance. "I've no doubt it will show to advantage," he said. "Such a prize would tempt anyone, no matter what they must marry to gain it."

It was beyond rude of him to say such a thing. But he wanted to see whether she had backbone, and insults were the quickest way to reveal it.

She drew herself up. "The Briarleys are a proud and ancient house, your grace — one that any family in England should aspire to join."

"Is that true, Lady Maidenstone?" he asked her companion. "Are the Briarleys a good match?"

Lady Maidenstone had watched him, fascinated, throughout this exchange. She shrugged. "Lord Maidenstone's pedigree was never in question."

The girl could have been a diplomat with that kind of answer. He smiled. "Unfortunately, it's not the Briarley pedigree that any of us are here for. I wish you good fortune at this party, Miss Briarley — provided it doesn't conflict with my own."

Lucretia's flushed cheeks and bright eyes were pretty enough. But Anthony was right — she was provincial. Her dress, her hair, even the room she greeted them in — it was all too perfect, as though she'd seen a fashion plate and copied it exactly rather than letting her own sense of style prevail. Anthony would prefer a girl who set the fashions of the day, not one who slavishly followed them.

But he observed her potential, looking her up and down in a cool, distant sort of way. She might make an interesting wife for someone, someday, if she gained a bit of humor and lost of a bit of stiffness.

She wasn't his problem. A few moments of conversation had already told him all he needed to know. Unless Anthony's tastes changed, Lucretia wasn't the heiress who would save them.

As he returned his gaze to her face, her back stiffened further — how, when it already seemed close to snapping, he couldn't begin to guess. But she took a deep breath and looked him dead in the eyes. "Would you care to take a turn on the balcony before dinner, your grace? I find I'm rather too warm at the moment."

That set him back, unexpectedly, on his heels. No proper woman would ask him, a man they all believed was capable of compromising innocents, to take a turn on the balcony with her.

Had he missed some clue about her? Lucretia didn't have the look of a fortune-hunter or a social climber. She was too forthright — too forthright for flirtation, or any of the other tricks Ariana had used. But from the way her hand fluttered to her stomach, as though adding support to her diaphragm as she held her breath, he sensed her nerves.

And a dangerous chasm opened up at his feet.

He took a step back from her, instinctually. But even though he could say the most appalling things to the nicest individuals, he still felt a twinge of remorse when her eyes flickered.

"You wouldn't want to walk with me, Miss Briarley," he warned. "I have a reputation."

"Yes, I know," she said, even though she shouldn't have acknowledged it. "Lady Maidenstone, will you accompany us?"

Lady Maidenstone leaned in and whispered something to Lucretia. Lucretia shook her head sharply and stood up, holding her hand out until the girl took it. When Lady Maidenstone finally gave in, Lucretia turned to Thorington expectantly.

There was nothing for it. He escorted the women from the room, knowing that every eye followed them but acting supremely unconcerned by that fact. But as soon as they were through the French doors and standing far enough from the open windows to avoid eavesdroppers, he turned back to Lucretia.

"I should warn you, Miss Briarley, that if you think to trap me into marriage, I shall refuse to offer for you. You'll be ruined if you attempt it."

Lucretia's mouth dropped open. "Do you really think me capable of that?"

Thorington shrugged. "I think most people are capable of most anything, given the right pressure. You are under pressure, are you not?"

She exchanged a glance with Lady Maidenstone. The blonde gave her a speaking glare before turning away from them to look out over the formal gardens. She didn't leave them unchaperoned, but it was clear she wanted no part in whatever Lucretia planned.

Lucretia sighed. "I wouldn't trap you. But I'll admit that I would like to marry you. Would you consider offering for me?"

Thorington, for once, was outflanked. "I beg your pardon, Miss Briarley?"

She turned to face him. The sunlight in her eyes showed he hadn't cowed her. Instead, she was determined, even though there was something in her face that suggested she'd taken a strong dislike to him. He'd heard enough about her to understand her desire to save Maidenstone for herself. But the purely mercenary set of her mouth, so unusual for a sheltered woman of her age and class, was a shock.

"You may ask me for my hand as though I hadn't offered it, if you prefer," she said. "I know some men would take offense at being offered for. But I've heard you aren't stiff with tradition."

"I am flattered," he said. "But I've no wish for a bride."

"Even if it brought you enough money to save your estate?"

"My estate isn't in any danger."

He said it easily enough. But Lucretia didn't seem convinced. "You asked for an invitation to this party, which must mean you need to marry one of us. What I've read about you suggests you've had a run of bad luck. And you were the only guest whose correspondence from his business manager preceded him. Marry me and your luck will change."

"I make my own luck," Thorington said. "Marrying you isn't in the cards."

She looked up at him, shading her eyes with her hand. She looked as young as she was for a moment — only twenty-three, and a rather sheltered twenty-three. He didn't have a conscience, but he had enough imagination left to speculate about her — about how her upbringing, and too much time with the irascible Earl of Maidenstone, might make her too bold in some ways, too innocent in others.

But helping her wasn't his plan, unless Anthony decided she was the one for him.

She still hadn't spoken. He shifted his weight and tried for a smile. "I would eat you alive, my dear. Find a boy who will worship you. Any number of guests at this party would fit the bill."

She dropped her hand and shook her head. "They are mostly ineffectual or incompetent. Maidenstone needs someone stronger than that."

"And your needs?"

"I need Maidenstone," she said.

Lucretia didn't embellish her statement. That flinty look was back. If she was too bold for her own good, it came from a vast reservoir of determination. And all her determination was focused on Maidenstone, to the exclusion of all else.

"I wish you happy with the man who may help you to save it," he said, more gently than he was usually capable of. "But I am not the one for you."

Lucretia sighed. She looked beyond him, toward the house that loomed behind him. A shadow of emotion moved over her face, passing so quickly that he wouldn't have seen it had he not been observing her closely.

And he wouldn't have recognized it if he didn't feel the same need.

"I can't lose," she said, almost to herself. "I mustn't."

Lady Maidenstone rejoined them. The girl had taken a few steps away from them during Lucretia's attempt to proposition him, but she must have heard everything. She took Lucretia's hand. "Come inside, dear," she said, sounding older than Thorington knew her to be. She had glared at Lucretia before, but now she was soft, sympathetic. "We shall find someone better able to appreciate your virtues."

He stayed outside as they returned to the party. For a moment, he considered the idea of marrying Lucretia and giving Callista to Anthony — if Rafe would consent to marry Octavia, they were guaranteed to win Maidenstone Abbey.

But he dismissed that thought as soon as he had it. Rafe didn't need a wife — he needed something that would soothe his demons, and Thorington didn't think any of the Briarleys could do it for him. And Lucretia's dowry couldn't pull Thorington out of debt for more than a few months.

Still, he sympathized with her, if only a little. She couldn't have taken it well when her grandfather had set up this contest. She must have taken it even less well that she was forced to play the hostess for the gathering that might see her lose the house.

She was not his concern, though. He needed to capture Callista and convince Anthony to marry her — between Callista and Lucretia, there was no contest. Every fortune-hunter at Maidenstone would target Callista as soon as they saw her.

And he was enough of a fortune-hunter to know she wouldn't be pleased to be hunted.

CHAPTER FIVE

At a quarter to five, Callie stood outside one of Maidenstone's drawing rooms and willed herself to focus. Her hair, mostly dry after a bath that had felt woefully quick, was stuffed into the most secure chignon Mrs. Jennings was capable of. She wore her best white muslin, spangled with an intricate design in silver thread down the front and around the hem. Her dressmaker in Baltimore had cut it according to a fashion plate from one of Ackermann's 1811 volumes. She had never been invited to something to which she might have worn it in Baltimore, and she had looked forward to wearing it here.

But now, she took a deep breath as she stared at the carved door frame. She realized, suddenly, horribly, that if she let it out all at once, she might scream.

Between Lucretia and the man in the woods — a *duke*, because of course he was a duke, and not someone she could avoid for the duration of the party — she'd used up her bravado. She pictured herself walking into a grandly perfect drawing room, with a lot of grandly perfect people, wearing a dress that had once been perfect but was now at least two years out of fashion...

She had thought she was ready for whatever she would have to do to marry someone appropriate for her ends. But the reality of it — the crowd, the surroundings, the man from the woods — wasn't something she had prepared for.

She let her breath go slowly, through lips pursed tight enough to keep her scream inside. She wasn't going to let herself fall apart now.

She could do this. She had successfully managed a shipping company. She had run the British blockade. She had survived a sea battle.

Surely she could walk into a drawing room.

Surely she could ignore the way the man — the *duke* — preferred to look at her, as though luring her to her doom.

Callie walked through the open double doors. The sound in the room fell away, then renewed itself with more sibilant undercurrents.

She could tell herself that they weren't whispering about her. But she didn't believe it.

"Miss Callista Briarley," the butler announced in his stiffest, most disapproving tones.

The whispers doubled. They were a current that carried the tidings of her arrival into the farthest reaches of the connected rooms, rippling away from her, uncontrollable.

She instinctively started to twist her hands together in front of her, a defensive posture fit for a penitent instead of a conqueror. But she took a breath and touched the sapphire pendant at her neck instead. It was the bauble Captain Jacobs had promised her from *Crescendo*. It hadn't convinced her that privateering was a safe endeavor, but she was rather fond of it.

She was more daring than anyone in the room. Surely she could take another step.

She didn't know where she was going. But she couldn't hide in the corner. Nor could she avert her eyes from those who examined her as though she was a hideous curiosity in the most macabre curio cabinet.

Briarley contra mundum. She walked straight ahead, nodding politely at anyone who caught her gaze, proceeding as though she knew what she was doing. She passed through the first drawing room without anyone stopping to greet her.

The second drawing room was no better. The only people she recognized were the Duke of Thorington's siblings. She steeled herself to join them, hoping Lady Serena and Lady Portia, at least, would be friendly. They hadn't seemed friendly earlier, but anyone was better than Lucretia.

But before she reached them, a different party intercepted her.

"Miss Briarley," the first man exclaimed. He grabbed her by both arms and kissed first one cheek, then the other. "I had begun to fear for your health."

His greeting shocked her, but she reminded herself that this wasn't Baltimore and she didn't really know what to expect. So she smiled rather than pushing him away. "No need to fear for my health. I've a strong constitution."

"You very nearly missed the start of the party. I thought I'd given you enough time to reach us, but travel can be so unpredictable."

She didn't have any idea who the rest of the party were — another man, who had rolled his eyes as the first man had kissed her, and two beautiful brunettes in exquisite evening dresses. But Callie guessed who the man who'd greeted her must be. "Are you the Duke of Rothwell?"

He bowed. "At your service, cousin."

Another duke. Maidenstone Abbey was positively rotten with them. He seemed friendly enough, despite his overly proprietary treatment of her cheeks. He was taller than her, but not so tall as to be domineering. An uncharitable person might have said that his hair was red, but in the soft light of an English summer evening the auburn strands were charming rather than unfashionable.

After a pause, she curtsied for him. It was brief, but it was more than she'd done for Thorington. The Duke of Rothwell was family, after all, in a tenuous sort of way — he was her grandmother's brother's grandson, which made them second cousins. And she didn't have a dark urge to do him violence like she did with Thorington.

"You aren't much for ceremony, are you?" he asked.

"I only find it appealing when it's deserved, your grace," she said.

Everyone in his party laughed. To her ears, they sounded charmed rather than judgmental. She unbent another fraction of an inch.

"Spoken like a true daughter of the republic," the duke responded. "I can't abide ceremony myself. You must call me Ferguson if you don't wish to use my title."

She must have looked startled — such intimacy was usually reserved for only the closest friends. The woman next to him laughed. "Don't let yourself be shocked by him, Miss Briarley. He asks everyone to call him Ferguson."

The other man in their party sighed. "You can be shocked, Miss Briarley. I am shocked every day when I remember I am related to him — it must be worse for you, knowing you share bloodlines."

Ferguson didn't look offended in the slightest. "I forgot myself. Miss Briarley, allow me to present to you my wife, Madeleine." He gestured to the woman who had just spoken, smiling as though he couldn't help but do so when he said her name. "Her cousin is, unfortunately, Lord Salford, but I accept him as the cross I must bear. And he has somehow claimed the lovely Lady Salford as his new wife."

Madeleine, the Duchess of Rothwell, gave Callie a warm smile as she embraced her — again more affectionately than Callie expected, but genuine enough that Callie slowly began to relax. "I look forward to knowing you better, Miss Briarley. If you Americans can give us advice on how to overthrow our ducal masters, I would appreciate it."

There was a vaguely French lilt to her voice, but it was her warmth that made her irresistible. Ferguson pulled her close to him. "Careful, Mad," he warned her, with fake severity. "I think you like being a duchess too much to advocate treason against me."

"Madeleine should have considered treason before she agreed to marry you," Lord Salford said drily.

"It's lucky for us our wives didn't think too hard about their situations, or you never would have won Prudence," Ferguson retorted. "Begging your pardon, of course, Lady Salford."

Prudence, Lady Salford, shrugged. "There's no accounting for taste, as you like to say."

For all that they were insulting each other, it was clear that the four held each other in the highest esteem. They were older than her — the women were perhaps in their late twenties, and the men in their mid-thirties. Was it their age that made them so confident? Their titles? Their wealth?

Or was it the bond they shared — some connection that seemed strong and unassailable?

Callie didn't have that depth with anyone. She smiled and hoped her sudden jealousy didn't show in her eyes. "Are you truly responsible for this affair, Ferguson, or did someone steal your name for the invitations?" she asked.

She had heard of his name even before she'd received his invitation. Anyone who had stumbled across a newspaper from London the previous year knew his name. He had inherited the dukedom unexpectedly, after losing his father and brother in a carriage accident, and the gossip sheets from early 1812 were full of rumors about his family's insanity.

Ferguson lifted his hands in a gesture of innocence. "The party rests on my shoulders. But your grandfather deserves the blame."

Then Ferguson really was insane, even if the rumors had died down after he'd married. Having a party to settle the will was not a common endeavor. "There must have been a better way to divide the estate than this," she said.

"Your grandfather was eccentric in the extreme," Ferguson said.

"As is Ferguson," Salford muttered.

"Quiet," Ferguson said to him. "You'll ruin my reputation." Then he returned his attention to Callie. "As I was saying, your grandfather was eccentric in the extreme. If he could have, he'd have had you fight to the death for it. Said it was the family tradition."

"I've heard nothing to dispute that," Callie said. "There is a special symbol in the family Bible for Briarleys who died at the hands of a relative."

"Have you already sought out the library?" Ferguson asked. "You might find Salford tolerable if you like books so much."

"No, the Bible is in one of my trunks. My father stole it when he left England. He was rather fond of it."

Rather more fond of the family Bible than he was of most of the other things she'd had as a child. A keen tracker could have found them in Baltimore by tracing the dolls, dresses, and books Callie had been forced to leave behind in their hasty maneuvers across Europe and the West Indies. But Tiberius had always managed to keep the Bible with them.

"There won't be any blood shed when the estate passes this time. A duel would have settled it all faster, but we shall have to endure a party instead."

"I hope the party won't be a chore for all of you," Callie said.

Salford sighed. "House parties are rarely entertaining."

"Cheer up, Salford," Ferguson said. "If one of the ladies finds herself compromised, I'll let you do the honors and force the man to own up to his faults. You excel at it."

Salford brightened perceptibly.

"How likely is that to happen?" Callie asked suspiciously.

"You're quite a prize, Miss Briarley. I'd set the odds at one in three," Ferguson said.

Madeleine shushed him. "You'll scare her."

"Yes, but she should know the chances," Ferguson replied. "I only invited gentlemen, but they might be tempted to do something unforgivable in order to inherit Maidenstone."

"You can make it understood that anyone who compromises one of the Briarley heiresses won't win," Madeleine said.

"True," Ferguson mused. "But then again, if all the suitors are boring, how am I to decide which one would have most impressed Lord Maidenstone? The old earl probably would have preferred any man who took the estate by force."

"This sounds positively medieval," Callie interjected. "I don't want to be fought over or forced into anything."

"No one does," Ferguson said. "But there it is. You have three months to find the right consort before I judge them. The party won't last that long, but if you'd all settle this before I return to London in September, I'd be much obliged. There are plenty of potential husbands for you to choose from here. As long as the suitors behave themselves and don't kidnap you, of course."

Callie looked beyond him to the other people in the room. She didn't see anyone, immediately, who struck her fancy, let alone anyone who seemed capable of kidnapping. They all looked entirely dull.

But then, she should be looking for dull. Someone so dull that he wouldn't notice her running a privateering company under his nose, for example.

"Who would you recommend I marry?" she asked. "If you want speed, I'll take your advice on how to win."

Ferguson arched an eyebrow. "Attempting to influence the judge?"

"It's the best strategy I have at the moment," she said. "I'm at a disadvantage to Lucretia and Octavia."

"Lucretia and Octavia both abandoned London years ago, after Octavia's brother died — his death is what started this whole mess," Ferguson said. "But I wasn't in London when they were. I know them as little as I know you. So you aren't at a disadvantage with me, even if you're less knowledgeable about society than they are."

"Do you know where they are?" Callie asked as she looked around the rooms again. She didn't particularly care to see them, but she needed to better understand her competition. "I haven't seen Lucretia since I arrived, and I've yet to meet Octavia."

"Octavia hasn't arrived — I assume she will at some point, but I've heard no confirmation from her either way," Ferguson said. "Lucretia went out onto the terrace with Thorington and Lady Maidenstone. She's probably being compromised as we speak."

Thorington. "Is he such a devil, then?" she asked.

"The very worst," Ferguson assured her.

Salford flexed his fingers. "I'm ready to do the honors if you need someone to teach the man another lesson, Ferguson."

Prudence shushed them both this time. "You don't have anything to fear, Miss Briarley," she said. "But I would recommend not going about without a chaperone. Did someone accompany you downstairs?"

Captain Jacobs' wife had been the nearest thing to a chaperone she'd had, and the woman had refused to come to England. Callie suddenly felt uneasy. "She wasn't able to make the voyage."

"Did you travel alone?" Prudence asked.

"I had my maid. She was previously my governess."

Madeleine nodded. "Good enough, although not ideal. I shall chaperone you for the duration of the party."

"I'm sure I don't..." Callie began to say.

Ferguson interrupted her. "And I shall act as guardian."

"I'm sure I don't..." Callie started to say again.

"Someone must negotiate your marriage contracts," Ferguson said. "I shall be honored."

"I'm sure..."

Salford interrupted her this time. "You're taking on rather a lot, Ferguson. Guardian *and* judge of this contest? I know you like matchmaking, but this is a bit much even for you."

"It's no burden. And I can use the practice so that I may negotiate better contracts for my sisters when the time comes."

Callie finally cleared her throat. The sound was unladylike, but it stopped them from talking about her like she wasn't there. "I don't need your assistance," she said, when Ferguson finally looked at her. "I have negotiated my own contracts for the last five years. I'm capable of seeing to my own affairs."

"I'm sure you can, Miss Briarley. But I am your nearest male relative — or at least as near as any of your other cousins on your grandmother's side. You're my responsibility now."

He said it as though it was an immutable fact. And she was sure he meant it as something noble. To men like him, everything was their responsibility.

Even if she had dreams that she was perfectly capable of achieving on her own.

But she couldn't achieve those dreams if she was transported for assaulting a duke.

Before she could do something regrettable to the man who would decide whether she won Maidenstone, Thorington stepped through one of the open French doors. He was alone. If he'd compromised Lucretia on the terrace, there were no screams or tears to indicate it.

She saw him an instant before Thorington saw her. But then he met her gaze unerringly, as though he had known exactly where to look for her. Had he seen her through the window, or did he just always know where to find his prey?

She dropped her gaze, discouraging him. But he joined them anyway. "Miss Briarley," he murmured, nodding at her. "You should know better than to converse with dukes and duchesses."

Ferguson's eyes turned cold. "Thorington. I didn't expect to see you here."

He said it as though Thorington really was the devil himself. Thorington nodded at him, utterly composed. "Rothwell. Duchess. Lord and Lady Salford. You all look well."

They all stared at him. Finally, Salford nodded. "Thorington. Good to see you again."

He sounded like he wasn't sure he meant it. Callie didn't understand the undercurrents, but the chill would freeze her if she stayed there.

"I can't seem to help but stumble across dukes and duchesses, can I?" she said to Thorington. "I'd rather find an honest farmer or ship captain."

"I ran out of invitations before we sank that low on the guest list, Miss Briarley," Ferguson said. "Besides, Madeleine will tell you dukes aren't so bad. Thorington excluded, of course."

His tone was completely friendly to her, but his comment about Thorington had a ring of truth to it. Thorington ignored it and offered her his arm. "I'm sure you'd prefer to converse with my sisters. You're of an age, I believe."

She looked past him to where his sisters sat with their heads bent together, watching them. "I don't believe they are interested in conversing with me."

"Don't pay Thorington any attention," Ferguson said. "His siblings are all charming enough, but he's not a candidate for your hand."

Thorington gave him a cool, assessing stare. "It was my understanding the ladies could choose whomever they wish for this contest."

"They can. But I can choose whomever I wish as the winner."

Neither of them said anything more. Anything else might have been an insult too great to remain unanswered. In any physical contest between them — whether it was swords, pistols, or fisticuffs — Callie guessed that Thorington would come out the winner. He wasn't substantially bigger than Ferguson, having only a couple of inches on him in height. But his cruel determination made him far more dangerous.

Still, he seemed to know when it wasn't in his interests to force a battle. He nodded instead. "I wish you luck with your meddling, Ferguson. You do excel at it."

Salford snorted at that, but managed to cover it with a cough.

Thorington walked away and joined his siblings. Lady Portia, Lady Serena, and Lord Anthony didn't look like him at all — they might have been three strangers who'd drawn lots and then been forced into his company. Serena, at least, had his eyes, if Callie remembered correctly from their earlier introduction — bright, inquisitive green, but topped with blonde hair rather than brown. But Portia's red hair and Anthony's blue eyes matched nothing about Thorington.

When he reached them, the girls pulled their heads away from each other as though he wouldn't notice that they had been gossiping. Anthony scowled at something Thorington said to him. They all looked mutinous, not amused.

Callie should have been appalled. His siblings, Ferguson, the other members of Ferguson's party — none of them seemed to like Thorington very much.

But the memory of his green eyes, and the realization that he didn't laugh very often but had laughed for her, still dazzled her.

"Do not pay him any mind, Miss Briarley," Ferguson said. "He's not suitable."

Ferguson's tone made her itch. "If I decide he is suitable, though, can I choose to marry him?"

All four were silent, as though the very idea made them vastly uncomfortable. Finally, Ferguson shook his head. "You can marry any other man at this party. You can even marry a farmer, if you can find one. But if you marry Thorington, you'll be condemning yourself to a life of misery. And I won't reward you for it with this estate, even if he fits your grandfather's ideals."

Where Thorington never seemed to laugh, the lines around Ferguson's eyes suggested that he always did. But he wasn't laughing now.

And Callie was left to wonder how Thorington had earned his enmity — and how she was going to follow through with her plan to win Maidenstone while Thorington's gaze followed her.

CHAPTER SIX

"You're holding the stick like you plan to club someone over the head," Rafe said as he walked into the billiard room after dinner.

"I must have known you planned to interrupt me," Thorington said.

Rafe shrugged. "If you're in one of your moods, you shouldn't have come to the billiard room. Not my fault you didn't seek solitude somewhere more private."

Thorington raised an eyebrow. Usually that gesture was as effective as slamming a door — particularly when accompanied by an icy, uninviting silence. But rather than leave, Rafe leaned against the wall and smirked at him, as though he knew the exact reason for Thorington's ire.

That was the problem with these blasted house parties. There was no solitude anywhere. He could hide in his room, but the only entertainment waiting there was the stack of letters from his creditors.

And hiding never suited his purposes. He had to stay, to watch, to further his goals.

But staying in the drawing room and watching Callista examining the other men like so much breeding stock made his heart cold, even as it made his blood hot.

"Make yourself useful and play with me, if you won't leave me alone," Thorington said.

"Are we putting money on the outcome?" Rafe asked as he selected a billiard-stick from the rack on the wall.

"Your pot of nothing for my pot of nothing? Not much excitement there."

"Better than going back to the drawing room," Rafe said. He shuddered in an entirely exaggerated fashion. With his flair for drama, one might have thought that Rafe, not Portia, was the bastard their mother had gotten off a Covent Garden actor.

But Rafe shared Thorington's blood. And Thorington couldn't dispute Rafe's assessment of the drawing room. Dinner had been an interminable affair. The food had been as delicious as could be expected when the kitchens were too far from the dining room, and the flowers Lucretia had arranged were an inspired touch. But all of Lucretia's preparations couldn't save the conversation from being insipid.

Nor did the flowers block the sight of Callista, sitting with the Duke of Rothwell. *That* corner of the dining room had enjoyed itself, even if no one else had. Thorington had been stuck between Lucretia and Lady Maidenstone — unpleasant, to say the least, since he had rejected Lucretia's suit. There hadn't been time for her to change the seating arrangements. He suspected that he would spend the next dinner in some hellish position, stuck between whatever poor neighborhood spinsters Lucretia had dug up to balance the table. Watching Callista with one of his sworn enemies, too far away to know what he said to her, required something far stronger than the claret in his glass to ignore.

Lucretia and Lady Maidenstone weren't inclined to talk to him. But that only made it easier for him to hear Callista's laughter — true laughter, the kind women in the ton were too well-bred to give voice to. Lucretia had made a whispered joke about Callista's American manners to the man on her other side. The dandy had snickered.

Thorington hadn't punched anyone since a youthful brawl at Cambridge, but he was tempted to relearn the skill.

He put Callista out of his mind and arranged the balls on the table. "Youth before talent," he said, gesturing Rafe toward the table.

"Don't be an arse," Rafe said amiably.

But he took the chance to make the first shot. Not that it helped him; Rafe was no longer much for billiards. The ball didn't fall his way.

Thorington lined up his stick. He saw the shot he wanted to make, saw how the ball would roll into the pocket. He couldn't control his fortunes. But he could still shoot billiards.

Or so he thought. Just as he pulled back, Rafe said, "Callista Briarley is something, isn't she?"

Thorington flinched, just enough to send the stick knocking into the table and the ball going wide.

"Unsporting," he said.

"You know I'm no billiards player," Rafe said.

Thorington watched Rafe line up his stick. His hands shook, just slightly, but enough to send the ball wide of its target.

Thorington nearly said that they didn't have to play billiards. His nerves weren't steady enough to watch Rafe's shaking hands, to wonder whether there was something that might be done to steer him away from the path to ruin.

But Rafe had his pride. And Thorington didn't have a plan to save him. So he picked up his stick again.

Rafe didn't wait for Thorington to set up his shot before pursuing his line of conversation. "How many days do you think it will take to marry Anthony off?"

Thorington didn't respond. He took his shot instead, sending a ball careening into the pocket. "The boy will come around soon enough," he said as he moved around the table. "If I am forced to stay for the entire month of this house party, I will not be a pleasant companion for any of you."

"Are you ever?"

"You wound me," Thorington said, lining up his next shot.

His brother laughed. "If I live to see the day when anything wounds you, I'll probably die from the shock of it."

Thorington aimed.

"I saw the way you watched her at dinner," Rafe said.

Thorington missed.

"Do you have a point in mentioning her, other than to distract me?" he asked.

Rafe smiled. "Seems to be working, doesn't it?"

Distractions might ruin Thorington's game, but they couldn't improve Rafe's. He missed again, with a muttered curse.

Thorington should have put his brother out of his misery, but he stood away from the table, leaning on his stick. "Shall we finish your discussion before I take my shot? Wouldn't want to distract you from my victory."

"Do you wish to discuss her?" Rafe asked.

"No."

Rafe tossed his stick back onto the rack and tugged the bellpull instead. "Then we should discuss her. Over whisky, I think."

Thorington stayed at the table, dissecting the angles, ignoring how Rafe's too-eager tug of the bellpull seemed to tug at his own heart. "There is nothing to discuss."

There wasn't. Callista would be Anthony's. That was the beginning, middle, and end of the story.

He just had to convince her. And Anthony.

And himself.

His shot went wide again. Why did the memory of her standing in the forest, in a skirt that belonged on the rag pile, choose that moment to return to him?

Why did he *like* that memory?

Why did he imagine stripping her out of that skirt? That she would laugh as he slid his hands over her hips, eager, happy? That she would look up at him with those infinitely dark eyes, eyes that would hold some secret promise for him? And then those eyelashes would flutter closed, and she would lean up so he could kiss…

No. Not the plan. Since Rafe had abandoned the game, he aimed another shot, wildly, inelegantly. The ball careened into the side of the table and launched itself over it, landing on the carpeted floor with a thud.

"I see your luck isn't improving," a voice said from the doorway.

Thorington would recognize that voice anywhere. He didn't bother to look up as he retrieved the ball from the carpet. "Come to gloat, Salford?" he asked. "It's unbecoming of you."

"I'm in an unbecoming mood," Salford said as he walked into the room. "I didn't expect to see you at Maidenstone Abbey. This doesn't seem to be your brand of mischief."

Thorington shrugged, placing the ball back on the table. "I didn't expect to see you, either. Shouldn't you and Prudence be setting up house somewhere?"

They had married only three months earlier. Salford sighed. "My sister and her husband show no signs of vacating my London townhouse. And anyway, Prudence wanted to see Devonshire. I told her that Stonehenge is more impressive than the ancient rocks here, but she insisted."

Thorington had said the same thing to Callista. He lined up another shot. "If you let her manage you like that, you'll never control her."

"I can manage her a damn sight better than you could have," Salford said mildly. "Not that I need to, since she loves me, etcetera. But I forget myself. I didn't come to gloat."

Thorington didn't miss this time. The ball fell into the pocket. "If you think I'm jealous, you should disabuse yourself," he drawled. "I wish you very happy, you know. Prudence was nothing but a convenience for me."

Rafe coughed. "Shall I leave this charming reunion undisturbed?"

"No," Thorington and Salford said simultaneously.

They had been friends before — the best of friends, when they were both pursuing their studies at Cambridge. Neither of them should have been there; Thorington didn't have the money for it, and Salford's father wanted him to give up his books and learn how to manage the estate instead. But they'd shared a love of history that had fueled any number of late-night conversations.

Granted, whisky and women had fueled those conversations too.

Until the night they'd found an Egyptian dagger that was reputed to grant wishes. Thorington had accepted the consequences that came with his wish — the security for his family had been worth the effects of marrying Ariana. But the curse's impact on Salford had been worse, and he'd spent the next decade searching for a way to break it.

In May, he'd finally found it.

And then he'd married Prudence — the woman Thorington had just decided to marry, in a purely mercenary scheme. By all accounts, they'd had a blissful summer together. In the meantime, Thorington's fortune had drained away.

So it was little wonder Thorington wasn't pleased to see his former friend at Maidenstone.

"Have you come to plague me anew?" he asked Salford. "Believe me when I say I don't need any further annoyances at the moment."

A footman interrupted them. Salford waited while Rafe ordered whisky, then shut the door behind the departing servant. "As I said, I didn't expect to find you here," Salford said. "But I'm glad to see you. I thought I might help."

"Help?" Thorington laughed. "Do you have another cursed dagger in your possession? I'll buy it on credit — rather low on funds at the moment."

He wouldn't have told anyone else about his finances, but Salford knew where he'd gotten all his money, and so Salford could guess that he'd lost it just as quickly.

Salford shook his head. "Cannot help you there, I'm afraid. But if it's a loan you need, I could provide one."

Thorington's grip tightened around the stick. "I don't need your charity, Salford."

"I said a loan, not a gift. But you'll get a better rate from me than you will from the usurers in London."

Thorington had never dealt with the money-mongers, even in his leanest days at Cambridge before his father had died. He'd come close when his oldest sister, Cynthia, had made her debut. Their father was still alive at the time, but he couldn't — or wouldn't — give her a dowry. Thorington had realized she'd never marry well without it.

But before he could borrow the money, and ruin himself in the process, he'd found the dagger. It had saved him from ruin, given Cynthia and Pamela the chance to make brilliant matches, given his other siblings every comfort...

He couldn't have saved those who depended on him without the curse. And he couldn't borrow enough money to make everything better now.

"It's good of you to offer," he said. "But the situation is too far gone for that."

Salford paused when the door opened. The footman deposited the whisky, and Rafe made quick work of pouring glasses for all three of them as the servant left. Salford waited until his glass was in hand before speaking again.

"I wish you luck, old friend," he said, raising his glass to

Thorington. "But my offer will always stand."

"Gav doesn't want luck," Rafe said, sipping his whisky. "He wants to end it all."

Salford's gaze turned sharp. "What do you mean by 'end it all'?"

"I won't commit suicide, if that's what you mean," Thorington said.

Rafe shrugged. "Near enough. Leaving us all here while you wallow in your poverty abroad sounds like a slow form of it, doesn't it?"

He considered the glass in Rafe's hand. His brother knew something about slow deaths.

Salford, meanwhile, didn't know Rafe well enough to catch that subtlety. He was still frowning. "There must be a way to right your estate even without the curse."

Thorington tossed back his whisky. "It's exceedingly doubtful. If you want to help me, convince Ferguson that Anthony is the best match for one of the Briarley heiresses. I can't save myself, but I can set up my siblings so that they are comfortable."

"Ferguson isn't easily persuaded. Especially by me."

"He seems to have warmed to you," Thorington said. "Help him warm to my brother."

Salford sighed. But he eventually nodded. "I'll do what I can. But the boy needs to charm Ferguson himself."

"Anthony's charming enough," Thorington said.

Rafe snorted. "I've changed my mind. You'll have better luck trying to find an Italian shepherdess."

His comment broke the dark mood. And for the next hour, Thorington enjoyed something close to congeniality with them.

But the odd, rather pleasant feeling of enjoying himself wasn't enough to fully distract him from his purpose. And so while they drank whisky and played billiards — the former well, the latter terribly — he schemed.

He had to secure Callista for his brother before anyone else won her affections.

And there was no time like tonight to start.

CHAPTER SEVEN

When she heard the scratching, she thought it was a rat.

"Of course there would be rats," she muttered to herself. Lucretia had probably instructed the servants to release a plague ship's worth of rats into the Tudor wing — it seemed like something her cousin would do.

But Callie had seen enough rats in the dockyards to be unconcerned. And anyway, it hadn't awoken her. Despite her exhaustion, her cot wasn't comfortable enough to lull her racing mind into sleep. Still, she turned toward the wall and tried to think of something else.

There wasn't anything better to think of than the rat. What else should she think about? Whether her ships had been captured yet? Why Lucretia seemed to hate her? Why Thorington was so intriguing?

Definitely not Thorington. Never mind that she'd sensed him watching her throughout dinner.

Never mind that some perverse part of her wished she'd been seated next to him.

It was good that she hadn't been. She might have tried to catch his gaze, to see if she could surprise a laugh out of him. She might have hung on his words, waiting to see whether he said something titillating. He was the most aggravating man at the party — but he was also the most interesting.

She was being a ninnyhammer. Thorington was the devil. And Ferguson had made it clear that she couldn't win Maidenstone with him at her side.

She punched her pillow and vowed to sleep.

The scratching stopped — to be followed, a moment later, by the door handle turning. Only a servant would enter like that. "Did you bring me a warming pan, Mrs. Jennings?" she asked, still facing the wall.

Compared to the sweltering heat of Baltimore, Devonshire was frigid. But it wasn't Mrs. Jennings who answered. "If it's warmth you need, I might be of service."

Thorington. His voice, dark and commanding, was already something she recognized instinctively, different as it was from all the hesitant second sons and half-grown whelps she'd met that night.

He stepped inside and shut the door before she could gather her thoughts. "Why are you here?" she asked, sitting up and pulling the covers around her.

"Still not willing to call me 'your grace'?" he responded.

That winnowed out the pleasant feelings and brought her anger to the fore. "I'd sooner toss you into the harbor and declare independence again than do so," she said.

He smiled. "Willful wench. Your strength might be commendable were it not set against me."

She wasn't frightened — in fact, if she were being honest, she was vastly intrigued — but she knew better than to encourage him. "My strength will remain set against you. Now take your leave before we're ruined."

Thorington placed his candle on the table and pulled the rickety chair forward. "I do not plan to ruin you at the moment. I came with a business proposition."

Callie knew enough of the world to guess what he meant. A

business proposition from a man of his status could only mean one thing. "I won't be your mistress, no matter how much you offer."

His frown was visible even in the shifting darkness. "I wouldn't dishonor you like that."

"What else would you offer?" she asked. "I can't think of any other business between us. And Ferguson made it clear you're not to be trusted. So you must be here to ruin me."

Thorington sighed. "I am disappointed to find you have the morality of the middle classes. But you're not screaming yet, so there's that. I may be able to make an aristocrat of you after all."

She gaped at him. Why had she wanted to sit by him at dinner? The man was mad. No, he was worse than mad. He was entirely amoral. And she was even more so — she was too wrapped up in delicious anticipation of his next move to be offended.

"Of course, I cannot make an aristocrat of you if you're incapable of speech," he said, examining his cuticles.

She couldn't let him know how much he intrigued her. "I find I dislike you too much to speak to you."

He laughed. "Charming. You and Lord Anthony have something in common. Marriages have succeeded with less."

The speed with which he changed topics kept her off guard. "Lord Anthony?" she repeated.

"My brother. Similar to all the rest you met today, but distinguished by his *au courant* rose-colored waistcoat. Don't judge him for it. He's quite proud of the thing, for reasons that remain unfathomable to me."

"I remember him," she said. "But what do you mean about marriage?"

"He is the proposition. I want you to marry him."

She gaped at him for another moment. Then her eyes narrowed. "I wish the scratching at my door had really been a rat."

"You can't do better than Anthony. He is eminently eligible as a match."

"And you aren't?" she asked.

She regretted saying it as soon as the words were out of her mouth. But he didn't seem to take any meaning from it. He leaned back in the chair, with a creak that could bring every Tudor ghost down on their heads. "I am not interested in marrying."

She rubbed her fingers against her temples, trying to stave off the first throb of a headache. She forgot that she had been holding the covers up around her until Thorington cleared his throat. "No need to tempt me, Miss Briarley."

"I'm sure you won't do anything you don't wish to do," she said, leaving the covers bunched around her waist as she continued to massage her temples. "With your complete disregard for others, you're likely incorruptible."

"That is true," he said. "Allow me to explain my position. I find you interesting, albeit untutored, and I wish to save you from the clamoring hordes. Better to arrange a marriage now than risk being caught up and ruined by someone else."

"Is it really so likely? Ferguson put the odds of me being ruined at this party at one in three," Callie said.

"Ferguson is a meddling fool," Thorington said, with an oddly amiable voice for such a statement. "But he knows the marriage mart. I'd guess his odds are accurate."

"You claim you don't want to ruin me, and yet you're in my room unescorted. Your logic is senseless."

"You're utterly alone up here. Anyone could ruin you if they knew where to find you. It only took me a guinea to buy the information from a footman, and I could have had it for less if I hadn't had to buy his silence as well. Take it from one who knows — it's better to arrange your own fate than to wait for someone to trap you."

"And you think I should arrange to share my fate with your brother?"

Thorington leaned forward again. His tone had been negligent, but the intent in his posture was obvious.

"Marry Anthony," he said softly, like a devil offering her a prize. "He has a good heart and a strong character. You won't find a better man at Maidenstone."

Thorington didn't sound much like a devil then. He sounded like he truly loved his brother. And she wondered, for a moment, how her own life would have been different if any of her brothers had survived infancy — if she had grown up with them, rather than with fuzzy memories of which foreign cities she'd lost them in.

Perhaps one of them would have taken care of her. But if one of them had survived, he would be the new master of Maidenstone, and Callie wouldn't be confronted with this mess.

As usual, she had to solve this for herself. No one was coming to her rescue.

She inhaled, but she didn't scream. Instead, she leaned forward and met Thorington's gaze.

"I'll consider marrying your brother. But only if you agree to my conditions."

*   *   *

"What do you mean by 'conditions'?" Thorington asked.

He watched Callista draw herself together. The girl had a backbone. If she were anyone else, she would have crumbled under his regard as soon as he'd pulled a chair up next to her bed.

He'd grant that she amused him. That was all he could afford to grant. Any other emotion he might have examined — any memory of the swell of her breasts beneath thin linen, or thought of how that saucy mouth might feel wrapped around…

He had enough control to squash that thought before it finished.

"I want to retain full control of my father's shipping company. And Anthony must offer for me himself."

Both conditions surprised him. "I'll indulge you for a moment," he said, dropping into a drawl and feigning disinterest. "Why do you want to retain full control of a shipping company, of all things?"

She shrugged. "My father built it himself. I wouldn't want to see it neglected. Give me that as my portion and Anthony can have the rest of my fortune."

He thought her disinterest was just as false as his. No woman would demand a shipping company just because her father built it.

"You would rather stake your security on a shipping company than on a pile of money? Your managers could leave you with nothing."

"I shall manage it myself," she said. "I already do."

"Intriguing," he murmured, still sounding bored even though she'd shocked him. "I didn't know the Americans had grown so lax in their business habits in the years since our countries parted ways."

He'd said it to annoy her. Annoyed people usually became careless, and carelessness usually encouraged them to say too much. But Callista smiled sweetly. "If my father hadn't died on another one of his larks, I might have had time to become the featherbrained female you men seem to prefer. Unfortunately, I had to provide for myself."

Thorington rubbed his hand over his mouth to cover his sudden smile. It wouldn't do to show amusement. She might think she was gaining an advantage. "And when you win Maidenstone Abbey — what provision will you make for that?"

She shrugged, sublimely indifferent to the prospect of inheriting one of the grandest estates in Britain. "Anthony can use it however he desires, so long as I retain the shipping company and my Baltimore house."

"Will you run away to America at the first opportunity?"

"I don't plan to. If the war progresses badly, I may not be able to return at all. But this is an arranged marriage. I'm sure Anthony wouldn't mind my occasional absences."

Thorington had a brief moment of misgiving. Anthony wouldn't want a loveless match, even if Thorington thought it would be safer for him.

But it was Anthony's safety, not his heart, that mattered. "You will have to discuss Baltimore with Anthony," he hedged.

"I don't care so much about living in Baltimore," she said, giving up the point more quickly than Thorington had expected. "But Anthony must agree to support me in whatever I decide to do with my shipping endeavors."

"That's far more to ask than just letting you have your way," Thorington pointed out.

"There have been occasions when I could have made a better deal if a man had seemed to be at the helm," Callista said slowly. "But Anthony won't have to trouble himself with it. I just need a *roi fainéant* on occasion to sign the papers."

A king with no power. Callista was strong-willed; she could turn most men into *rois fainéants*, and they would happily yield just to win a smile from her.

The thought didn't make Thorington happy — not for Anthony's sake, and not for Callista's. She deserved something better than an empty marriage and the power of her husband's name.

But winning Maidenstone for Anthony was more important than what Callista deserved.

"Very well," Thorington said. "You have my word."

She exhaled. It was a sound that signified victory, more subtle than a trumpet on a battlefield but no less audible when he listened for it. "Then if Anthony offers for me, we have an agreement," she said.

"Anthony is capable of making pretty speeches when he feels so inclined. I'm sure he'll make you quite happy."

He was lying through his teeth. Anthony still might not accept Callista. If that happened, they would need to leave Maidenstone and look for an heiress elsewhere. And finding an heiress in the dog days of August would be as difficult as making his fortune back by working in a lead mine. Unless he wanted to sell Anthony to an industrialist or a banker, someone looking to advance a cow-faced daughter in society, he needed Anthony to accept Callista as soon as possible.

But at least he'd gained Callista's acceptance. That gave him time to work on Anthony, without worrying that she would marry someone else in the next few days.

Callista drew her knees up to her chest. "This isn't about happiness. If it was, Anthony would have come here murmuring love words rather than sending you. But I thank you for pretending it figures into your calculations."

A knife dug into his side. "I cannot promise you happiness, Miss Briarley. But I vow you'll be safe. And I'll do whatever it takes to help you win Maidenstone."

She laughed. "I'm under no illusions that you're doing this for me."

The knife twisted. She was magnificent. Why would she accept a deal like this, when she deserved a love match? Her heart was too big, her smile too ready, her eyes too bright, for something as mercenary as what he proposed.

But she had agreed to it. And as soon as she had Anthony's ring on her finger, she wouldn't be Thorington's problem.

"Sleep well, Miss Briarley," he said. "And shove the chair under the doorknob if you cannot lock the door. We wouldn't want some foul fortune-hunter sneaking up here in the dead of night."

"No one could be as audacious as you," she said.

She smiled as she said it. Thorington ignored the smile. He focused instead on how good she would be for Anthony, on how important her dowry was for their family. He could find a pretty smile in any brothel in London, as long as he wasn't too particular on the number of teeth.

But he didn't sleep well that night. And it wasn't victory that made him restless.

CHAPTER EIGHT

It took fifteen minutes for Callie to find the breakfast room. If she inherited Maidenstone, her first task would be to commission a map of the entire house. It seemed likely that there were rooms no one had entered in living memory.

It wasn't quite seven in the morning when she finally stumbled into a room that contained foodstuffs. She had thought she might have it to herself. Mrs. Jennings, with a sniff of disapproval, had made it clear that Callie's early hours would be deemed unfashionable, even in the country. But she found Lord Anthony there, alone, with his head bowed.

She hovered at the door. He hadn't seen her yet. She could still leave.

But there was something about the contemplative way he pushed his eggs around his plate that interested her. She squared her shoulders and stepped into the room. "Good morning, Lord Anthony," she said. "It appears that we shall have another lovely day, doesn't it?"

He looked up when he heard her voice, coming to his feet in a gesture of respect. But if his reaction was polite, his eyes seemed disapproving. "Good morning to you as well, Miss Briarley. I did not expect to see you here."

"I cannot stand to stay in bed while the sun shines," she said. "Do you also arise earlier than most?"

"The ladies usually take their breakfasts on trays in their rooms," he said, ignoring her attempt at conversation.

She hoped his comment was an observation rather than a mandate. She couldn't spend another minute in that tiny cell, especially when the memory of Thorington's presence still filled it. "I find my room too dark to properly enjoy my breakfast," she said. "May I join you?"

She had wondered how to interact with Anthony when she saw him next. It was one of the thoughts that had kept her awake long after Thorington had left her. But she hadn't expected that he would disapprove of her.

That disapproval wasn't a trick of the light, though. It rolled off of him like fog rushing over a headland. "I was just finishing. If you insist on staying, I cannot stop you."

Was it her imagination, or was there a 'yet' implied after that statement?

She picked up a plate. The sideboard held chafing dishes full of tempting selections — perhaps even more tempting than dinner the night before, since the dishes were better equipped to keep the food at the proper temperature.

"When I inherit Maidenstone, I shall have to retain the cook Lucretia's hired. Do you think he's French, or is he merely masquerading as a Frenchman?" she asked as she sat down.

He'd stayed standing while she served herself — it wouldn't be proper for him to sit until she did. But when she sat down with her plate, facing him with her back to the door, Anthony didn't move. And he didn't answer her question. He just stared at her as though he had been confronted with something that appalled him.

"Won't you join me?" she asked, gesturing at his unfinished plate. "It would be nice to converse with you."

Nice. Nice to converse with her future husband.

"I don't think it's proper for us to be alone together. Are you going to trick me into marrying you?"

Callie snorted. "We aren't hiding — anyone could join us. And I don't need to trick you, do I?"

"Why do you say that?" he asked.

She coughed. "I don't mean anything by it," she said, trying to recover. "Don't mind me — I rarely make sense before I've had my breakfast."

"He asked you, didn't he."

Anthony's voice was flat. Callie looked off to the side, not quite able to meet his eyes. "I thought you were in agreement," she said.

His hand clenched over the back of his chair. "When did he talk to you?"

"Last night."

She still watched his hand. His fist was the only sign of tension. His voice was calm, albeit cool. "And should I congratulate us on our good fortune?"

She finally met his eyes. "You should."

"Damn him," Anthony swore.

Callie carefully placed her fork on the table. "Do you not want to…accept our arrangement?"

Anthony finally took a seat. "What arrangement did he make? Did he already sign the papers?"

"No," she said, making a mental note to get a contract from Thorington before progressing further. "But the agreement won't be finalized until you offer for me yourself. He did say you are capable of pretty speeches."

"Did he?" Anthony shrugged. "He never listens to them."

That statement sounded resigned, not petulant. Anthony was three or four years younger than her, and the mix of bravado and uncertainty hadn't settled yet into whatever mature face he might wear someday. Callie appraised him like she might a ship — he had good lines, a good record, and enough opportunity for improvement that he would be worth an investment. In a few years, with the right woman, it was quite likely he would be a very good man.

He didn't make her heart swell. He didn't make her cheeks flush. He would be stable like a merchant ship, not swift and risky like a sloop or caravel.

But she needed safe, not sorry.

"I would listen," she said. "We can pretend that no arrangement exists, if that suits you. Then you can make your pretty speech whenever you desire."

She saw him smile for the first time. "There is no need for that, Miss Briarley. But I appreciate the offer."

"Are you sure?" she said. "I might prefer to listen to a pretty speech if it meant you wouldn't leave me to eat breakfast alone. How do you find Devon?"

His mercurial smile faded. "I still don't think you should be here."

"Are you really that proper?" she asked.

He nearly snorted. "I don't have to be. But with ladies it's different. Your reputation is all you have, really. I wouldn't want to cost you yours."

"Your brother doesn't seem to care for his. Do most people in the ton hold your view, or are they lax like him?"

Anthony laughed shortly. "Thorington is a duke. He doesn't have to care. But ask anyone else — they'll tell you the ton has no pity. And the lower your rank, the worse the risk. I must be more careful than Thorington is. And if you were to make a single social mistake, it would rapidly turn into complete disgrace."

She stabbed her fork into a slice of ham. "Are you concerned about my well-being? Or are you concerned that I'll embarrass you?"

He flushed. With his blond hair and fair skin, he couldn't hide his discomfort as his brother could. "Your conversation is too forthright for a lady."

Had no one ever been direct with him? "If it's merely a matter of learning some archaic rules, I can learn them well enough to avoid disgrace. But you must tell me what I should know."

"I am not a governess or a finishing school," Anthony said. "I haven't the first notion of what you should do. I merely recognize when you're not doing it — such as now."

She reminded herself that she needed safety, even if Anthony's judgment was the cost. "How should I learn it, then?"

"Find someone to teach you," he said, dismissal implied in his voice. "One of your cousins, perhaps."

"Why should I trust them? We are in competition for Maidenstone. They might tell me that all proper young ladies practice calisthenics on the front lawn in the nude, just to make me ineligible."

His smile returned, the one that made her think he might have some capability for humor buried beneath that starched cravat. "One of my sisters, then. Lady Portia and Lady Serena know their manners, even if they don't always use them."

"If I had known lessons were required, I would have asked for a better marriage settlement," she said.

He didn't take it or her conspiratorial smile as a joke. She saw a flash of steel in his eyes, just enough to make her wonder if he could someday turn into Thorington. "There won't be a marriage if you embarrass me in front of my friends."

When Thorington made a threat like that, she felt some odd sense of heat — some unwelcome but oddly appealing knowledge that she was dealing with a man rather than a boy. Perhaps Anthony hadn't mastered his tone yet. She only felt irritation, the kind that made her want to rebel rather than roll over.

But before she said something regrettable, Anthony's gaze flickered to a point over her head. "You're awake early," he said to whoever stood behind her.

"Not early enough," Thorington said.

There was that odd sense of heat.

Anthony scowled. "You should have sent a note informing me of my upcoming marriage."

Callie resolutely refused to turn around, but she could picture Thorington shrugging. "I decided to give you my felicitations in person."

"I'm not sure felicitations are in order," Anthony said. "Not until I know she's capable of behavior suitable for my wife. I told you I didn't want to marry an American."

Anthony hadn't even bothered to look at her when he said it. "May I also have the opportunity to assess whether you are capable of behavior suitable for a husband? I hadn't planned to marry a knob-kneed aristocrat," she said.

"Children," Thorington said sharply. "Mind your manners — anyone could walk by. If you cannot be civil, we must discuss something else."

Anthony stood up. "No need. I was leaving anyway."

Callie rose as well. "Please, stay. I'm sure the two of you would appreciate time alone together."

Anthony snorted. "I make it a point to never be alone with him. Harder for him to order me about if I'm not nearby."

She turned toward the door, but Thorington blocked her. He couldn't have slept any more than she had, but he looked perfectly composed and completely unruffled. "The two of you will marry even if I must toss you into a locked carriage bound for Gretna Green. Coming to an agreement here would be far more comfortable."

"She doesn't know the first thing about society," Anthony complained. "I could never host a house party with her, even if I did inherit Maidenstone. And if I become the Duke of Thorington someday, what kind of duchess would she make?"

"Rafe and I aren't dead yet, my boy. But since you asked my opinion so nicely..." He looked down at Callie. His quiet scrutiny should have unnerved her, but she was too mesmerized by the flash of humor in his eyes to be uncomfortable. "Miss Briarley would make the very best sort of duchess," he said.

That odd heat returned.

She dropped her eyes. "I've no desire to be a duchess. I want to marry a third son and run a shipping company."

"A *shipping company*?" Anthony asked.

He sounded like he had choked on something — probably his own pride. Thorington's lips thinned. "We'll discuss it later."

"No, I've a right to know what you've signed me up for. She wants to run a *shipping company*? She might as well say she wants to run a string of Cheapside brothels."

Callie drew herself up. "The company was respectable enough for my father, and he was the son of an earl. I can manage it just as well."

"An exiled son of an earl is a world apart from an unmarried granddaughter of an earl," Anthony shot back.

Thorington intervened. "Anthony, go to your room if you are incapable of being civil to Miss Briarley. Miss Briarley, a word?"

"Do you plan to explain to me what you meant when you claimed your brother is willing to marry me?" she asked sweetly. "Because I begin to believe that he was not entirely informed."

Thorington looked behind him, through the open door to the hallway beyond. "No. But if you don't wish to be rescued, I shall leave you here. A fortune-hunter would be happy to find you alone, I'm sure."

Callie thought of a number of setdowns for him — thus far, he was the only fortune-hunter who had found her alone. But Anthony didn't let her talk.

"If she disgraces me, I shall never forgive you," he said to Thorington.

She switched to thinking of setdowns for Anthony instead. But Thorington's steady, assessing gaze drew her attention back to him — and she wasn't sure she liked the direction her thoughts took as she considered the crystalline brilliance of his green eyes.

"She won't disgrace anyone," Thorington said. "I will make sure of it."

CHAPTER NINE

He had retrieved her from the breakfast room before she'd clawed Anthony's eyes out, but it was a near thing. The boy would have deserved it — even if he didn't want to marry her, he could at least be charming — but Thorington wanted to leave him unmaimed.

They had walked outside for five minutes — two minutes longer than he expected — before Callista finally balked. "Say what you wish to say," she said. "I'll go no farther. And if you need a reminder of how business is conducted, sirrah, know that even though we have an agreement, it does not give you leave to treat me like a child who must be contained."

They were somewhere in Maidenstone's vast ornamental gardens, which were large enough that it was easy to find a spot where they could talk without being overheard. Callista's maid, whom he'd forced her to call as a chaperone, walked behind them, out of earshot but adding a thin veneer of respectability in case anyone saw them from the windows of the house. He glanced around the vicinity and pointed to a nearby bench. "You may be assured that I do not see you as a child. Please, be comfortable, Miss Briarley."

She stayed standing. "You have one minute, sirrah."

"Am I keeping you from something more important?" he asked.

She lifted her chin. "My correspondence is very important."

"I'm sure your needlework is as well," he said drily. "But humor me for a moment while we discuss the more mundane topic of your future."

She walked to the bench, holding her hands behind her back as though she was being walked to the gallows. When she sat, her shoulders rounded — not quite a slump, but not the fortified posture he was accustomed to seeing from her.

"Are you feeling well, Miss Briarley?" he asked.

Callista nodded. "What do you wish to tell me?"

He sat beside her. The stone bench was still cool, although the morning sun had burned away the worst of the dew. "Are you warm enough?"

She waved her hand impatiently. "If you are going to go back on your word, please do not keep me waiting. Say what you came to say."

Thorington shook his head. "That is not what I came to say. I take my vows seriously."

"Is that so?" she asked. She lifted her head, and he sensed the moment when her fire came back to her. "Then if you intend to uphold our bargain, you should be talking to Anthony, not me. He is the one who is likely to put everything at risk."

He should have talked to Anthony as soon as he'd left her room the night before, even if it had meant waking his brother up. He hadn't anticipated that the chit would reach the breakfast room before him — he hadn't anticipated that she would be there at all, since the women of the party would take trays in their rooms. And so he had indulged his rare desire to avoid a confrontation and chosen to delay his conversation with Anthony until morning.

His self-indulgence had cost him, as it always did. He wouldn't make the same mistake again.

And so even though there was a disused part of him that wanted to see Callista remain exactly as she was — an impulse he refused to examine — he crushed that desire and replaced it with determination. "I will talk to Anthony. But the boy has a valid concern. You must develop your social graces if you are to survive the ton."

"If this is because I have refused to call you 'your grace,' do not fret. I will behave myself with other dukes."

"What will your title be if you marry my brother?" he asked.

She looked at him blankly. "I beg your pardon?"

"Excuse me. What will your title be *when* you marry my brother?"

He had slipped, just a bit. But that wasn't what she had taken issue with. "It is your question that surprises me, not how you phrased it."

"Do you know the answer?" he asked.

Callista frowned. "I don't see how it signifies."

Her hesitation told him all he needed to know. "I will give you three choices. Will you be Mrs. Anthony Emmerson-Fairhurst, Lady Callista Emmerson-Fairhurst, or Lady Emmerson-Fairhurst?"

She watched his face carefully as he said all three, as though she might be able to read the answer there. "Lady Emmerson-Fairhurst?"

Her voice tilted up at the end, questioning. He smiled. "You need me, Miss Briarley. I will teach you all you need to know."

"I wouldn't think you'd have patience to play the governess," she said.

"I have infinite patience when it suits the situation."

She nipped at her bottom lip with her teeth. He thought, briefly, that he might be able to have infinite patience for her. But he stabbed that thought in the heart and laid it to rest with all his other inconvenient emotions.

"I will admit that my education wasn't designed to make me a lady," she said.

"I'm sure you were educated to foment revolt and lead rebellions, not waltz and pour tea."

She laughed. "Is that what you think of American educations?"

"I've no idea. But I would not be surprised if you told me that you'd only learned how to shoot muskets and skin rabbits."

Callista pursed her lips in mock reproof. "I learned to shoot a handgun, not a musket. It is more difficult to hide a musket in one's reticule."

"And the rabbits?" he asked.

"I prefer to clean fish," she said.

"My little colonial," Thorington said. "So skilled, aren't you?"

"I'm not a colonial," Callista retorted. "I am an American."

She didn't dispute that she was his, though. That thought hung over his head like a noose. If he let it drop another inch, he'd be caught by it.

"I'm sure your skills are perfectly suited to your old life," he said smoothly. "But if you wish to have a chance at winning Maidenstone, you must learn to live in this world."

"Do you have any character references?" she asked.

Thorington snorted. "There isn't a man alive who would give me one."

"Then how am I to know whether I should hire you as my governess?" she said.

He laughed. She'd tricked the sound out of him again. "If you aren't paying me, I do not think it should be considered employment. Not that I'd dirty my hands with work. Consider it a favor."

"But you aren't doing it for me, are you?" she asked. "You're doing it for your dynastic ambitions."

"Everything is for my ambitions."

Her eyes held a hint of judgment — the same judgment others may have felt for him in the past, but everyone else was better at feigning respect for a man of his means. "That is a sad reflection, sirrah."

"First lesson: do not say 'sirrah' again unless you wish me to rap your knuckles for it. And my ambitions are not so different than yours."

"I'm not wholly focused on what I need to get from others," she said.

"Possibly not. But you accepted this arrangement with as much avarice as I did. Now, if you want to keep what you're trying so hard to win, you'll allow me to instruct you on how to behave."

Her jaw clenched in a decidedly unladylike way. But eventually she nodded. "Teach me whatever you feel you must teach me. But if your brother continues to see me as a pariah rather than a possible partner, I will find someone who will appreciate me as I am."

"You cannot go back on your word," he said.

"I never do. But I won't have to. Your brother isn't as willing as you led me to believe last night. I will do my best to win him over — it's in all our best interests. But if I cannot entice him with the prospect of gaining Maidenstone in exchange for giving me my freedom, he may break the deal despite our efforts."

"I will take care of Anthony. Let me escort you back to the house. You should change into something more appropriate for this morning's activities."

She looked down at her blue cotton dress. "What is wrong with my gown?"

"It's more suited for working in a garden than sitting in a drawing room sparring with your cousins. And that sapphire pendant is wholly inappropriate for daytime. Wear something white — you want to look as pure and unattainable as possible."

"I don't have any white day dresses," she said.

He raised an eyebrow.

"They are difficult for the laundress," Callista said defensively. "And anyway, I prefer color."

"Of course you do." She would look stunning in something jewel-toned — something meant for seduction and sin. Something that matched her necklace, not something designed for a debutante.

He shook his head and regained his focus. "White is required. You are approximately the same height and shape as Lady Portia. She will make a loan of her dresses until we can buy you a better wardrobe."

Callista frowned. "I don't want to waste my money on clothing."

"And I don't want to waste my time on arguments. I'll have one of her dresses sent to you within fifteen minutes of our return to the house. Then you must go through her wardrobe and take whatever you need. I sent a messenger to London — a modiste should arrive within the week."

He'd also asked the messenger to learn what he could of Callista's shipping endeavors before returning to Maidenstone. Her desire to run the company herself was no concern of his — but she was rather more eager for the task than anyone, man or woman, of their social circle should have been when given the option of living an idle life in the country.

In the past, with his old luck, Thorington wouldn't have considered the risks. Risks always came out in his favor. But he couldn't forget that his investment in Callista — in choosing her, training her, and convincing Anthony to accept her — could go as sour as everything else he'd touched recently. Investigating Tiberius Shipping and what it meant to her was prudent. Perhaps the most prudent decision he'd made in an age.

He knew better than to tell her that, though.

"Willful duke," she muttered.

Thorington smiled. "Only because the world runs more smoothly if I arrange it."

Callista stood. He stood with her, offering his arm. She knew better than to spurn it, but she couldn't seem to resist digging into him. "I will learn so fast that I shan't have to spend more than a few hours in your company."

"Of course, Lady Anthony."

"I beg your pardon?" she asked.

"Lady Anthony. Your title after you marry my brother will be Lady Anthony."

"That wasn't one of the choices you gave me."

"It was a test. I couldn't risk you guessing correctly and not telling me it was a guess."

"Then if I am Lady Anthony, no one will call me by my own name again, will they?" she asked.

"No. Not unless they are very close companions and you invite them to."

Callista's hand tightened on his arm. "This marriage business isn't very fair, is it?"

Ariana's claws had dug into his arm like that on many occasions. Then, it had felt like a trap — one he walked into again, and again, in some self-loathing desire to fulfill his vows to the wife he hadn't wanted.

Now, with Callista, it felt like she was trying to anchor herself to him — trying to find safe harbor in the treacherous seas of the ton.

He shook his head. He was ascribing feelings to her that she likely didn't have. And he was letting himself imagine things that might only torture him.

"No, it's not fair. But the ton is like a game of chance. If you learn the rules, you have a better chance of beating the odds."

They walked around a hedge and onto the lawn, approaching the house from the side, with Callista's maid still trailing behind them. Maidenstone loomed ahead of them. In the morning light, with a breeze blowing in from the sea, it looked more mystical than it was. The vaults and arches of the mostly abandoned Gothic wing, off to the side but never demolished, were magical, not a looming architectural disaster. The Tudor wing, remade from the abbey, looked ready to house a queen, not a passel of fortune-hunters. The Palladian rooms, built in the 1600s by Inigo Jones, still showed off their grandly symmetrical loggias and porticoes. Light streamed into the modern rooms of the Georgian wing, airing out the haunted corners.

The Briarleys may have spent centuries killing each other, but they couldn't seem to let go of the rooms their ancestors had built. Any other owner with their wealth would have torn it all down and rebuilt in the latest style. But he had to admit the abbey had a certain charm, even if it made no attempt to blend harmoniously with its surroundings.

"Is your house as magnificent as this?" Callista asked.

"Fairhurst is a manor house. It was all rebuilt in the last decade. It's more commodious, but less interesting."

It also had suddenly developed a leaking roof and a bad case of rot in the basements, according to the latest letter from his land steward. But Callista didn't need to know that.

"It must be nice to have so much history around you," she said. "I like my house in Baltimore, but it isn't the same."

"If you want history, I should take you to Bath. It has been used for its waters since Roman times."

"I think I shall be quite content exploring Maidenstone for the moment. From my father's stories, it must hold any number of secrets."

"Then you will have to learn your lessons well so that you may win it. Unmarried ladies cannot go exploring alone."

She tilted her face up to him. "What if you went exploring with me?"

A dark moment of tension hung between them, at odds with the brilliant morning sunshine. They were both talking of the future — of a future in which they sought out amusements together — that could never happen.

"You wouldn't want to go on an adventure with me, Miss Briarley," he said lightly. "With my luck, we'd find a dragon instead of a treasure."

"Dragons are more interesting than treasure," Callista said.

He let himself wonder whether she'd find *him* more interesting. But then she laughed a little, as though she were joking, and he knew it could not be.

He had a week, perhaps two, to teach her everything she needed to know to be a good wife for Anthony. And he had the same time to convince his brother that she was the most delightful woman he would ever meet. Surely once Anthony had spent a few hours with her, he would see how lovely she could be.

Once they were settled, Thorington would return to London and complete the messy business of dealing with his creditors. Better for Anthony and Callista both if they were on their honeymoon — preferably someplace far removed from the City — when that happened.

And better for Thorington if the marriage happened as quickly as possible. The cemetery where he buried all his inconvenient emotions was filling up too fast for comfort.

CHAPTER TEN

"The dress suits you," Thorington said to her two hours later.

Callie smoothed her gloved hands over the stark white muslin, feeling self-conscious in Portia's borrowed dress. "This is entirely impractical for a walk along the cliffs."

"Nonsense," he said, offering her his arm. "If you fall into the sea, your body will be perfectly dramatic."

They were setting off on an expedition to explore the cliffs with Rafe and his sisters. If Anthony had been invited, he had refused. No one else would come with them — after the first suitor had expressed an overly-jovial interest in joining them and been skewered by Thorington for it, the rest had kept their distance.

"I am not afraid of heights," Callie warned. "So if I faint or fall to my death, it will only be because you pushed me."

"There has not yet been a rumor of me killing a woman. I would prefer to keep it that way."

"We could have our first lesson in the library," she pointed out. "It is less likely that either of us would die there."

He ushered her through the front door instead, out into the brilliant sunshine. "Wouldn't want the servants to overhear me quizzing you on the titles and estates of everyone in attendance," he said as soon as they were out of earshot of the footmen. "They would take word to Lucretia, and she would use it against you at the first opportunity."

Portia had been trailing behind with Rafe and Serena, but she caught up to them before they reached the edge of the lawn. "Hold a moment, Miss Briarley," she commanded.

"What is it?" Callie asked. "Have I already ruined your dress?"

Portia came around to face Callie, untying the green ribbon on the poke bonnet that she had included in the loan of the dress. "It's the fashion to tie the bow on the side, not directly under the chin," Portia said, making a quick adjustment. "Tell your maid to talk to my maid about how to dress your hair. It would be better with a bit of curl."

The thought of Mrs. Jennings making herself over into Portia's highly-trained French lady's maid nearly made Callie laugh. "I will tell her," Callie said. "And I must thank you again for the loan of the dress, Lady Portia."

Portia waved a hand. "It's nothing. Thorington paid for everything I have. If he wants to dispose of it, it's his right."

She shot a look at her brother when she said this — a look that Callie thought was sincere. But she felt Thorington's arm tighten. "It's a loan, not a disposal. You'll have everything back and more once you marry."

Portia sighed. "Let us talk of something more pleasant, please? You can play the autocrat in the drawing room, but I'd prefer to enjoy the fresh air without a lecture."

Thorington nodded. "You can help educate Miss Briarley about our fellow party-goers, if that pleases you. Or you and Serena can take turns trying to push each other into the ocean."

Portia's eyes lit up. "I've always thought Serena would make a lovely sacrifice."

She stopped walking, letting them pass her as she waited for her sister and Rafe. "Are your sisters always so interested in sororicide?"

Callie asked Thorington.

"Usually they can be convinced to go after my blood instead. I'm sure only their mutual animosity toward me has kept them from murdering each other these many years."

He said it lightly. But something about his tone made her wonder. "Lady Portia seems to adore you," she said.

"Adoration is not a concept with which I am familiar," Thorington said.

Callie thought back to Portia's words. She had taken them as a bit of sisterly teasing. But Thorington sounded like he had felt something else — something like guilt, if it was possible for him to feel guilty about anything. "I think your family loves you more than you realize," she said.

He shrugged. "Love and need are not equivalent, Miss Briarley. I need my estate manager, but I do not love him."

Callie would have laughed if she had thought he was jesting. Instead, she said, "I thought I felt the same about my father, until he was no longer there. Your feelings may surprise you."

"They rarely do."

She had come to recognize the tone he used when he thought a conversation was over. On another day, with another person, it might have angered her.

But today, filled with perfect light and fresh sea air, was made for banter. It was made for a lazy afternoon stroll and sweet, sultry laughter.

He was made for sweet, sultry laughter. She saw it in his eyes occasionally, on those rare moments when she startled him into amusement — saw the man he might have been, half-starved behind his indifferent mask.

What had happened to make him so dark?

And why did she care, when he was not hers to rescue?

"Perhaps you should let your feelings surprise you," she said.

"Feelings are not particularly useful for my ambitions."

She nodded. "Nor are they for mine. And yet I would rather indulge occasionally and pay the price for it than live forever without them."

"Is that so, Miss Briarley?"

The way his voice wrapped around her name made her shiver. "I will spare you my feelings so that they do not inconvenience your plans," she said. "Do not worry yourself."

"This would be a good time to call me 'your grace,'" he murmured.

He had surprised her this time, and she laughed in spite of herself. "Never, sirrah."

He tapped the fingers she'd wrapped around his arm. "Next time it will be a ruler across the knuckles, my dear."

She laughed again. Some of the tension between them ebbed — but it was tension at low tide, not a complete retreat. "We're sufficiently away from the house," she said. "Tell me everything I must know about titles. I am in such suspense that I cannot think for the excitement of it."

Thorington looked down at her and smiled. She had tilted her head up to look at him just in time. At any other moment, the stiff sides of her bonnet would have kept her from seeing that peculiar light in his eyes as he regarded her.

"I live to serve, Miss Briarley. We begin with the barons."

*　　*　　*

Callista was a quick study. She knew the rudiments of British noble titles and forms of address from reading months-old editions of *The Times*. And she seemed to have a good recollection of faces and mannerisms. It was easy enough for him to describe other members of the party and have her recognize the person in question, even if she didn't yet know every nuance of their social and political lives.

After almost two hours of exploring the cliffs and going over titles, though, she seemed to have tired of their lesson. Thorington had sent servants ahead to the cliffs with a few chairs and some light foodstuffs. He'd also left word for Anthony that he was to join them, but it didn't take a keen mind to guess that Anthony had disobeyed him.

Callista still sat dutifully in her chair, but she watched the swell of water on the horizon. The bonnet gave her away — it was too easy to see that her head was oriented toward the sea rather than toward his voice.

"What are the proper addresses of Ferguson's sisters?" he asked.

"Lady Catherine and Lady Maria are in attendance with him, although I've yet to meet them. They are the blonde twins who are of an age with Lady Serena. His other sister is Lady Folkestone, a marchioness."

He hadn't mentioned Ellie, although he was acquainted with her. "How do you know of Lady Folkestone?" he asked. "She isn't due to attend."

"Her husband, Lord Folkestone, is in shipping," she said shortly.

"Who is the Duchess of Rothwell's cousin?"

"Lord Salford. He's the earl with the pretty dark-haired wife — you can tell they're newly wed by the way he smiles at her."

"Where is Salford's family seat?"

"Why on earth do I need to know that?" Callista asked.

Rafe, dozing on the blanket next to them, yawned. "Indeed, why do any of us need to know that?"

"Because knowing the enemy makes it easier to defeat them."

"Do you consider everyone your enemy?" Callista asked.

At least he'd regained her attention. "No. But friends can turn to enemies and enemies to allies. Easier to change course at a moment's notice if you are educated about everyone on the field."

Rafe yawned again, more obviously this time. "Miss Briarley, ask his grace who Lord Salford's pretty dark-haired wife is."

"Is there a story behind that question, Lord Rafael?"

She addressed the question to Rafe, but she turned to Thorington as she said it. Thorington interrupted before his brother could cause more trouble. "Lady Salford was formerly Miss Prudence Etchingham. Her father was Lord Harcastle. What rank must he have been if he was a lord and she was a mere miss?"

"A baron or viscount," she snapped. "What else is interesting about her?"

"There is absolutely nothing interesting about her," Thorington said.

Serena and Portia were playing cards on the other blanket, but that quelling tone brought their interest rather than scaring them away. Serena looked up. "Lady Salford would have made a good duchess."

"Is that so?" Callista asked. She still looked at Thorington, but now her eyes narrowed. "Did you have a *tendre* for Lady Salford?"

"No. What will Salford's son be called, should he have one?"

"I don't give a fig for Salford's son," Callista said.

His siblings laughed. Thorington tapped his walking stick. "He will be Viscount Whitworth. And their daughters?"

"Should I not focus on people who are alive and able to cause me problems?" Callista asked. "Or do even infants earn your enmity?"

Portia tossed a card aside and picked up another. "Thorington doesn't have enemies. No one is allowed to disturb him long enough to reach that status."

Rafe shifted up onto his elbow so that he could look at Callista and Thorington more easily. "That's not quite true, Portia. Salford was his enemy for ages. How Gav managed to forgive him for winning Lady Salford is still a mystery to me."

Thorington refused to be baited. "What, if anything, was wrong with how Lord Rafael just spoke?"

Callista was frustrated — he saw it in the way her eyes flashed. "Lord Rafael should have told me what he was about from the start, rather than whetting my curiosity."

"My apologies, Miss Briarley," Rafe said.

He didn't sound contrite. Thorington ignored him. "Correct. But he was also impertinently improper. As you've not been given leave to call me or Lady Portia by our given names, he should have been more formal as well despite his closer acquaintance with us."

"Miss Briarley is to be our sister, though," Serena said, sounding quite sensible. "I'm sure the rules can be relaxed with her."

Portia shot her a look. "We weren't supposed to tell Thorington that we knew. Anthony will be unhappy with you."

"As though it isn't obvious," Serena sniped. "Why would Anthony refuse to come with us today? He usually loves the sea. And why would Thorington care to teach her anything unless he was grooming her to be Anthony's bride?"

Callista looked down at his sisters. "Perhaps the duke is being friendly."

His sisters both laughed. "Thorington doesn't do anything without some purpose," Serena said.

Thorington couldn't see Callista's face, so he could only guess what she was thinking. But her words surprised him. "Then should I assume that he wished to marry the new Lady Salford for some purpose as well? Or do you think it was a love match?"

Portia and Serena glanced at each other. "We wouldn't want to gossip," Portia said.

Rafe snorted. "Tell us another fairy tale."

Thorington cleared his throat. "It is time to return to Maidenstone. Miss Briarley has learned enough for one afternoon."

Callista held up her hand in a gesture he recognized — it was something he might have done. "A moment, if you please. I am curious about Lady Salford."

"Curiosity is highly unseemly for a gentlewoman," Thorington said.

"Then it is lucky for me that you chose to start with titles instead of manners," Callista replied.

Rafe sat up. Thorington didn't like the way his eyes moved from Thorington to Callista and back again. "We are all lucky, Miss Briarley," he said. "I wouldn't want to see you change at all."

From the smile on Rafe's face a moment after that sentence, Thorington guessed that Callista's grin must have been radiant.

He damned the hat that blocked his view of her. He thought of telling her that poke bonnets were sorely out of fashion and that she should only wear caps to their next lessons. Instead, he stood and offered her his arm. "Shall we, Miss Briarley?"

She looked up at him, and he finally saw her eyes again. But the light there wasn't quite what he expected.

If she were interested in him as a man, she might have been jealous. If she were interested in his life as fodder for gossip, she might have been curious. He'd seen every emotion across both spectrums from Ariana.

Instead, she rose from her chair and took his arm, squeezing it in a gesture that another would have called comforting. "I am sorry she didn't marry you, your grace. I'm sure you would have made her happy."

She couldn't have stunned him more if she'd hit him over the head with a rock. And it wasn't her unexpected use of his proper address, after all her refusals, that had startled him.

He knew why he hadn't recognized that light in her eyes before.

It was compassion.

For him.

He stared into her eyes, saw the invitation there. Her mouth tilted up into a tentative smile.

He couldn't bear it.

"I would not have made her happy," he said.

She tilted her head. "Oh, I'm sure…"

"No, *I'm* sure," he said, cutting her off. "I had kidnapped her and was on the verge of marrying her by force when Salford rescued her. She would have hated me for the rest of our unfortunate lives. Deservedly so. But I would have had the revenge I wanted from her."

Callista's mouth dropped open.

"Do not make me into a hero, Miss Briarley," he said, his voice low. "I assure you I will never be one. I will do what I must to uphold our bargain. And I will see that Anthony gives you the best of everything. But don't look for kindness in me. I do not have it to give."

She pulled her hand away from his arm. "I see," she said.

Her eyes dimmed. He forced himself to watch, to make sure she really *did* see. Only when wariness had fully replaced compassion did he turn away from her.

"Rafe, see the ladies back to Maidenstone. I need some air."

Rafe stood and offered his arm to Callista without comment. Thorington strode away, not waiting to see whether the rest of them obeyed him.

It was better this way. Better to groom her, and walk away, than to make her think he was something he wasn't. She needed security and someone who could preserve her fortune. He couldn't give her either.

But damned if he didn't wish he deserved her.

CHAPTER ELEVEN

An hour after they'd returned to the house, Callie walked into the drawing room to join the other guests before dinner. She wanted to go straight to Thorington, but some unusual reticence held her back. The warning in his eyes that afternoon had been real, though she didn't understand it. But even if he hadn't warned her, she couldn't thank him publicly for what he'd done without inviting gossip that might ruin her.

When she had returned from their aborted walk to the cliffs, Lucretia's butler had escorted her to a spacious room in the Georgian wing, one with a real bed, a pair of delightful chairs, and room for its own bath. It even had a dressing room. Mrs. Jennings was already unpacking Callie's trunks, humming a happy little tune at their changed circumstances.

"Please send my thanks to your mistress," Callie said to the butler.

"Miss Lucretia did not arrange this," the butler said.

He had left without saying another word. But her maid handed her a note, sealed with red wax. Callie opened it to find two sentences scrawled across the center of the paper.

Lock your door and beware of fortune-hunters. I will suffer the rats.

It wasn't signed. But she would have laughed if Thorington hadn't been so foul at the end of their walk. He must have arranged to exchange rooms before they had gone out. Before he told her that he had no kindness left to give her.

But this wasn't the gesture of a villain.

Thorington was just visible in the next drawing room, but she did her best to ignore him. Instead, she walked to one of the open windows and looked out over the lawn. It was better than looking around the room and realizing that she had no friends with whom to converse.

It was an odd reaction. She was accustomed to solitude. It had been nearly constant in Baltimore, since her father had died before she'd come out there and she'd had no female relatives to ensure that she was received properly by society. Captain Jacobs' wife had escorted her occasionally, but her social status didn't match Callie's. Callie hadn't minded at the time; she was more interested in shipping, and she didn't mind that most of Baltimore considered her eccentric in the extreme. But there was so much she didn't know about this world — so much she didn't know about how to have a conversation that meant nothing and went nowhere.

If she was honest with herself, the possibility of finding friends and moving in society had been part of her desire to return to England. But if this endless line of dull house parties was the ton's definition of friendship, she wasn't sure she wanted any part of it.

"May we join you, Miss Briarley?" a woman said behind her.

She turned. Prudence, Lady Salford — the woman Thorington had, so very recently, tried to marry — smiled, her brown eyes seeming friendly enough. Madeleine, the Duchess of Rothwell, stood next to her, wearing an equally warm look.

"We thought you might like a bit of company," Prudence continued. "It can be difficult to find one's bearings at a party such as this."

"Thank you," Callie said. "But there is no need for you to put forth any effort for my sake."

Madeleine waved a hand. "I'll own up to being a negligent chaperone — you were nowhere to be found this afternoon. But that doesn't mean I don't want to be friendly with you."

Did they know she had spent the afternoon with Thorington? Callie hadn't made any effort to let Madeleine or Ferguson know about her excursion to the cliffs — the thought hadn't even crossed her mind, accustomed as she was to setting her own schedule. And with Thorington's sisters as company, Callie had thought she was safe enough.

But the ton had its own rules. And Callie didn't know if she had just broken one.

"I wasn't aware that I was needed here," Callie said, sidestepping the implied question of where she had been.

Prudence grinned. "Are any of us needed here?"

That grin wasn't the smile of someone who sat in judgment of Callie's actions. Callie smiled back, still slightly wary. "I suppose not. But this is all very unusual."

"Don't worry yourself too much," Madeleine said. Then her eyes turned serious. "But I would suggest not leaving the house with Thorington again."

"His sisters were with us," Callie said.

"Yes. But he could have absconded with you in an instant."

Callie snorted. "You make him sound like a villain in a Gothic romance."

Prudence and Madeleine exchanged glances. "That's not so far from the truth," Prudence said.

"Yes, I heard he abducted you," Callie said. "But it appears that it all came right in the end."

Prudence looked shocked. "Who told you that?" she asked, dropping her voice.

"Was it a secret?" Callie asked.

"I would prefer that no one in London knew, if that's what you mean," Prudence said in a low whisper.

"I see." Callie paused, wondering how to proceed. But she had never been good at subterfuge. "Thorington confessed to it this afternoon. He seemed to want me to know how dangerous he is."

Madeleine grabbed Callie's arm, pulling her closer to the window and farther from the nearest guests. "He is dangerous," she said flatly. "He may have a title and vast wealth, but he would be a horrible husband."

"Who said anything about marrying him?" Callie said in the drawl that an afternoon in Thorington's company had drummed into her.

"In my experience, you don't have to say anything about marrying him. He'll decide it for himself," Prudence said.

"He's a villain," Madeleine declared. "I find it difficult to believe he escorted you to the cliffs as a mere social excursion."

"Lord Rafael and his sisters were with us as well," Callie said. "I like them all well enough. And as you said, it can be difficult to get one's bearings at a party like this. At least they offered to pass the afternoon with me."

Something like guilt passed across Madeleine's face. "I should have thought to invite you to join us in the library this afternoon."

"A walk to the cliffs sounds vastly more interesting than the work we did with our correspondence," Prudence said. "Especially with a villain."

And then she winked at Callie in an entirely conspiratorial manner.

Callie smiled. "I must admit I would take the sea over the sitting room any day."

"That's a fine preference for America, I'm sure," Madeleine said. "But you must be careful here. Especially with Thorington."

She sounded worried enough that Callie decided not to take offense at the implied slight on her American ways. "You don't need to worry, your grace. I shall be careful."

The conversation moved on to the weather, Callie's impression of Devonshire, and Prudence's assessment of the history of Maidenstone. It was all pleasant — more than pleasant. And Callie slowly began to relax, to let herself be charmed by them.

But that comfort wasn't destined to last. Lucretia approached them.

"Miss Briarley, may I have a word?" she asked stiffly.

Callie eyed her cousin, feeling her hackles rise even before Lucretia finished speaking. "Must you?" she said.

Lucretia flushed. "I only need a moment."

Madeleine and Prudence were gracious enough to leave without being asked — more gracious than Callie had been. Callie had enough awareness to feel just a bit of shame at that.

And her shame grew after Lucretia drew her onto the terrace and began speaking. "I wanted to apologize for yesterday," Lucretia said. "I was rude, and I am sorry."

Callie's stomach shriveled, twisting on itself. She didn't like Lucretia.

But was it possible that Lucretia was a better person than she was?

"I am sorry as well," Callie said. "I shouldn't have stolen your horse."

"No, you shouldn't have. But I should not have kept you waiting for a room. I'm sure you needed more time than you had last night to make yourself presentable for dinner."

Lucretia's dark eyes, so similar to Callie's own, seemed contrite enough. But there was an edge to her voice that didn't match her apology.

In fact, it almost sounded like an insult.

"I thought I looked presentable enough," Callie said. "Particularly after the voyage I had."

She'd thought she looked more than presentable the night before. After she'd calmed her nerves in the drawing room, she'd enjoyed wearing her white dress. And her hair hadn't fallen out of its pins — Mrs. Jennings had surpassed herself.

But Lucretia sniffed. "You looked well. But you don't know the first thing about Maidenstone."

Callie stopped feeling guilty. "Is this still an apology?"

Lucretia didn't say anything for the longest time. She turned toward the gardens instead, looking out over the formal shrubs and paths to the remnants of Maidenstone Wood in the distance.

Callie should have looked at the landscape as well. But she watched Lucretia instead. Her cousin could be quite pretty. Her complexion was clear, and her figure was trim enough to show advantageously in the straight, simple dresses that were so in fashion. She wore white, with a set of pearls around her throat and another rope twined through her hair.

She could have been one of the fashion plates that Callie used to look at, before she realized she didn't need fashionable attire to manage a shipping company.

But while Lucretia was beautiful when frozen like this, the despair in her voice marred it.

"Do you remember anything about Maidenstone?" she asked, still looking at the gardens.

"My father told me..."

"No," Lucretia interrupted. "Do you remember anything personally? From when you were a girl?"

Callie shook her head, but Lucretia wasn't looking at her. So she said, "No. I had a moment on the staircase in the Tudor wing yesterday when I thought I remembered playing there once, but nothing beyond that."

"You don't remember me or Octavia?" Lucretia asked.

"No. But I wasn't even five when we left England. I do not recall my father spending much time here in the years before that."

"Tiberius never liked my father. He was still alive then, and still at Maidenstone, so it makes sense you wouldn't have come."

Lucretia's father would have inherited, if he hadn't died when Lucretia was a child. But all of that was decades ago. "I am pleased to see Maidenstone now," Callie said. "It's more charming than I expected."

"You say it as though it's a mere curiosity," Lucretia said. Her voice developed a slight, but very perceptible, edge. "I took my first steps in the nursery. I rode my first pony on the drive. I took my first communion in the chapel. I had all my lessons in the schoolroom. I played at being princesses with Octavia in Maidenstone Wood."

Lucretia paused again. Her voice had dropped off on the last statement, into something that almost sounded mournful.

"Where is Octavia?" Callie asked. "I thought she would have arrived already."

"Octavia will not be attending," Lucretia said, in a final sort of way that left no room to ask why. "Which leaves you."

She turned to Callie as she said this. Her voice was shored up again, supported by some reservoir of will.

"I will give you five thousand pounds if you give up your claim to Maidenstone."

Callie laughed.

"It's an earnest offer," Lucretia said.

"You must do better than that," Callie said. "I have lived abroad most of my life, but I know the value of a pound. And I know the value of an estate. Five thousand pounds is nothing compared to Maidenstone."

"But it isn't about the money."

"Everything is about money," Callie retorted.

Lucretia had made a fine effort of seeming contrite earlier. But now her eyes narrowed. "Maidenstone's legacy isn't about wealth. But you don't know anything about that, do you? You've never cared for the family, only your own needs."

Callie was too confused to be offended. "What are you going on about?"

"Grandfather was most put out that you didn't come home after Uncle Tiberius died. You should have obeyed him."

"Obeyed him? I can't say I even remember him, save for the miniature my father kept of him. What cause did I have to obey him?"

"He was the head of the family," Lucretia said impatiently. "I never would have dreamed of disappointing him."

Callie frowned. Her cousin seemed truly upset that she hadn't danced to the old earl's tune. As though it would have changed anything — the title still would have died at his death. There was nothing any of the girls could have done to avoid that fate.

But while Callie didn't particularly like Lucretia, she didn't want to further upset her. So she said, with more care than usual, "Would you like an apology? I did not know that I had caused any of you pain."

Lucretia snorted. "It's late for an apology. You can give it to Grandfather the next time we decorate the mausoleum. It's traditional for Briarleys to apologize to the dead, since we don't do it to the living."

"I would offer one to the living, if it would make a difference," Callie said.

She could very nearly taste the bitterness in the air as Lucretia paused. The other girl still looked lovely — but there was such a depth of darkness in her eyes that Callie wondered, suddenly, what tragedy she had suffered.

Callie would wager it was something far beyond losing their grandfather at the natural end of his days.

"It wouldn't," Lucretia said finally. "And it's not necessary — you did nothing to cause offense, save for ignoring us. Perhaps I would have been happier if I'd done the same."

"It's not too late, you know," Callie said. "You aren't tied to Maidenstone any more than I am."

If there had been a bit of wistfulness and something approaching understanding in the previous moment, Callie's encouragement killed it. "You don't know the first thing about Maidenstone, or its history, or the people who depend upon it for their livelihood," Lucretia snapped. "If you win, you would destroy it all just to turn a profit. I won't beg your forgiveness when I say that I'll do whatever I can to make sure it stays out of your hands."

Lucretia didn't wait for Callie to respond. She returned to the drawing room instead, stomping more than a lady should have.

Callie should have followed her. But she was still too stunned to face anyone.

She looked back out over the gardens instead. Had her instinct to put down roots been killed by Tiberius's perennial wanderings? This land, with the ancient forest ahead of her and the magical house looming behind her, was built for roots. It was saturated with history — both the bloody kind and the sweeter, simpler ties of tradition that stretched across generations. And it was so very different from Baltimore. Maidenstone Abbey was a place that would *stay*, not a place still finding its footing in a new world.

She wanted roots.

She just wasn't sure she was capable of growing them. Already Baltimore seemed so far away. She had spent over seven years there — seven times longer than she'd spent in Jamaica, which was the longest she'd remembered living anywhere. She had thought it was home. But her house there was just a house. Her things there were just things. She couldn't remember anything she'd left behind, beyond a few books and trinkets. The things that mattered to her — the Briarley Bible, her mother's jewelry, the only doll that had survived her wandering childhood — had come with her. The rest of it could be abandoned if necessary.

Lucretia would fight for this place. She probably would have welcomed their grandfather's original idea of a duel — for all that she was too stiff with propriety, Callie could still see Lucretia trying to put a sword through her throat to keep her from winning Maidenstone.

But Lucretia didn't fight for wealth or status. She fought because it was the only thing she could do for the place that meant everything to her.

And Callie knew, then, that she was jealous of her cousin, and a terrible person besides. Because she wanted *that* — that conviction, that desire — more than she wanted Maidenstone. She wanted a place to care about.

And she was willing to take Maidenstone from Lucretia if it helped her to feel it.

CHAPTER TWELVE

"You may demonstrate singing or pianoforte," Thorington said the next morning, as soon as Callie had walked into the music room. "I have no preference."

"If you want to see my best talents, I should demonstrate knot-tying," Callie said. "My father said I was quite proficient."

Thorington didn't smile. In fact, his expression exactly suited the displeased, disapproving governess he'd offered to become for her. "Unless your knot-tying is for the purpose of fashioning a purse, forget the skill. You'll have no need of it as Lady Anthony."

Thorington and Portia had been waiting for her in the music room when she arrived. Thorington may have offered to teach Callie what she needed to know to survive the ton, but she still knew that if anyone caught her alone with him, society would bury her for it. Not that Portia was an adequate guard for Callie's morals, even if her presence could help stave off a scandal. The girl seemed a little too eager to seek out mischief.

"I would quite like to learn how to tie knots," Portia said.

"Your enthusiasm is noted and declined," Thorington said.

"Unfair," Portia said as she returned to the stack of sheet music she'd been leafing through. "Wouldn't you like for me to know how to tie knots when I run away with a cavalry officer?"

Callie could almost hear Thorington counting silently in his head. But the man's voice was as cool as always when he finally responded. "If you are pea-brained enough to run away with a cavalry officer who won't tie knots for you, you'll deserve your fate. And don't encourage Miss Briarley. You are the daughter of a duke. She is not."

"Even daughters of dukes can learn how to tie ropes," Callie said. "Lady Portia might prove quite good at it."

Thorington turned his green eyes upon her, with a look that said he wanted to throttle her. "Of course Lady Portia could learn to tie knots. As a duke's daughter, she might even bring it into fashion. But you, my dear, are a mere colonial. It would behoove you to remember that and not treat us to any of your provincial talents."

His voice seemed meant to slide down her spine like a fillet knife. But she didn't feel the effects. She smiled instead, ready to bait him further. "I should show you scalping, if you think barbarism is all we're capable of."

This time, unexpectedly, he laughed. "Save your scalping knife for Lucretia. Now, will it be pianoforte or singing?"

The mercurial nature of his moods kept her off-balance. She could never guess when he would turn cold or when he would warm up. But when he warmed up — when he was like this, not the man he warned her he was — she melted with him.

She couldn't let herself think like that.

"Why do you care about my musical talents?" she asked. "They have no bearing on my dowry."

"No, they do not. But they do have bearing on how well you are perceived by your peers. A proper lady should be able to play music at an impromptu party, produce a passable watercolor, embroider daintily, and dance competently. I can't hope to train you in all of those skills before your marriage. But I need to assess your deficits before planning how we can make you into a lady."

Callie frowned. "This is a waste of your time and mine. All that matters is pleasing Ferguson. And that duke, unlike you, doesn't seem too particular about my skills."

Thorington sighed. "I cannot begin to guess how Ferguson will decide this contest, save for knowing he would never choose me. Which is just as well, since I've no intention of saddling myself with a Briarley."

She supposed she was meant to take offense at that, so she smiled sweetly instead. "Which is just as well, since none of us would have you."

"That's not precisely true," he said. "But I wouldn't betray a lady's trust by telling you of the offer I received when I arrived."

Callie gasped. "Don't say Lucretia asked you to marry her?"

He examined his cuffs, flicking an invisible piece of lint aside. "I believe she realized her error. But she means to play to win, my dear. If you don't want my help, perhaps I should secure her for Anthony instead."

His threat might have sounded more serious if Portia hadn't laughed. "Anthony is even less likely to marry Lucretia than he is to marry this one."

Thorington gave his sister a withering glare. "Save your observations until you are enough of an adult to know when to share them."

Portia didn't seem offended. She returned to her music, humming a few bars of whatever sheet was in her hand.

Really, Thorington's family was strange — perhaps too strange to align with. "Where is Lord Anthony?" she asked. "He is just as necessary to my plans as Ferguson is."

He was also the family member she'd seen the least of, even though he was the most crucial to her plans. Thorington flipped open his watch. "Late, as usual. I had asked him to join us, but he must still be abed."

"Unlikely," Portia said.

"Have you seen him this morning?" Thorington asked.

Portia didn't respond.

"Well?"

The girl looked up, smiling insincerely. "I wasn't sure I was adult enough yet to share my observations. But since you asked so prettily...I saw him walking with Lady Maidenstone in the gardens."

"Bloody hell," Thorington said.

Callie didn't know whether that was directed at Portia, or at the knowledge that Anthony had defied him. She tilted her head as she met Thorington's gaze, striving for an innocent look. "How am I to follow through on our bargain if you can't deliver what you promised?"

She took more glee than she should have at the frustrated look on Thorington's face. As far as she was concerned, the man deserved to be thwarted just a bit. He had all but ignored her the night before, staying away from her before dinner, avoiding the drawing room entirely after. And so his note this morning had surprised her.

Music room, ten o'clock. I pray your singing voice is sweeter than the one you use with me.

So like a man. He had likely already rewritten the story of their conversation on the cliffs the day before to make her into the villain. He had probably told himself that Callie, sad spinster that she was, had mistakenly set her cap for a duke. He likely believed he'd been nothing but proper — that he'd done nothing that might mislead her into thinking he had some interest in her.

Men could believe anything if they put their minds to it. And Thorington had the discipline necessary to convince himself even in the face of overwhelming evidence to the contrary.

So she was just a bit too pleased that his morning wasn't arranging itself precisely to his demands.

"I will deal with Anthony," he said. "Pianoforte or singing. Now."

Callie sighed. She thought of leaving; his tone had turned too preemptory to amuse her. But if she left, there was no better entertainment to be found in the house.

And she wouldn't examine the fact that she'd rather spend time with Thorington than return to her solitude.

"Come, Miss Briarley," Thorington said, in a voice he might use to cajole a child. "I'm sure you have some musical talent. This is not the time for cowardice."

She knew she had been manipulated into action, but that wasn't enough to stop her from reacting. She took the first sheet of music from the pile Portia had made — it was a Gypsy tune adapted by Haydn, difficult but by no means impossible. "Turn the pages for me, will you?" she said to Thorington.

He raised an eyebrow. "Forgetting the 'please' in addition to the 'your grace'?"

He hadn't mentioned the moment when she'd called him 'your grace' the day before. In fact, he hadn't mentioned the day before at all. It was as though it had never happened. Had she dreamed how his face had looked, in that moment before he told her that he was an awful person? Had she imagined that he was capable of something more tender than coercion?

She shrugged, knowing insolence piqued him more than anger. "You'll know within a few bars that this exercise is superfluous."

He smirked. She exhaled, bending over the keys.

Then she began to play. She wasn't a virtuoso. A former teacher had told her she had the soul for it, but she didn't have the patience for consistent practice. Still, she was competent enough to play straight through the first sheet of music by sight without missing more than a few notes.

When she stopped for wont of someone to turn the pages, she found Thorington staring at her. "Will that suffice for the third son of a duke?" she asked sweetly.

He waved a hand. "For now. I trust you'll teach your daughters better. They will be ladies when Anthony inherits my title."

It was her turn to stare. "Why wouldn't your son inherit?"

"Have you seen a son in evidence?"

Portia snorted. "Pay him no mind. He's being overly dramatic about his widower status."

"What?" Callie asked.

There was a beat of silence, then another. Portia flushed. "Did you not know…"

Thorington cut her off. "Another excellent example of why you must learn more about the ton, Miss Briarley. It wouldn't do to confess your ignorance about such matters in the future."

Callie felt like she'd been punched in the chest. "You've been *married*?"

"Yes. How is your skill with watercolors?"

She moved away from the pianoforte. "How did I not know you were married?"

"You should have read your *Debrett's* instead of engaging in whatever provincial entertainments you found in Baltimore. It's quite common knowledge, I assure you."

She wanted to slap the amused look off his face. Instead, she went for his gut. "Did you have to force her into marrying you like you tried to force Lady Salford? You don't seem the type to make nice to anyone."

As his jaw hardened, she immediately regretted the jibe. It was an ill-considered joke, especially as she knew nothing of the situation. And before he even had the space to answer, her conscience whipped around. She suddenly felt sick to her stomach.

"I am so…" she started to say.

"Before you apologize for something you fully intended to say, know that I do not care whether you are sorry or not," Thorington said. "At the moment, I only care about your skill at watercolors."

How could a voice that calm make her feel so small? "I am still sorry," she said stiffly. "It was unfair for me to make an assumption of your past based on your current behavior."

"An odd sort of apology," he said.

She shrugged. "You are correct. I intended to say it, although I didn't consider how it would sound. Still, while you've told me that you aren't a very nice man now, I should do better than to assume you were never one."

He didn't respond immediately. They stood only a few feet apart, with Portia there to protect her virtue. His green eyes sparked as he looked her over. And she wondered if the circumstances were different — if Portia wasn't there, if Maidenstone didn't stand guard over them like a prison rather than an inheritance — he might have closed the distance between them.

Might have shown her the man she thought he could be.

Instead, he inclined his head. "I accept your apology, Miss Briarley. Perhaps we can move on from watercolors and explore your dancing skills."

"I'm quite capable," she said.

That may have been a slight exaggeration. She had hired a dancing master in Baltimore, before she had realized that she would not attend very many assemblies, but she was out of practice. Still, she knew the steps of all the dances they were likely to have at Maidenstone.

"So you say," he said. "But I think there will be waltzing some night soon. Lucretia means to have a ball for the local gentry. And you must be able to waltz."

"Do you really think this is necessary?"

He nodded. "I had planned to watch you dance with Anthony. It would be easier to give you instructions if I watched from afar. But since he is late to our little party, I shall do the honors."

Portia took the place Callie had vacated at the pianoforte. "I'll play while you attempt the steps," she said.

There was something suspicious in her voice — something that sounded too eager. But then Thorington bowed to Callie and offered his hand.

She curtsied on instinct. When she looked up, his smile was back — a real smile, just for a moment, before he twisted it into something else. "I knew you could curtsey to me when given the proper incentive," he said.

She placed her hand on his arm. "Do not let it go to your head, sirrah."

He squeezed her other hand, rubbing his thumb over the knuckles he'd threatened before. "You play a dangerous game, madam."

Portia began to play. The music lifted around them and he pulled her into the heart of it, their steps perfectly timed to the beat of the waltz.

Callie had waltzed before. She had even enjoyed it. But this experience — the feeling of being held, surrounded, overwhelmed — was entirely different. She felt every brush of his leg against hers, every bit of pressure from his hand against her back.

The music swelled. She was no longer a girl in a borrowed dress, still slightly fatigued from her journey, uncertain in a new country. She was *herself* again. But she was the best version of herself — the confident, joyful Callie she had been on her ship during a sea battle, not the hesitant Callie she'd been when she had arrived at Maidenstone.

She made the mistake of looking up. Thorington was watching her. Their gazes locked, becoming a tether that was unbreakable even as they spun around the room. His green eyes had lost whatever hardness she'd expected to see there.

All she saw was heat.

He somehow pulled her closer. And still she didn't stop looking — she couldn't have stopped, even if she'd been told that she'd be condemned to death for looking directly at him. She was too fascinated by the man she saw lurking in those eyes.

All his outrageous words and mercenary schemes should have sent her running from him. But there was more to him than that. And none of his warnings were enough to stop her from wanting to see who he could have been.

When the song stopped, it took a moment before either of them remembered to separate. They took several steps in silence before he suddenly brought them to a halt. They stayed there for another few seconds — a few endless seconds, in which every emotion seemed to flash through his eyes, even as his face stayed remarkably impassive.

At least she remembered to step back before he did. She curtsied again. "Thank you for the dance."

He bowed. "You are more than I expected, Miss Briarley."

It didn't occur to her until later that it was a strange choice of words. He should have said that she was better than he expected, if he was talking about her ability to waltz.

But she didn't think that was what he had meant.

CHAPTER THIRTEEN

After dinner the next night, Thorington realized he had avoided her for over twenty-four hours.

It felt like twenty-four days.

Of course, house parties often dragged on interminably. Not that Thorington had been invited to one with proper ladies and gentlemen in an age. Society wouldn't trust him with their daughters, and he wouldn't have accepted even if they had. If this were any other August, he might have been at Fairhurst, tramping through the fields and woods, talking to his tenants. Or he might have been at another gentleman's country estate — some gathering of rich gamers and high-flying courtesans, with not a wife or debutante in sight. Either way, he wouldn't have been quite so bored.

Surely it was his own boredom, more than any of Callista's charms, that had made him want so badly, throughout the day, to see her.

He'd wanted to see her the previous day as well. They had parted ways after their lesson in the music room with an entirely proper farewell — and then he had burned for her the rest of the afternoon.

He had known she was magnificent already, but knowledge was nothing compared to the feel of her, strong and supple, as they waltzed together. The attraction of her body was something he could ignore — he'd ignored other attractions before, while keeping his vows to

Ariana. But he couldn't ignore how she'd made him laugh, or how her dark eyes had been so full of light.

Perhaps he'd cursed himself again just by touching her.

But he had resisted the temptation of her company through the previous day's annoying entertainments. And today he had pursued business instead of pleasure. While the rest of the party had spent their Sunday engaged in more pious endeavors, Thorington had spent the day with his financial ledgers, looking for a way out of his predicament.

It was a wasted effort. His ledgers merely reminded him that he was completely destroyed. He could slow his fall into ruin if he made the worst cuts — refused dowries for Serena and Portia, eliminated Anthony's allowance, stopped paying the extravagant pensions and annuities he'd promised former servants and retainers when his money had seemed limitless. But that would only slow the bloodletting. If his luck didn't turn around — and at this point, he had no reason to believe it would — he would still lose everything eventually.

So he had tossed his ledgers into his trunk and returned to the original plan.

"Anthony," he said, catching the boy as they walked out of the dining room after Sunday dinner. "A word."

If Thorington had been steadfast in his avoidance of Callista, Anthony had been just as determined to avoid Thorington. Since the moment Anthony had learned that Thorington had selected Callista for him, Anthony had barely said two words to him. He'd ignored or refused all invitations to spend time with him and Callista. And he was too deep in Lady Maidenstone's pocket to talk to before or after any of the dinners.

But the boy was still loyal enough that he couldn't ignore Thorington's direct demand. He sighed, though, to make it clear that he felt put upon. "What is it?" Anthony asked.

Thorington waited until the last of the men had passed them on their walk from the dining room to their next pursuits. Then, in a low voice, he said, "I have arranged a room in which you may become better acquainted with Miss Briarley."

Anthony turned to him with a scandalized glare. "Don't say you mean for me to compromise her?"

"Of course not," Thorington said. "I mean for you to have a conversation with her. I think you'll quite like her once you speak to her properly."

"Is she capable of speaking properly to me? I must say she didn't seem to know the first thing about propriety at breakfast."

"She's a quick study."

Anthony snorted. "Why would I marry someone who still requires lessons? In fact, why would I marry anyone at all? I'm too young for it."

"You're the same age as Lady Maidenstone. You seem interested enough in her."

Thorington didn't want to encourage that connection, but he needed Anthony to see the situation from a different vantage point. Anthony wouldn't be baited, though. "Lady Maidenstone is entertaining for now. But she has even less desire to marry than I do, from what I can judge. Widows are fair game, are they not?"

It was a common viewpoint — one Thorington might have even subscribed to when he was Anthony's age. But hearing his younger brother say it, when Thorington still sometimes thought of him as a child, was shocking.

He tried to remember that Anthony was a man now. Still, there was too much at stake to let Anthony pursue pleasure instead of prudence. "You need money more than you need entertainment. Now, come upstairs with me."

He laid a hand on Anthony's arm.

For the first time, Anthony shook it off.

"I promised Lady Maidenstone I would attend to her," he said.

Thorington's first instinct was to drag Anthony upstairs by the ear. But Anthony wasn't a child anymore. His jaw was set — perhaps not as firmly as Thorington was capable of, but there was pride and determination there that Thorington recognized.

Anthony would never marry Callista willingly.

And if Thorington forced the issue, Anthony would never forgive him.

"Are you sure you can't give half an hour of your time?" he said. "She is a better prospect than you would imagine on first meeting."

"If she's such a good prospect, marry her yourself," Anthony retorted.

Thorington sighed. But he let Anthony proceed on to the drawing room as his plans churned in his head. He could ask Rafe to marry Callista...

He dismissed that idea immediately. Rafe was too far gone for marriage, and Callista didn't deserve the task of fixing him — or the pain of burying him.

Or Thorington could marry her himself.

He dreamed of it for a moment. In truth, he'd dreamed of it the previous day as well — he never would have gone back to his ledgers, looking for a new path, if he hadn't. She was magnificent. And she would be even more magnificent as a duchess.

Perhaps she would be so magnificent that she could change his ruined luck.

He shook his head to dislodge the thought and walked toward the Gothic wing and the rendezvous he'd arranged. Ferguson would never let him win Maidenstone. And her dowry, if that was all he gained from her, wasn't enough to cover his debts. Granted, her ships might be worth something, but he couldn't count on them to survive the war. She'd be left impoverished, and leg-shackled to him besides.

Callista didn't deserve that fate. She'd hate him for subjecting her to it.

And he couldn't bear for her to hate him.

*   *   *

Callie was almost glad it was Sunday. Lucretia had suggested, after less than an hour in the drawing room, that they all retire for an evening of quiet contemplation.

Quiet contemplation was good. Callie could quietly contemplate murdering Lucretia. Or she could quietly contemplate how to shock the party into talking about something other than the weather.

Or she could quietly contemplate Thorington.

That path led to madness. He hadn't come into the drawing room with the other gentlemen after dinner. In fact, he had seemed to avoid her all day. As much as she thought their lessons over the previous two days had been farcical rather than helpful, she found that she'd already begun to look forward to them.

And she was just the slightest bit hurt that he'd made no move to teach her something that day.

Callie didn't let herself wallow. She'd spent her time in the drawing room staring out the window and trying to name every flower she could see. Unfortunately, she wasn't much for gardening. She thought she saw some roses, and perhaps some kind of ivy, but it was really too difficult to tell.

She was going to go mad before Anthony ever got around to offering for her. Not that it seemed likely that he would, now. When he'd arrived in the drawing room after dinner, he'd immediately lured Lady Maidenstone out into the gardens. The two of them probably knew every flower for miles. Their blonde heads were bent together as they walked, and he kept whispering things that made Lady

Maidenstone laugh.

Lord Salford had been right the first night — house parties were awful. She needed the sea, or a dockyard misadventure, or even a badly balanced ledger to set to rights.

Where the devil was Thorington?

Like a besotted fool, Callie had been reading old editions of the *Gazette* all afternoon, seeking more information about Thorington's past in the society pages. What she'd read so far hadn't put him in the best light. She thought she might as well return to the library and continue her studies, even though she felt a vague sense of shame that she was so interested in his past when he seemed to have no interest at all in her. But as everyone filed out of the drawing room after Lucretia sent them to bed, Lady Serena trailed after her.

"Will you walk with me, Miss Briarley?" Serena asked.

Callie didn't want to engage in the hundredth inane conversation of the day. She kept walking. "Lucretia has the right idea — Sunday is better for contemplation."

"If Lucretia is as pious as she claims to be, I will give you all the remnants of my pin money. I think she sent us all to bed so she wouldn't have to think of yet another way to entertain us."

Callie laughed. "That isn't very charitable of you."

"Little annoys me more than inhospitable house parties."

Callie could think of a whole host of issues that annoyed her more than inhospitable house parties. The war's effect on shipping, for one. Or the lack of current knowledge about where her ships were and what trouble Captain Jacobs might have gotten himself into. But if Serena's life had been so sheltered that house parties were the worst of her problems, Callie tried not to begrudge her that fact.

Still, Serena seemed very intent on conversation. She let Serena take her hand and direct her away from the modern rooms. If nothing else, she didn't want to have this argument in the main hallway, where

other guests might hear them. But Serena took an unusual path —
toward the darkened halls and disused rooms of the Gothic wing.
Warm, painted walls and carpeted floors gave way to cold stone.
Evening light still streamed through the windows, but the openings
were narrower than those in the main wing, illuminating ancient
tapestries.

This was a part of Maidenstone she hadn't seen yet. And she was
charmed despite the chill.

But she was more curious about what she'd find in the *Gazette*
than in Maidenstone's oldest rooms. "This is lovely, but I would rather
return to the library," Callie said.

"I don't know why you would. There are far better things to do,
even at a house party like this one, than hide yourself away with some
books. And my brother doesn't want to waste the evening in quiet
reflection when he could drill you in your hostess skills."

She had seen Thorington at dinner, but they hadn't spoken.
Lucretia had seated her between a baronet who was missing half his
hair and a viscount's nephew who was missing half his brain. But
much as she wished she'd seen him earlier in the day, her temper was
too frayed now to be safe with him.

"I don't wish to have any lessons tonight," she said. "Please give
my regrets to your brother."

"Tell him yourself, if you're so insistent. If he's in the mood to
shoot messengers, as he so often is, I want no part of it."

"I played hostess for my father. Testing those skills isn't necessary."

Serena shrugged. "Then take five minutes to prove it to him and
retire for the evening."

"Must I?" she asked.

"You must."

That was Thorington's voice, not Serena's. He stepped out of an
open doorway, still wearing his proper dinner attire. But his smile was

decidedly improper as he held out his hand to her.

He was a devil. She was becoming sure of it. His odd manner and autocratic demands intrigued her — more than she cared to admit, if she were being honest. But she couldn't afford to be intrigued. Her company couldn't afford for her to be intrigued.

She touched the pendant on her necklace, hidden by the swell of a borrowed white dress over her bosom, and tried to remember her responsibilities. "If I tell you all the steps of making a proper cup of tea, will you leave me be tonight?"

"I'm afraid I require a demonstration. A future duchess must be able to serve tea with ease. And all I know of your kind is that you are capable of tossing tea into harbors, not steeping it."

Callie scowled at him. "That was nearly forty years ago. If we're all to judge each other on such time frames, I should ask where your powdered wigs and knee breeches are."

Thorington wiggled his fingers at her. "Come, Miss Briarley. We can insult each other more comfortably over tea."

His hand was tempting. His voice was more so — something dark and devilish.

She was being overly dramatic. He was just a man. But that didn't do justice to how much *more* of a man he was than the others at the party.

Serena pushed her between the shoulder blades, causing her to stumble forward. "How clumsy of me," Serena murmured, not sounding apologetic in the slightest. "Go about your lessons without worrying about your reputation, Miss Briarley. I'll keep watch across the hall."

"You aren't staying with us?" Callie asked.

Serena grinned. "You can thank me later when you realize you won't have to pour tea for me."

Thorington frowned. "It would be better if you stayed."

"No, I'm sure you can train Miss Briarley more effectively without me," Serena said brightly. "I'll be within earshot if you need anything."

The girl very nearly shoved them into the room, pulling the door shut between them.

And that left Callie looking up into Thorington's eyes and wondering if he was really, truly, a devil.

"A proper chaperone wouldn't leave me alone with the duke," Callie said.

"If it would make you feel more comfortable, you may pretend that I'm not a duke," Thorington said. "For tonight, I'm your governess."

Callie laughed despite herself. "The very idea is ludicrous. I'm sure that if we are caught, no one will think to believe that you are tutoring me rather than ruining me."

"We won't be caught," Thorington said. "Lady Serena will watch for intruders and keep them away. But from my reconnaissance of Maidenstone, it seems that this floor is entirely disused."

She gave into the tide and let him pull her into the room. "Now, Miss Briarley, show me how you prepare tea."

There was a tea cart near the window, completely out of place when most of the furniture was swathed in dustcloths. Someone had uncovered two chairs and a settee, along with a pair of small side tables. This room faced south, toward the sea, and an open window admitted a refreshing breeze to the disused space. The sun was setting, but the air was still warm — warm enough that Callie would rather be out in the garden than trapped in one of Maidenstone's older rooms, with one of Maidenstone's more dangerous guests.

"Won't the footman who arranged this tell Lucretia what you're about?" Callie asked.

"I gave him two guineas for his troubles. If he tells her, he will never get such a handsome reward again."

"I hope your assumption is correct. I wouldn't want to be forced to marry you."

Thorington's smile was menacing. "No, you would not. Put your mind at ease, Miss Briarley. I've no intention of compromising you."

The entire situation was compromising. Their bargain was very nearly compromising — and would certainly be compromising if anyone guessed how much time they were spending alone together. But Callie nodded. "And if I pour tea to your satisfaction, will you let me take my leave of you?"

Thorington waved a hand toward the teapot. "I'm sure you don't wish to miss all the quiet reflection you could be enjoying," he said drily. "Show me what you are capable of."

Callie sat next to the tea cart. Everything she needed was there. The box of tea leaves was smaller than the ornately carved chest she used in Baltimore, but it was also unlocked — there wasn't enough tea in it to be overly concerned about theft. A teapot, cream, sugar, spoons, and four teacups completed the scene.

"Shall we wait for our other guests?" she asked.

Something dark flashed over Thorington's face as he sat down across from her. "No. I'm afraid you'll have to make do with me."

She couldn't tell him that she didn't mind.

Callie made a show of pouring hot water into the teapot to warm it, then draining it to make room for fresh water. Then she spooned leaves into the pot — one spoon for every cup she intended to make, along with an extra spoon to make the tea slightly stronger — before pouring more hot water over it and replacing the lid.

As she waited for the tea to steep, she folded her hands in her lap. "I told Serena this was a waste of effort. I've been pouring tea since my mother died."

"Pouring tea for merchants is a far cry from what's expected in an English drawing room," he said.

She smiled sweetly. "Indeed. The merchants can pull their own weight rather than living off the labors of others. Much easier to satisfy them when they know the efforts involved in producing tea."

"I am a merchant as well, you know."

"Are you?" she said. "Or are your business managers the merchants? I can't see you dirtying your hands with trade."

Thorington smiled. "On that, you are correct. I'd rather save my hands for more…delicate endeavors."

The man seemed intent on teasing her. She refused to blush. Instead, she checked the tea in the pot and considered her words. She had wondered why Thorington was so intent on making Anthony marry her, when he seemed to have enough wealth to take care of the boy indefinitely. What she'd read in the *Gazette* made her question his motives.

But she wasn't one for considering her words. "Does Lord Anthony stand to inherit any of your wealth?"

He looked at the teapot. "Are you sure you haven't steeped it for too long?"

"Another minute, I think. Does that not give you enough time in which to answer my question?"

"I should have moved on to manners rather than mechanics, I think," Thorington mused. "You're more proficient at basic skills than I suspected, but your conversation is still woefully imperfect."

She arranged their cups on the tray. "I should likely hire a new governess for conversational lessons rather than relying on you."

"I am a master at conversation," Thorington said.

"That, sirrah, is a gross overstatement," she retorted.

"You will call me 'your grace' again someday, you know," he said. There was a promise in his voice that made her suddenly feel warm, as though his words were enough to pick up her heart and hold it close. "And I will find it sweeter because you've waited."

"Are you this evasive with all of your conversational partners?"

He smiled. "Most of them never arrive at the point where they dare to ask a question."

"Charming," she murmured. "Do you take milk or sugar?"

"Milk, no sugar. Who gave you the necklace?"

She dropped the sugar tongs with a clatter. "I beg your pardon?"

He reached forward before she could think to lean back, hooking a finger around the chain and pulling the pendant from its hiding place. "It's a lovely piece, Miss Briarley. But it isn't suited for this gown. Nor was it suited for any other gown you've worn it with. I wouldn't think you would wear it unless it meant something to you."

She swatted his hand away and covered the pendant with her palm. "There is no meaning to it that you could comprehend."

"Humor me, my dear."

"As you humor me?" She tucked the necklace back into her bodice. "You aren't very sporting."

Thorington smiled. "No, I am not. What does the pendant mean? Some secret lover waiting for you?"

"Of course not."

"No one who will jeopardize your agreement with my brother?"

"No," she said. It was time to go on the offensive and lure him away from a dangerous topic. "I won't say another word until you tell me why you are so set on marrying Anthony to me when he doesn't seem to have any interest in the proceedings."

"What gave you that impression?"

Callie shook her head. "I know that tactic. I want an answer, not another question."

He stayed silent as she poured milk, then tea, into his cup. Then she added a lump of sugar to her own cup, pouring tea over it and stirring until the sugar dissolved. When she handed him his cup, he lifted it in a toast. "To grand alliances, Miss Briarley."

She met his eyes. "You are a devil."

He sipped his tea. "I've been made aware of that fact before. Now, shall we discuss what topics would be appropriate for an afternoon gathering? The list is quite short."

"I'm afraid I cannot concentrate on anything at all. My poor female brain is completely befuddled trying to guess why you want Anthony to marry me."

Thorington snorted. "Your poor female brain hasn't met a problem it couldn't solve, I'd wager."

"How flattering of you to say," she said.

And she *was* flattered. But she didn't want to be. And even if he meant it, it was likely just another tactic — just another means to distract her.

"Do you play cards, Miss Briarley?" he asked.

"Why do you ask?"

He took another sip of his tea. "You have proven yourself adept at dancing, music, and serving tea. But if you are to survive in the ton without ruining yourself, you should know how to play cards — or how to avoid them. And you should know how to hold your drink so that you don't disgrace yourself."

He reached into his jacket and pulled out a small flask, setting it on the table with a flourish. And then she noticed the pack of cards that rested, unnoticed but out of place, on one of the side tables. "You told me I would be free to leave after I poured tea."

Thorington gestured at the door. "I haven't locked you in, Miss Briarley. But I thought you would want an adventure instead of a night of quiet contemplation."

There was some intent, searching look in his eyes — something that seemed almost like a dare. "You warned me that I would find dragons if I went on an adventure with you," she said.

"So I did." He paused, then turned over two fresh teacups and splashed the contents of his flask into them. "But you seem better suited for dragons, Miss Briarley."

He pushed a cup toward her. She stared down at it, considering.

Thorington wanted something. He didn't do anything without a plan. This plan, though, left her in the dark.

"May I ask why you want to test my tolerance for spirits?" she asked.

He picked up his cup, looking serious enough that she wasn't tempted to laugh at the incongruous spectacle of his large hand wrapping around such a dainty piece of porcelain. "We both want information from each other. And we both seem disinclined to give it. If you'll agree, though, we could play for it."

"You'd bet your information against mine?" she said.

He nodded. "As long as we both vow to tell the truth. I'll even give you one answer for free, in case your skill at cards doesn't match mine."

She knew that his thinly veiled insult of her skill was meant to lure her into the game. But she didn't care. "Very well — I'll play. Is the minimum bet one question? Or something else?"

"One question seems appropriate," he said. He set his whisky aside and took up the pack of cards. He shuffled them expertly, manipulating them with complete confidence. "You should be warned that I never lose."

"Is that so?" she said coolly. She picked up her teacup and sipped the whisky he had poured for her. She noted, over the rim of her cup, a flicker of surprise in his eyes. "Did you know that Lucretia has saved hundreds of old issues of the *Gazette* in the library?"

"I did not," he said, setting the cards aside so that he could arrange a table between them.

"I read the May and June society pages this afternoon," she said. "And I was quite interested to note that you lost a vast sum at Wattier's this spring."

"Indeed? I wouldn't consider a few thousand pounds a 'vast sum'."

"No doubt," she said. "The papers were also breathless over the fact that you spent fifty thousand pounds on an antiquity at a private auction recently. A few thousand pounds would be nothing to you."

Thorington picked up his cup again. For once, so unusual that she was almost convinced she'd misinterpreted, he seemed flummoxed — moving from his cup to the cards and back again as though she'd stunned him. "You have been very studious, Miss Briarley. As your governess, I find your knowledge commendable."

She smiled sweetly. "Shall we play, then? I have a great number of questions for you."

CHAPTER FOURTEEN

This was not a good idea.

In fact, as Thorington dealt the cards, he realized that it was the worst idea he'd had in quite some time. Betting against Callista Briarley wasn't part of the plan. He shouldn't have even continued with his plan to have tea with her after he realized that Anthony wouldn't join them — and especially after Serena, that little traitor, had coerced them into being alone.

Not that Serena's actions surprised him. When he had asked for her help in arranging this, she had seemed delighted — until she had realized that Thorington intended for Anthony to attend.

"She would be a wonderful duchess," Serena had said that afternoon. "Her hostess skills aren't the question. The question is what you are going to do about her."

"I am not going to do anything about her, save for making sure Anthony appreciates her."

He had been examining his nails, which was usually warning enough. But Serena pressed her point. "Ariana has been gone for months now, rest her soul. And you deserve more happiness than she gave you."

Of all his siblings, Serena had been the kindest to Ariana. Portia had despised her, Rafe had kept his distance, and Anthony had ignored her completely. "This has nothing to do with my former wife."

"No," Serena agreed. "Nothing ever did. The two of you could have lived the whole of your lives without being in the same room again — it's a wonder you've even noticed she's gone."

He and Ariana had parted ways less than six months into their marriage, when it had become clear to her that he wouldn't waste his time letting her become a preeminent hostess — and that his peers would never fully accept her in that role anyway, given her ties to the trade. She had decamped to Brighton, then Bath, then a separate townhouse in London, meeting only occasionally when one or the other of them thought that it might be time to try again for a child.

It had been a cold, bloodless union. And she had probably deserved better from him. But he'd never thought himself capable of the coddling Ariana needed — only the cool, calculated arrangements he made to take care of everyone in his life.

Until Callista. He didn't feel cold and bloodless with her.

But he knew better than to admit such a thing to Serena. "Just fetch Miss Briarley after dinner. You and Portia can talk all you want of my failings amongst yourself, but don't waste your breath bringing them to my attention."

Serena had flounced away when he'd said that — and the little smile she gave him that night, as she'd left Callista alone with him, said she had found the perfect way to pay him back.

He shouldn't have let himself stay there alone with Callista. It was neither safe nor wise. He could justify it — barely — with the claim that he needed to observe her skills.

But drinking whisky and playing cards?

There was no plan for the future that required her to know how to drink with him.

He finished dealing. When he looked up, ready with some cutting remark to make it clear this was just a game, he inadvertently looked straight into her eyes.

He should have looked anywhere else.

She grinned at him. Her smile was too honest for the ton — too honest for the games he usually played. There was a playfulness to her that he felt like he'd never seen, not even when he was young enough to know what playfulness was.

He didn't want to be the reason why she lost that playfulness. So he stopped the insult he might have tossed her way and smiled. "The game is *vingt et un*, Miss Briarley. Shall I recount the rules for you?"

She shook her head. Not a single curl fell out of place — and Thorington was enough of a fool to regret that she'd taken his advice about her hair. "I should have warned you that I played *vingt et un* all the way from Baltimore to Havana," she said, as sweetly as if she had claimed that she'd spent the voyage knitting socks for orphans. "I hope I won't embarrass myself."

She picked up her cards with all the easy grace of a gambler. "I'm sure you'll acquit yourself adequately," he said.

And she did. Not just adequately — comprehensively. The first hand wasn't even a contest. His pride wanted to blame his defeat on his ruined luck, but she had enough skill to beat him fairly.

She also had enough naïveté to take the win for herself, rather than letting him have it. A girl trying to make him fall in love with her would have made a pudding of her cards, then asked for his help.

When the last card fell, Callista smiled as though she was eager to sweep the floor with him again.

He raised his teacup in a salute, then downed half of the whisky remaining within it. "I begin to suspect I shouldn't have spotted you an extra question, my dear."

"No, you shouldn't have," she said, agreeably enough. "And now I've added another to it. Shall we ask as we play, or stockpile them until the end?"

He tilted more whisky into her teacup. "Ask. We can enjoy our drinks while I answer."

His only hope to compensate for his bad luck and her unexpected skill was to even the playing field by getting her foxed. It was an unwholesome plan — but better than answering every question that lurked in the gorgeous shadows of her eyes.

She picked up her cup, took a sip like she'd been born drinking whisky, and said, "Why did you try to force Lady Salford to marry you?"

This was *really* not a good idea.

"She was the best of a bad lot," he said briefly.

Callista leaned back in her chair with her whisky, fixing him with her best glare. "I thought you prided yourself on keeping your vows. What's the truth of the matter?"

"The truth?" He stared into his teacup. He hadn't given much thought to Prudence since the night Alex had rescued her from him. Beyond a fleeting sense that she might have been a good influence on him and some grudging admiration over the fact that she rarely bowed to his whims, he hadn't particularly cared about her. "The truth is that my enemy at the time was in love with her, and she would have been a good enough companion for my needs."

"And what were your needs?"

"Is that your second question?" he asked.

She looked him over. Then she shrugged. "I can win another. What were your needs?"

"At the moment I need another flask of whisky."

Callista scowled. "That wasn't the…"

He held up one hand in surrender. "It was a jest, Miss Briarley."

He paused. Deciding to go after Prudence Etchingham had been a bad plan. But he had needed influence over Alex, his former best friend, and using the woman Alex loved was the most obvious solution. And then, when influence was no longer enough, Thorington had needed the money he could get from marrying her. Prudence was the seller of the antiquity he'd bought in the auction Callista had read about — and when the curse was broken, he desperately needed to regain the fifty thousand pounds he'd given her.

Alex and Prudence had returned the money to him, but it had disappeared along with the rest of his fortune. And he couldn't explain all of that to Callista without explaining the curse he and Alex had suffered from, and how Alex had broken it. So, giving Callista the rest of the truth, he said, "I needed a wife who wouldn't embarrass me, one with whom I might have a somewhat intelligent conversation with. Miss Etchingham, as she was before she became Lady Salford, had impeccable manners and a sharp mind. She also had a decent sum of money in her possession. A man could do worse."

Callista didn't say anything. She looked him over again, then took another swig of whisky. "I have more questions. Deal the cards."

No one dared to order the Duke of Thorington like that. He arched a brow.

"Sirrah," she added.

He laughed in spite of himself. That laugh seemed to shake something loose within him — something that ached to touch her, to tease her, to make her laugh in return. To capture and keep all her innocence and all her insolence.

To make her his.

But that was *not* the plan. She was to be Lady Anthony. And never, in his lifetime, the Duchess of Thorington.

He reached across and poured more whisky into her cup. But he didn't let himself touch her hand, as he wanted to. Didn't let his hand drop to her shoulder, then graze across the swell of her breast — to touch silk, then skin. Didn't let himself free her from her bodice. Didn't run his thumb over her nipple, didn't take the pleasure of watching it tighten in need for him. Didn't shove the table aside. Didn't pull her into his lap. Didn't feel his cock hardening against her backside, didn't shift her to straddle him, didn't run his hands through her hair, didn't whisper his need for her against her throat, didn't hear his name — his real name, not his title — on her lips…

He pulled the flask away, then looked into her eyes. She looked dazed, meeting his gaze over the rim of her cup, as though he'd said his fantasy aloud.

Their gazes held. It was only a moment.

But it was long enough for Thorington to wish that he'd been another man. A better man.

"Careful what you wish for, Miss Briarley," he said, his voice low. "You might not like the answers."

She drew a breath, as though it could release her from their enchantment. "I'll take my chances with your dragons."

Thorington pushed his whisky aside. He needed a clear head with her. But a clear head didn't help. He dealt, arranged his cards, plotted his course — and she beat him just as quickly as she had before.

When the last card fell, she leaned back again, sipping her whisky with complete confidence.

"What's your question?" he asked.

"I need a moment," she said. She considered him, tapping her finger against her cup as though counting all the ways she could annoy him. Finally, she set her cup on the table and straightened her shoulders.

"If this is too painful, you may refuse to answer. But what were the circumstances of your marriage to your first wife?"

That was as broad a question as she could ask — as though she intended to get the whole of his ten-year marriage into one question. "Curious little minx, aren't you?"

Callista wouldn't be thrown off by a comment like that. She

smiled instead. "I'll confess I find you more interesting than anyone else I've met. And this game was your idea, not mine."

"I should hope I'm more interesting than whatever miscreants you might find in Baltimore."

Insulting America usually did the trick, but she still wasn't swayed. "That doesn't sound like an answer to my question."

"Willful wench," he said.

She just looked at him expectantly.

Thorington sighed. "Ariana wanted a title. I needed money. She used some...unorthodox methods to convince me to marry her. I probably wouldn't have looked at her otherwise. But at its heart, our marriage was a business arrangement."

"Then you didn't love her?"

It was a second question, one he wasn't obliged to answer. But he wanted her to know the answer. "No."

"But..."

He cut her off. "You'll have to win again before I say anything more."

Callista smiled. "Of course. Deal."

He should have stopped their game then. But he liked the reckless look in her eyes. And he liked the reckless pounding of his pulse.

Thorington was never reckless.

He dealt. Her recklessness must have turned to cockiness, because she didn't pay attention as closely as she had before — misplayed so badly that even his ruined luck couldn't lose. Her shock at losing was almost adorable, even though it tweaked his pride.

She looked up and met his gaze with all the preparation of a battle-hardened veteran ready to defend against a cavalry charge. "Your question, sirrah?"

He wanted to ask why she wouldn't give him the title that was his due, but he suspected she had said 'sirrah' to turn his mind to that instead of other, better lines of inquiry. He paused, letting his gaze rove over her face, then down the column of her neck.

"What is the provenance of your necklace?"

She put a hand over her heart. He didn't think her flush came from the whisky. "My necklace?"

He tsked. "I answered your questions directly. Don't say Americans have less honor."

Her flush deepened. "Of course not. One of my captains gave it to me."

"And will this captain jeopardize your future marriage?" he asked.

"That's another question, sirrah," she said prettily.

He grinned and shuffled the cards. "So it is, Miss Briarley."

They played again. And he won again. But he didn't ask the question she expected. "Do you think you are capable of loving Anthony?"

Her shock was evident. She leaned back again, but this was more of a slump, as though the very thought overwhelmed her strength. "Why do you ask?"

"That's my question," he said, more gently than he intended.

She closed her eyes. He waited. He could be patient in those rare moments where everything seemed to hang in the balance. Finally, with her eyes still closed, she said, "No. This is a business arrangement, not love."

It was the answer he expected. Maybe even the answer he wanted. But now that he had forced her to say it, he wished he could take the question back. "You can still be comfortable in a business arrangement. Perhaps, in time, you'll feel differently."

"Perhaps." She opened her eyes again. The room was growing dark, with the last bit of sun starting to fall. He would need to light candles soon if they continued playing, but there was still enough light to see the faint, incongruous uncertainty on her otherwise resolute face. "Were you comfortable in your business arrangement?"

He wanted to reassure her. But even though she hadn't won the right to ask him that question, he didn't believe in sparing people the truth. "No. But Ariana and I were not suited for each other. She wanted to be a duchess from a fairytale."

"You seem to be the right duke for a fairytale," Callista said. "Were you not so arrogant when she met you?"

Her insult sounded like a compliment. He smiled. "I've been arrogant since I was in leading strings. But she was disappointed, after she'd trapped us both, to find I would far rather read a book than go to a ball."

"Poor girl," Callista said, shaking her head. "Did she never learn it's more fun to live in a book than in a ballroom?"

Thorington shrugged. Anything he might have said to that would strike too close to the core of him, to whatever storm was brewing within his heart and threatening to sweep all his plans aside.

So he stupidly dealt the cards again. And as the sunlight faded, Callista won.

She looked up at him. "Have you ever been in love?"

There were only shadows between them. But he could still see her face. Etched as it was in his memory, he might have been able to see it in total darkness, but there was enough light left to see the sweet, tentative curve of her lips as she waited for his response.

He couldn't bear it.

"'In love'?" he repeated. "I don't understand. Is that French?"

She laughed. But it was a soft, wistful sound — not a response to his jest, but an agreement. "I didn't think you had been. But I hoped you could tell me how it feels."

*　　*　　*

She never should have agreed to stay with him. She should have poured the tea and been done with it.

But Callie had never been good at *shoulds* — only *wants*. And she wanted to stay with him. She wanted to see what he could be like when he forgot his title, when he wasn't surrounded by people toad-eating him, when he let himself laugh.

She shouldn't have, though. Because it just made her *want* to see him more, when every rational thought said she *should* see him less. He wasn't the husband she needed. No matter how humorous he could be in some moments, he was too autocratic to ever let her run her company herself.

Still, she was enough of a fool to want to hear his answers to her questions. So she drank far more whisky than she should have, took courage from it, and ignored how her courage turned to recklessness.

He had turned reckless as well. He tipped the last bit of whisky into his cup. "Why are you thinking of love?" he asked, setting his flask aside. "Do you no longer want a business arrangement?"

Either the whisky or the conversation suddenly made her tired. She tucked her legs up underneath her — not what a lady *should* do, but she needed to feel comfortable somewhere in this awful house. There wasn't enough light left to read the nuances of his face, but she thought he tensed up, as though her casual pose somehow caused him pain.

"A business arrangement is what I should do," she said.

"It's the curse of our class," he said. His voice was sympathetic — more sympathetic than she might have judged him capable of. "But I would rather take that curse than a different one. Love doesn't pay the creditors."

"Nor does it buy ships," she agreed.

"Or whisky."

Callie laughed. "We make quite the pair, don't we?"

She had meant it in reference to their mercenary natures — they were sitting there talking about money like two misers in a counting house. But Thorington didn't laugh. "If I could wish it different for you, Miss Briarley, I would."

"I thought you told me to be careful of wishes."

He fell silent. She tried to fill in what she couldn't see in the low light, imagining he looked cool, concerned — more concerned about making sure she married his brother than anything else, she imagined. Thorington was difficult enough to get one's bearings around without losing the visual clues.

"What would you wish for?" he asked.

"Peace between our nations, of course," she said, somewhat flippantly.

He snorted. "You can be more selfish than that, my dear."

There was something about the fading light that made her feel secure in his presence. He was the opposite of safe. But his voice didn't sound dangerous. And he hadn't made a single move to touch her.

Heaven help her, it wasn't proper, but she wanted him to.

That reckless fuel was still in her veins, burning. She had a whole lifetime to do what she should. A whole lifetime to live by the cold rules of business rather than what her heart wanted.

"I want my first kiss to be something other than a business arrangement."

It was a stupid thing to say. But in that moment, she wanted it more than any other wish she might have made.

Thorington didn't say anything for the longest time. She almost didn't want him to. When she thought of her words in the morning, she would be mortified. Now, in the silent shadows, she could pretend their conversation was perfectly normal as long as he didn't say anything to break the moment.

When he finally spoke, his words weren't what she expected.

"Come here, Callista."

Her given name, the one no one ever used now that she didn't have family or intimates, caressed over her, more of a dream than a demand. She hadn't given him permission to use it. But Thorington wouldn't wait for permission. The thought should have scared her. Giving anything to a man who could take everything was always a fool's bargain.

But there was a note to his voice that she hadn't heard before. Tender, almost.

Briarleys were known for their stupid decisions.

She circled the table between them. He sucked in a breath — even though he'd sounded assured, she guessed that he hadn't expected her to obey his command.

There was no time to change her mind. He grabbed her wrist and pulled her into his lap.

Should not. That thought was lost to her.

He'd heard her wish. Perhaps he was the only one who could grant it.

He cupped a hand around her neck, stroking his thumb over the sensitive ridge behind her ear. She closed her eyes, leaning into his touch.

This wasn't love. But it felt like it. And that was enough.

Still, she didn't quite know what to do. Her hands lay stiff and still in her lap. His, bolder, held her in place with pressure that felt more protective than punishing. He shifted underneath her and she tilted, instinctively, toward him.

But just when she expected his lips to find hers, he stopped.

"Callista," he whispered.

She opened her eyes. He was inches from her, close enough that she could still see him in the twilight. He was heartbreakingly beautiful in that moment, pure strength and dominance sheathed, temporarily, in soft shadows.

She understood, then, what to do.

She curled one hand over his chest, seeking the strong, steady beat of his heart. The other reached up to trace, wonderingly, over the angular line of his jaw. His breath hissed. His eyes turned to fire. He caught her wrist again, but he didn't pull her hand away — he wrapped her fingers in his, as though they were partners.

As though they had all the time they needed for whatever might come next.

His words, though, didn't match the invitation his body gave her. "This is not the plan," he said.

He almost sounded like he was talking to himself. She shrugged. "Plans can change, can't they?"

He met her eyes, searching for answers. She met his without a trace of fear. Perhaps she should have feared him, feared what he could do to her, to her company —his reputation, his title, and his usual demeanor all marked him as someone with whom one shouldn't trifle. But she suddenly felt like an explorer granted access to a strange and mysterious land — the first outsider to see the secret heart of the kingdom, not just the fearsome walls surrounding it.

Callie stopped hesitating. She leaned in and kissed him.

When her artless softness met his unyielding experience, she should have lost. But he was the one who crumbled. His reserve vanished. His hands turned possessive. His mouth, momentarily stilled by shock, turned hungry, then ravenous.

Ravenous was the only word for it. He slanted his mouth over hers, pressing, seeking, demanding. She tried to breathe, and he seized the opportunity. Their mouths fused together. His tongue, the weapon he wielded expertly in conversation, became something wholly different — something she welcomed.

She couldn't think. She only felt — felt the heady rush as they melted into each other. His hands caressed over her shoulder, over her spine, over the silk that kept them apart. His mouth, never stopping, could have conquered her even without the expeditionary force of his hands.

Even without her sudden belief that she had been born for this.

She moaned at that thought. All her wants, all her secret dreams — all the women she wished she could have been — waited just below the surface. He would uncover it all.

He was right — she should have been careful with her wishes.

"Thorington," she whispered, pulling away from him.

"Gavin," he said, shifting her in his arms so he could claim her again. "Call me Gavin."

She heard the need in his voice, recognized it as the match to her own. So she let him kiss her again. She might have begged him to if he hadn't.

But it was bittersweet this time, undercut by the knowledge that he was right — that this wasn't part of the plan. And when she pulled away a second time, he didn't follow her.

Her hand still pressed against his heart. She let it trail over his shirt, then over the buttons of his coat. He caught it then, holding it back against his chest.

And then they were silent.

She stayed still for as long as she could bear. She wasn't sure she could look into his eyes and see everything she felt reflected back to her. She wasn't sure she could bear the knowledge of what she'd seen. Thorington — Gavin — was so much more than she had thought he was.

And like a traveler coming home from a foreign land, she wasn't sure that even she would believe what she had seen.

"I trust I was adequate for your first kiss," he said.

In his usual dry, disdainful tone, that would have sounded like an insult. But there was just a hint of uncertainty. And his hand, still holding hers against his chest, didn't seem willing to let her go.

"Adequate enough, sirrah," she whispered.

The darkness wasn't complete enough to hide his smile. His fingers squeezed hers. "Don't doubt I'll rap your knuckles someday for your insolence, my dear."

"Such a gentleman, aren't you?"

She said it teasingly, but she realized, too late, that it was the wrong thing to say. He dropped her hand. "No. I'm not."

"Gavin."

One word. She tested the weight of it and found it pleased her to say it. He should have been Gavin, not Thorington. In the dark, she could make it so.

But only if he agreed to it. And suddenly he didn't seem so agreeable.

"We should return you to your room, Miss Briarley."

She frowned. There was still recklessness — or whisky — in her veins. "But we haven't finished our tea."

He laughed. She could still surprise him. But she couldn't entirely sway him when his mind was made up. "Your skills are commendable. But it's dark now. You should go to your room before some villain ruins you."

"You're the only villain I've seen at Maidenstone," she said.

"Precisely."

The heat in his voice gave her a hint as to what ruin she might find if she stayed with him. And part of her — the woman she might have been — wanted to stay.

But she had stopped kissing him for a reason. He would be a horrible husband. He would grind her underfoot while she, dazzled and stupid with need for him, gave in to his every demand.

Not to mention that he had never said he wished to marry her.

He'd sold his brother to her, after all. That wasn't the action of someone who wanted her for himself.

In the calculus that made up her life, she could choose love or freedom.

And, as he had reminded her, love didn't buy ships.

So she gave up the safe haven of his lap. "Thank you for the lesson," Callie said.

Thorington — for he was no longer Gavin — inclined his head.

She left him alone in the dark. Left before she could change her mind.

Left before she could find out any more of what might have been.

CHAPTER FIFTEEN

When Callie left — fled — Thorington's presence, she discovered that Serena had abandoned them. So much for Serena's claim that she would protect Callie from ruin.

Callie was less concerned than she likely should have been. They hadn't been caught. Still, she dashed down the darkened stairs and through the gloomy passageways that would take her back to Maidenstone's modern rooms. The darkness wasn't absolute yet, but twilight made the house feel unsettling. Any number of foul deeds had happened in those halls — it wasn't so hard to imagine that she could be another.

But she would rather be caught in a near-run than go back to Thorington and beg for a candle.

She didn't want a candle anyway. She wanted to go back and kiss him again. Just the thought of it made her smile — a silly smile, one that made her try to control the upturn of her mouth even though no one was in sight. He might still be up there, in the dark, thinking of her.

Thinking of her as she thought of him. Maybe it was the whisky that made her smile. It couldn't be that their kiss had been more than she'd imagined a kiss could be. It couldn't be that *he'd* been more than she'd imagined he could be.

She wasn't surprised that he had kissed her — some instinct, one she mostly ignored, had known that he desired her. But she was surprised that he had been so tender. And their conversation before that kiss had somehow felt easy, even as they delved into secrets neither of them should have shared.

Thorington could never be described as easy. But for a few moments, for her, he had been.

Callie hesitated on the final staircase. If she returned, she might surprise a laugh out of him. He might become Gavin again.

No. He had made it clear that a kiss was all he could give her.

Callie rubbed her hand across her mouth and straightened her shoulders. She felt a bit woozy, either from the kisses or the whisky. She thought of going to her bed, lying there, and dreaming of Gavin.

She was a fool. He wasn't Gavin; he was Thorington. And succumbing to dreams when she needed to be making plans was not something she could allow herself to do.

She found the library again and was pleased that it was empty. There was just enough twilight left for her to see that the servants hadn't cleared away the newssheets she'd left on one of the heavy mahogany tables. Somewhere in the distance, she heard muted conversation; there were others in the house who still stirred.

But the library was perfectly empty. Her study in Baltimore sometimes felt like this, when she sought it out on cool, restless nights. She ran her fingers along the mantel above the empty fireplace until she found a tinderbox. She had become quite proficient with fire after her father's death, not needing someone else to strike steel against flint or coax the sparks into embers, then flame.

She showered sparks onto the tinder until it caught, then lit a candle before damping the tinder and closing the box. The candle seemed to be spermaceti, more expensive than tallow or even beeswax, and it cast a warm, steady light in her little corner of the library.

She returned to the table. She'd thought the newssheets had been left undisturbed, but she realized that someone had placed a recent edition of the *Gazette* on top of the pile. It took at least two days for papers from London to reach them, and the papers were then passed around the party until they were at risk of disintegrating.

This one was from over a week earlier. It wouldn't have any gossip about Thorington. But as she set it aside, a headline caught her eye. *AMERICAN PRIVATEERS A MENACE.*

She laughed. The British were so shocked that anyone could challenge them on the seas that the issue of American privateers had become a national disgrace. She skimmed over the article, looking for any news she might glean about her own interests.

And there, near the bottom, she read, "Ships from Baltimore, in particular, are causing havoc across the Atlantic, even daring to prey on British interests in the Channel and around the Irish coast. A single ship from Baltimore has, in its first cruise, taken over a dozen ships, including the British frigate *Adamant*. The captain of that unfortunate vessel, a Mr. Hallett, son of the Hon. Frederick Hallett, M.P., is now billeted at Dartmouth, assisting in the preparation of Channel defenses against both the privateering nuisance and the larger threat from Napoleon. We pray he is more effective in this endeavor than in his last command. We also urge the government to destroy these vipers in their nest, in Baltimore's harbor, rather than allowing them to prey on innocent merchants."

Callie snickered. She recognized Hallett's name — she had read the captain's log after they had captured *Adamant*. She wasn't surprised that the Navy had taken away his command, even in the midst of wars with France and America that left them continually desperate for men.

But the dozen ships that the paper referenced gave her pause. What had Jacobs been up to? Had he been caught yet, or were all those prizes safely distributed?

As she contemplated whether she might be rich or ruined, one of the terrace doors opened. Rafe emerged from the twilight. "I didn't expect to find you here, Miss Briarley," he said. "Has the party reduced you to such dire circumstances?"

He was beyond the reach of her lone candle and she couldn't see his face. But his voice, as always, sounded friendly. "I do read on occasion," she said. "You must be shocked to find literacy among the Americans."

He laughed. "I've never cast aspersions against the Americans. If you tell anyone I said this I'll deny it, but the lot of you are lucky you took your freedom from us long before we started this bloody business with Napoleon."

"I had nothing to do with it, of course," Callie said. She flipped the paper over, casually, hoping he wouldn't notice the headline. "I'm a mere female, and too young to have been a revolutionary anyway."

Rafe snorted. "I'll grant you're too young, but I vow that's all that would have stopped you."

"I shall take that as a compliment, my lord," she said.

She didn't invite him to join her, expecting him to leave her. But he dropped into the chair across from her. He wore a greatcoat over riding breeches and Hessian boots, and he carried a hat in his gloved hand. Callie vaguely wondered where he had been; she couldn't recall whether she had seen him at dinner, although it wouldn't have been remarkable for him to skip the event.

"You should not be here alone, Miss Briarley," he said. "You might perish of boredom."

"I was far more alone in Baltimore," she said, waving him away. "I believe I shall survive tonight."

Rafe stripped off his gloves, picked up a cold candle from the table, and leaned over to tip it into her flame. When it caught, he sat back, considering her. "Your self-sufficiency is admirable. But let's cut bait, my dear. You are too valuable a prize to be left unescorted."

Callie laughed. "That sounds entirely too medieval. I'm not a prize."

Rafe gestured around the room. "It fits the house, doesn't it? And anyway, you are a prize. Even if those who see it aren't doing enough to make you aware of it."

His voice hinted at something that Callie didn't want to examine. She tried to dismiss him instead. "I'm sure I shall be quite safe. No one has behaved with even the smallest bit of impropriety toward me at this party."

"Those who would are too frightened of Thorington to do so. But if they found you alone, they might seize the opportunity."

"Your imagination is vivid, my lord."

Rafe nodded, but he didn't smile. "Humor an old man, Miss Briarley. I wouldn't want to see you harmed. I shall keep you company until you are ready to retire."

Callie nearly laughed again. But there was something in his eyes that stopped her. He was younger than Thorington — thirty-three, according to the *Debrett's* she had finally read after being embarrassed over not knowing about Thorington's former wife — but at the moment, he seemed far older.

And far more aware of what dangers might befall her than she was.

So she nodded instead. "I thank you for your concern, then. But perhaps I should return to my room so I do not ruin your evening."

"Never mind that," he said. He crossed his legs at the ankle, elegantly. "My evening activities have come to an end. Was there something you were looking for in the library?"

She considered him. He didn't look like he was going to leave her.

"If you were looking for a novel, you mustn't feign propriety for my benefit," Rafe continued. "I've been known to read them myself."

"I do not think my governess would approve," Callie said. "I shall educate myself with the newspapers instead."

"And how go your lessons with your 'governess,' Miss Briarley?" he asked.

She shrugged. "I find the business tedious."

That wasn't true — not at all. And his laugh said he knew it. But even though Rafe was perhaps kinder than his brother, he was still relentless. "By the time you finish your lessons, I vow you could reach far higher than Anthony for a match."

She snapped one of the papers open. "I'm sure I have no desire to reach higher."

"A shame," he said. "You could be a queen if princes weren't so hidebound about royal ancestry. But I'm sure you could settle for becoming a duchess."

His words slapped across her face, stunning her for a moment. She felt blood rush to her cheeks. Unable to help herself, she looked over her paper and finally met his gaze.

"You do yourself no honor by teasing me, Lord Rafael," she said in a low voice.

"I am not teasing you, Miss Briarley," he said gently.

Something twinkled in his eyes — but it looked more like sympathy than cruelty. She shook her head, slowly, as though the gesture could erase the words that still hung in the air. "I have no designs on becoming a duchess. And you aren't being kind to Lord Anthony by suggesting it."

"Lord Anthony would be the first to dance with you if you announced your engagement to someone else," Rafe said.

Callie gathered her papers together. "I think I should retire, my lord. But I thank you for the conversation."

Rafe rose, coming around the table and offering her his arm. "I shall escort you, then. There could be any number of devils waiting in the corridors."

"I doubt it," she said crisply, putting her hand on his arm. "But I will humor you if it means we may part ways sooner."

"Yes, your grace," he said.

Callie glared at him. "I find your humor to be entirely inappropriate."

He was close enough now that she had to lift her face in order to glare at him properly. He sniffed, and something in his smile turned sly. "Whisky, Miss Briarley? What devil took you under his wing tonight?"

The gleam in his eyes said he knew.

Her anger hadn't subsided by the time they reached her room. She waited outside while he opened the door and checked for intruders, as though he really was concerned for her safety. When he came back into the hallway, his smile was contrite. "I apologize, Miss Briarley. I have come to admire you greatly, but I forget that you may not feel the same about me."

She unbent a little. "I admire you as well, Lord Rafael. But I do not think the subject of my marital prospects is an appropriate conversation."

He leaned against the wall, as rakish as ever. "It's not. But as it's the only conversation anyone at this party seems to have, you can forgive me for forgetting that you're the least interested in it of anyone."

"You cannot be serious," she said.

Rafe grinned. "There are bets being placed, Miss Briarley."

"There are always bets being placed," she said tartly. "Men can't seem to help themselves."

"It's not just the men. Portia has fifty pounds on you running away with a footman."

"She wouldn't," Callie said with a gasp.

"If it helps, she hedged her bet and put sixty on you marrying

Thorington. But the oddsmakers give that an even worse chance than you disappearing with a stable hand."

Callie shook her head. Her candle cast ominous shadows in the hallway. And again, she thought their conversation sounded medieval.

For a moment, she bitterly regretted that she had come to England. Not that she had entirely ruled her own life in Baltimore — Captain Jacobs' refusal to stop privateering had reminded her of that. But at least she had had the illusion of control.

Tonight, there were no illusions. She was on display, every move dissected.

And the only moments when she enjoyed herself were with a man who might cost her everything if she married him.

"I won't marry a stable hand, so I hope you didn't put money on that," she said, trying to direct Rafe away from talk of Thorington.

He couldn't be directed. "Of course not. I put money on my brother. I do hope I'm right — you would be the best thing that could happen to him."

He didn't say which brother. And Callie stepped into her room and shut the door before she was stupid enough to ask.

CHAPTER SIXTEEN

"How long have you been in Miss Briarley's employ?" Thorington asked.

The small sitting room Thorington had found for this interview was decorated with elaborately scrolling rococo woodwork from the previous century, too fussy to be imposing. But Mrs. Jennings twisted her hands in her lap. "Nearly twenty years, your grace. Lady Tiberius, rest her soul, hired me as a nursemaid to accompany them to Europe, and I stayed on after she passed."

She hadn't picked up the cup of tea he had insisted she pour for herself. She sat rigidly in her chair — the chair he had practically forced her into, since she didn't think it proper to sit with him. Thorington often used his power to overwhelm other members of his class, but he rarely did so with servants.

But now that he wanted a servant to give him a direct answer, his power and title thwarted him. Her answers thus far had been nearly monosyllabic.

And nothing she said could give him any clues to Callista's secrets.

He smiled encouragingly, a gambit he usually didn't employ when interrogating someone. "And are you happy to have returned to England?"

Mrs. Jennings nodded.

He debated the merits of plying her with whisky. It had worked with Callista the night before. But the thought of Callista, always dancing on the edge of his consciousness, distracted him. She had been so...alive, the night before, in a way he had never seen a woman be with him.

He wasn't a comfortable man to be alive with. And he hadn't realized, until she had left him in the dark, what he had missed as a result.

The memory of that dark, empty room haunted him. He had sat, perfectly still, after she left, staring into the shadows. It was as if her laughter slowly cooled into melancholy. He had dreamed of her — dreamed of wicked smiles and clever words, wickeder laughter and cleverer tongues, the wickedest things she could do to him, the wickedest joy he could wring from her.

There was no word for what he felt — or, at least, no word that he could allow himself to acknowledge. So he didn't try to identify it. He dreamed instead, until the twilight was completely gone and darkness reigned.

Until her laughter was gone and his heart had gone cold again. There was no future in which Callista would be better for having him.

Even if there was no future in which he was better for losing her.

Still, even though he knew he couldn't have her, he wanted to see her safe. And the suspicions he'd harbored about her — and, thus far, mostly ignored — needed to be assuaged.

Mrs. Jennings looked down at her folded hands. Thorington reverted to form. "You do realize, my dear Mrs. Jennings, that I must determine whether you are an adequate lady's maid for my brother's future wife. You've done little to recommend yourself."

She hadn't responded to kindness, but she bristled at his bored drawl and the threat behind it. "You'll find no more loyal servant than me, your grace."

He shrugged. "Your loyalty is to be commended, I'm sure. But your mistress is destined to be an arbiter of fashion when she marries into my family. She will need a maid who can meet the demands of London."

"An arbiter of fashion?" Mrs. Jennings repeated.

She sounded like she had choked on the words. Thorington rubbed in some salt. "Forgive my high-sounding speech. It means she shall be one of the foremost leaders in the ton."

"I know what 'arbiter' means," Mrs. Jennings snapped.

Thorington raised an eyebrow.

Mrs. Jennings flushed. "I apologize, your grace. But if you will allow me to speak freely, I must say that I do not see Miss Briarley choosing to play such a role."

He stayed silent, waiting to see what she might blunder into if forced to fill the pause.

"Begging your pardon, of course," she added hesitantly.

She was still too cowed by him to say what else was on her mind, but he'd seen her flash of annoyance — and, before that, what had sounded suspiciously like mirth at the idea of Callista becoming a member of the fashionable set.

"What other role do you think she would choose?" he asked.

He looked at his nails, feigning boredom. Mrs. Jennings hesitated, but again, he didn't rescue her from silence. Finally, she said, "It isn't for me to tell tales, your grace. But she would want the freedom to choose her course."

Thorington returned his gaze to her. The woman was in her forties, perhaps — she may have only been a teen when she had left England with Lord and Lady Tiberius to care for their daughter. She was a handsome enough woman, if a bit unrefined. She was more practical than the fashionable maids he'd hired for his sisters, chosen decades ago for her sturdiness as a child's companion instead of her abilities with a lady's hair and clothing.

He wondered, idly, whether there had ever been a Mr. Jennings. Not that it mattered. But the fierceness in her voice as she talked about Callista told him all he needed to know about her.

"You would want to see Miss Briarley safe, wouldn't you?" he asked gently.

She looked down into her cooling tea. "Of course, your grace."

"And do you think she would be safer in England than in Baltimore?"

She nodded, decisively enough that Thorington's suspicions grew.

"Is there anything that may make her less safe? Anything that I, as her future husband's guardian, should be aware of?"

Mrs. Jennings looked up. He'd startled her. "Why would you ask that, your grace?"

Her voice held some new note — either suspicion or guilt. He didn't move, not wanting to change the mood in any way when he sensed that he was closing in on his target. "Baltimore has become notorious for its contribution to the British Navy's woes of late. It strikes me that Miss Briarley's shipping interests may be in danger."

It was just a shadow of a suspicion — one that had occurred to him as he'd considered Callista's necklace the previous night, and what trouble she might have found on the voyage from Baltimore to Havana. If Mrs. Jennings had looked confused, he probably would have moved on from the idea entirely.

But instead, Mrs. Jennings scanned his face.

He didn't know her well enough to be sure. But the way her eyes moved gave him the hint he'd looked for.

"I admit I am relieved Miss Briarley has come back to England, your grace. But I'm sure I don't know anything about her ships."

The second part was a lie. He was sure of it.

The only question was how to arrange everything satisfactorily.

If she were his servant, he would have interrogated her until he knew everything there was to know from her. But her loyalty to Callista was twenty years in the making. He might get every answer he wanted from her — but unless he killed her after, she'd report their conversation to her mistress immediately.

Thorington couldn't kill her. But he no longer had the money to buy her tongue.

The realization that he couldn't buy her loyalty was another little dagger to his pride, pride that had already been shredded by similar limitations. But he kept his face neutral as he dismissed Mrs. Jennings. She'd already told him all he needed to hear.

There was something about her ships that merited further investigation. If his messenger to London didn't return soon, he'd have to send another — and perhaps send men to Portsmouth and Southampton as well, in case those ports held any other secrets.

Not that he could afford to send men running around the country. But Callista couldn't afford to marry the wrong man if it became clear that her shipping concerns were rather less legal than she had made him believe.

And if he had any money left to wager, he'd put it all on guessing that Callista was in quite a lot of trouble.

CHAPTER SEVENTEEN

Callie had felt like a lady when Mrs. Jennings dressed her in Portia's navy gown before dinner. Her maid had asked one of the laundresses to lengthen the hem slightly, and the woman had done it perfectly — no one could guess that the dress hadn't been made for her. And Serena had sent her own maid to help with Callie's hair, with admirable results — curled in perfect ringlets and caught up with a pretty silver ribbon, her hair was better than it had ever looked.

But were ladies always so…bored?

She drummed her fingers on the dining table. On her left, Sir Percival Pickett continued his monologue. "Of course Byron's cantos would get acclaim," he said, his voice dripping with disdain. "Our modern age doesn't appreciate the sublime beauty of the older poets. For my money, I'd rather be a Spencer than a Byron."

The man on her right, some baron whose name she still didn't remember despite days of repetition, shoved his peas onto his knife and then into his mouth. "With your money, you can keep trying to be a poet," he muttered.

It was a cruel jibe, made more boorish by the fact that he shouldn't have talked over Callie to the man on her other side — and he certainly shouldn't have talked with a mouthful of peas. Callie wasn't surprised at her seating arrangement. Lucretia would never put her next to anyone who might be a worthy match. She had been forced to endure Sir Percival at dinner twice already. But for all that she found him annoying, she also found him harmless. If he wished to spend his money printing poems no one would buy, it harmed no one but him.

Still, she couldn't give her other companion a withering setdown without attracting attention to herself. So she drummed her fingers on the table and thought dark thoughts.

The courses continued. Maidenstone Abbey's grand dining room was the same as it had been in her father's time. While most of the entertainments were hosted in the light, airy drawing rooms of the newest wing of the house, the main dining room was still situated in the Palladian wing. It could hold sixty diners with ease, or a hundred with additional tables set in the adjoining anterooms.

Tiberius must have endured any number of dinners here. He'd said that his father insisted on formal dinners even when it was just the family in residence. Callie thought she understood, now, why they all hated each other. If she'd spent years walled up under that chandelier, cloistered in by fake columns and arches, she might have taken a knife to a sibling just to ease her boredom.

The fish course was served lukewarm, like all the others. The journey from the kitchens to the dining room was too long to keep anything hot. When Callie inherited Maidenstone Abbey, she would raze the entire bloody thing and build a house where she could get a single blasted dish served at the right temperature.

"I say, Miss Briarley, are you feeling well?" Sir Percival asked.

Callie looked up. "Perfectly well, Sir Percival."

He looked entirely skeptical. And then he gestured at her hand.

She had dug her knife into the table without realizing it.

"Marrying a madwoman for Maidenstone would still be worth it," the baron said, to no one in particular. "Enough attics to lock her in."

She released her grip on the knife before she put it in his throat. "My apologies, Sir Percival," she said, ignoring her other dining companion. "I'm sure your poetic discourse set me dreaming."

He beamed at her, forgetting that he'd eyed her like a dangerous criminal moments earlier.

Then he resumed his monologue. And Callie resumed her finger drumming.

She could grow accustomed to parties like this. She could grow accustomed to wasting her mind on inane conversation rather than intellectual pursuits. To wishing other people would leave, rather than wishing for company.

She could grow accustomed to having roots. To feeling like those roots held her in place like a prison rather than giving her a foundation.

She could.

She had to.

*   *   *

Two hours later, Callie decided her boorish dinner companion was more intelligent than she had given him credit for. She should lock herself away in one of Maidenstone's attics forthwith. She *couldn't* grow accustomed to this.

Solitude was surely preferable to yet another evening trapped in a drawing room with these people.

A summer storm had swept over the house, forcing them to shut the windows. The conjoined drawing rooms were bigger than the entire main floor of her house in Baltimore. They were also still half empty as the men lingered over brandy in the dining room. But the space closed in on her. How could such beautiful rooms feel like the jaws of a bear trap?

She thought of retiring to her room, but it was scarcely eight o'clock. She wouldn't want to sleep for hours. And if she wished to inherit Maidenstone Abbey — if she wished to move in the circles that would give her security — she had to practice patience.

She stood near one of the windows, flicking open the drapes to watch lightning flash in jagged waves. The steady drum of rain against the glass was undercut by deeper timpani rolls of thunder. It was a symphony made up entirely of percussion — like horses' hooves or cannon fire — and Callie would rather listen to the beat than whatever melody Lady Portia was playing on the pianoforte in the next room.

The spectacle outside was far more interesting than the party within the walls. But no one else seemed to hear or care. Occasionally, some ninnyhammer would shriek when the thunder was particularly loud. Otherwise, the guests pursued their varied — and invariably dull — entertainments.

If she were in Baltimore, she might have gone out into the storm. Callie loved warm rain scouring over her face. She'd sought it out often enough, after Mrs. Jennings had given up trying to keep her in the house. She could tilt her face up, let the storm do its worst, and take some thrill in the knowledge that she'd still be standing in the morning even after the storm had faded to nothing.

She traced her finger over the glass, following a rivulet of water down the pane. She couldn't go outside. She would ruin her dress.

But if she didn't go outside, she might scream.

"Don't you look a picture," Thorington murmured beside her.

Callie's smile came unbidden as a fierce jolt of joy lit up from the vicinity of her heart. She shouldn't have smiled. She shouldn't have let her traitorous Briarley heart view Thorington as anything other than a dangerous, temporary partner.

But the sound of his voice — the compliment sounding true despite his habitual sarcasm — was enough to ease the metal teeth that had sunk into her heart. If the room was a bear trap, Thorington was the only one strong enough to pry it open and set her free.

It wasn't lost on her that he had sought her out immediately upon arriving with the men.

She turned to face him. The chaos of the storm was nothing compared to him. He stood before her, languid, bored — the devil couldn't appear to care. But the intensity of his eyes gave him away.

She couldn't appear to care, either. "If I look a picture, the credit goes to your sisters," she said. "I might have worn breeches and left my hair undone if it weren't for their intervention."

"Thank the gods you didn't. A lady of my family won't wear breeches in public."

"Trust a hidebound aristocrat to lean too much on propriety," she said. "I'm accustomed to more freedom than that."

She was teasing, of course. She wouldn't have worn breeches to a party in Baltimore, either. He smiled. "Have your freedom in private, if you dare to cross me. But be glad you didn't wear them in public. All the men would ogle you. Then I would have to kill them. And I am not dressed for butchering."

Though the words were pure Thorington — outrageous and entirely too domineering, driven by a need to protect his belongings — his voice and the light in his green eyes were fueled by something more. By the same thing that had fueled their kiss the night before. That voice, and that light, belonged to Gavin.

And Gavin belonged to *her*.

The thought shook her, even as another rumble of thunder cut between them. Thorington would never let himself belong to anyone. Any woman who tried to take him was a fool. She may not die in the attempt, but she would be crushed underfoot as surely as any other enemy.

Callie didn't feel like an enemy, though. Not when she looked into those green eyes and saw her own hunger reflected back to her.

For a moment, there was nothing and no one else. She only heard the little hitch of her own breath. She smelled only him, clean with just the barest hint of spice. Her fingers itched to touch him, the way she had the night before, skimming over his coat to find out whether his heart beat as quickly as her own.

Her fingers itched to touch a lot more than his heart, if she were being honest.

He seemed to know what she wanted. His hand took hers. He raised it to his lips, grazing a kiss over her knuckles, never breaking their locked gazes.

He could have asked anything in that moment and she would have done it.

Her head knew this was a horrible idea. Thorington would break her if she let him. And she would never win Maidenstone with him at her side.

But her traitorous Briarley heart wanted what it wanted, consequences be damned.

Mine.

She curtsied. He still held her hand, becoming her anchor as she dipped low, then lower still. When she returned to vertical, the jolt of surprise in his eyes was her prize.

"Willful wench," he said. His smile was softer than she'd seen it before. "Your curtsey is days overdue."

She shrugged. "I would ask my governess to teach me how to be biddable, but I fear it's a task beyond his skill."

"Have a care with your wishes, my dear. Your governess might relish the attempt," he said.

Could it always be like this? To always feel this delicious need, fueled by the way his voice promised any number of delights? He was both a storm and a haven — all the chaos was there in his eyes, but the way his hand held hers became her shelter.

If she were a sailor, his voice was the siren luring her to her doom. And her heart would rather see her dashed upon the rocks than let him go.

Callie retrieved her hand. "I thank you for the warning."

He paused. There was a quality to his silence that told her he was weighing something — no doubt tallying the advantages of one plan over another, as though every step of his life was governed by arithmetic rather than desire.

And she knew when the arithmetic was settled. He offered her his arm. His smile, when it came again, wasn't soft — it twisted, mockingly, as though he would rather do anything but escort her somewhere.

"Let us go find my brother. Unless you'd care for a lesson in propriety instead?"

She was tempted to choose the lesson. But he was Thorington now, not Gavin, and she knew the lesson wouldn't please her.

She wanted to run out into the storm, dress and reputation be damned. The mention of Anthony, when she wanted Gavin, turned her mood sour. But she was trying to win Maidenstone, not give it away. So she placed her hand on his arm and let him take her across the drawing room.

Lord Anthony's location didn't surprise her. He had taken up a place in the court forming around Lucretia and Lady Maidenstone. He seemed more interested in exchanging jests with his friends, but Anthony occasionally looked at Lady Maidenstone like she was the most beautiful creature he'd ever seen.

Callie didn't begrudge Lady Maidenstone her suitors. The girl couldn't have enjoyed herself with the old earl. She was sweet enough to deserve some happiness.

But Anthony had watched Lady Maidenstone for days. And he never once looked at Callie like that.

No one at the party looked at Callie like that.

Except, of course, Thorington. Thorington looked at her like he planned to snatch her up and steal her away, plans and inheritances be damned.

She wished he would.

She looked up at him out of the corner of her eyes, trying not to let her head turn in his direction.

And she caught him watching her with just as much intensity as she'd recognized before.

She returned to staring straight ahead. It was safer that way. Safer to look for stability within the crowd of suitors, if Anthony failed to come up to scratch. Safer to seek out someone who couldn't hurt her.

Thunder cracked again. Someone shrieked. Callie smiled but smothered it in the name of propriety.

"Are you frightened, Miss Briarley?" Thorington said in her ear.

"Petrified," she murmured.

He laughed. And his laugh reminded her of Gavin — the way he had been the night before, not the way he was tonight.

She ordered herself to be calm, to ignore his effect on her. Thorington was a devil. Callie knew she might always want a thunderstorm. But she *needed* a hearthstone. Needed someone safe and biddable, who would let her go her own way.

But maybe — just maybe — she could give herself to the storm before she sought safety.

CHAPTER EIGHTEEN

Thorington was a blithering idiot. And it had nothing to do with lost luck or broken curses.

Callista's hand still rested on his arm as they stood on the edge of the circle around Lucretia and Lady Maidenstone. Her fingers, the ones he'd kissed a few minutes earlier, were tucked into the crook of his elbow as though they belonged there.

He was finding it increasingly hard to remember that they *didn't* belong there.

He looked down at the top of her head. She'd met his gaze before, in a moment of haunting connection. Now her gaze was directed toward the conversation, but he sensed that her attention was somewhere else. Outside, perhaps, with the storm beating against Maidenstone's walls.

Or inside, perhaps — perhaps at the sensitive point where her fingers met his arm.

He was an idiot.

Anthony still hadn't looked at them. The boy's attention was entirely focused on Lady Maidenstone. He had gone to her straightaway after dinner. If this night played out like all the others, he would stay there until she retired.

Thorington's gaze passed over the other men like a dark angel, judging them all in an instant. Callista had been seated between Sir

Percival and Lord Webster at dinner — two of the least eligible men at the party, which must have been Lucretia's doing. But the other men weren't prizes either.

He'd grant they were all decent enough. None of them would ever beat a woman, or seek to embarrass her. They were all discreet and civil — solid citizens of the empire, with no scandals or secrets attached to their houses. Or they were boys, exuberant but trainable.

They were, in short, safe.

Safe unless they married Callista. She would probably shoot the unlucky winner of her hand within a fortnight of marriage, just to keep the boredom at bay.

Thorington grinned at the thought.

Then he remembered that he was an idiot.

It didn't matter that she'd shown no sign of moving her hand from his arm. It didn't matter that their kiss the previous night had so haunted his dreams — enough that he might have tried his hand at poetry over it, if his black heart could create sonnets instead of schemes.

He couldn't have her.

But he wasn't going to let her go until he was sure she was safe — from others and from her own activities.

The man who had created this debacle strode up to them. "Thorington," Ferguson said coolly. "A moment of your time, if you can free Miss Briarley from your clutches."

Ferguson's jaw was tense. Thorington thought of loosening it with his fist. Instead, he smiled — the smile that had too many teeth and too much of an edge to be viewed with anything other than alarm. "I am occupied. We can exchange niceties in the morning."

Ferguson was not alarmed. "The morning doesn't suit," he said. "Accompany me into the hall for a spell."

Thorington knew every tactic in Ferguson's arsenal. The pause, the assessing stare, the direct order — all were perfectly timed to spike Thorington's rage.

Thorington smiled instead. "Of course. I'm not mad enough to cause a scene."

The rumors of Ferguson's insanity, which had swirled around him in the first months after he'd returned to London to claim the dukedom the previous year, had all but subsided. But the flash of annoyance in his blue eyes was enough to tell Thorington he'd scored a hit.

Callista didn't let go of his arm. If he were a weaker man, he might have let himself believe that she wanted him, rather than guessing that she'd taken offense at Ferguson's proprietary treatment. "I'm mad enough to cause a scene," she said. "What's the meaning of interrupting us, cousin?"

Her voice was dry as she made reference to their relationship. Ferguson smiled. "Your grandfather would have liked your spirit. But don't trouble yourself — I mean to protect you."

Callista's fingers curled over Thorington's arm, as though she involuntarily made a fist. If Thorington were slightly more evil, he would have let Callista do the damage he was sure she itched to do. She could probably break Ferguson's nose if she were so inclined.

But they were drawing the attention of those around them. The three of them together were a powder keg. For once in his life, Thorington chose to defuse it rather than ignite it.

"Let us go to the hall, where we can converse more comfortably," he said. "Miss Briarley can come with us, if she wishes."

They walked into the hall as though they were all close friends, though none of them were happy with it. Ferguson seemed to know, for once, that he'd overstepped in ordering Callista to stay in the drawing room.

Ferguson stopped them in the hallway, near the grand staircase that led to the ground floor. "We'll be comfortable enough here," he said. "I'm sorry there is no chair for you, Miss Briarley, but this will only take a moment."

"I would offer you whisky in the library, but it's not my house yet," Callista said.

Ferguson's smile this time was real, not the goading grin he'd given her earlier. "I'm charmed, Miss Briarley. But allow me to warn your would-be suitor that he is not doing you any favors in your quest to win Maidenstone."

Her fingers were still on his arm, but Thorington felt them twitch — as though she debated whether to cut him loose immediately, or whether to annoy her cousin by holding onto him. "Thorington is not my suitor," she said. "But I've found him very helpful in my quest."

Thorington didn't like the statement, but he didn't dispute it.

Ferguson, however, arched a brow. "You have him wrapped around your finger, cousin. I can't walk more than fifty feet, it seems, without finding him trailing after you like a sheepdog."

"I prefer guard dog," Thorington said, cool as ever. "She would have been ruined by someone far more unsuitable than me were it not for my protection."

If this was a duel, it was the oddest duel that had been fought at Maidenstone Abbey. In this battle the weapons were words, leaving bruises beneath the skin. "I'm sure I am capable of protecting my family," Ferguson said, adjusting the cuffs of his shirtsleeves beneath his jacket. "And there is no one more unsuitable here than you. If you recall, I made the guest list — and you, friend, were not on it."

Thorington bowed. "An omission I'm sure you meant to correct."

Callista finally dropped her hand from his arm. "Don't tell me you had the audacity to come here uninvited?"

"I received an invitation. It just wasn't from Ferguson."

"Indeed," Ferguson said. "I only invited those who were unlikely to harm my cousins."

"Thorington hasn't harmed me," Callista said. "If you must know, we are negotiating for an alliance, but not between each other."

Ferguson considered this, then shook his head. "If you mean Lord Anthony, you should reconsider. The boy is too wet behind the ears, and too enamored with pretty young widows besides. Although I understand Thorington might want him to find an heiress to refresh his coffers."

Thorington shrugged off the implication. "It's not for my coffers. But I won't deny I'd like to see my brother settled, and settled well."

"I've heard the rumors about your finances," Ferguson said. His voice was silky now — a diplomat planting doubts, not a warrior going directly for the body blow. "I'll grant my sources are more effective than most, but by September I'd wager everyone in England will have heard them."

"You know better than to think a handful of losses at hazard would have any effect on me," Thorington drawled. "I am possibly the richest man in England."

"Possibly," Ferguson agreed. "But not probably. Not anymore. It's little wonder you've tried to win my cousin over to your family."

Callista had listened to all of this without saying a word. Thorington stole a glance at her. She seemed contemplative. Her dark eyes watched him, not Ferguson — as though she could judge Thorington on his own merits, rather than rumors.

He met her gaze and held it. Though pools of light from the wall sconces interrupted the shadows, it was hard to see exactly what she was thinking.

He desperately wished to know what she was thinking.

And that's when he knew he was really, truly a blithering idiot. When had he ever cared what someone else thought?

"Is this true?" she asked.

"That I'm possibly the richest man in England?"

She laughed. "I'm possibly the Queen of Spain. Your phrasing is not lost on me, sirrah."

The tension in the pit of his stomach unwound itself just a little. "Careful, my dear," he said. "I still owe you a rap across the knuckles for that."

She offered him her hand. "Do your worst. I assure you it won't be the first time I've had my knuckles rapped for speaking out of turn."

It was still too bloody dark to see exactly what was playing out in her eyes. But her voice, all laughter and warmth, brought sunshine to the dim hallway.

He thought of taking her hand. Of pulling her into his arms so he could see her better. Or, if he couldn't see her, he'd pull her closer, then closer still, until he could feel her — feel whether she was really more interested in him than his fortune.

More interested in him than in winning Maidenstone.

Idiot.

He was still aware of their audience. And he was aware that he couldn't do the things he dreamed of with her. So he brushed a kiss against her knuckles instead.

Ferguson cleared his throat.

Thorington turned to him. "Is there anything else you wish to discuss? Or shall we return to the illustrious guests you've assembled here for our pleasure?"

Ferguson had his quizzing glass out again. Not that the man could see any better with it in the dark than he could with his own eyes. But Thorington knew his affectations — Thorington, after all, was a master at similar misdirection. Either Ferguson wanted to throw them off balance with his regard — or he was so thrown off balance himself that he needed to buy a moment to regroup.

Finally, Ferguson dropped the glass. "There is no accounting for taste," he said sadly. "A shame, really. Miss Briarley, I wish you much happiness in your poverty."

The air changed — and it wasn't just the sudden gust of wind up the stairs, as though the door in the entryway below had been opened to the storm. Callista turned to Ferguson. "And what, precisely, do you mean by that?"

"I cannot abide the possibility of being linked to Thorington by marriage," Ferguson said. "The man is too meddlesome for my tastes."

"Coming from you, that seems rather rich," Callista said. "As though this house party wasn't an attempt to meddle in all our lives."

Downstairs, the front door slammed shut, though not even that could interrupt Ferguson's posturing. "I prefer to say I'm helping," Ferguson said loftily. "But you won't find favor with me if you marry him. And trust me when I say that his finances are too tenuous for you to place faith in his ability to care for you."

Thorington saw red then. Usually, when his rage came, it was black and cold, something that could be channeled into a cutting retort rather than a left hook to the nose. Never a burning red.

But he was very tempted to punch Ferguson in the face.

Instead, he yawned. "This conversation grows tedious. You sound like a matchmaking mama, Ferguson. Never thought I'd see the day."

He would have liked to see the look on Ferguson's face — the man had gone from rake to reputable citizen in less than a year, and few men handled reminders of their settled status well. But a movement at the top of the stairs distracted him.

A woman climbed the last steps. Two footmen scurried behind her, one with a lamp and the other with three portmanteaux and a hatbox gripped precariously in his hands. She was backlit, and the torch added a burnished glow to her wet brown hair — and an improper level of transparency to her damp evening dress.

"Where is Lucretia?" she demanded when she reached them.

They all stared at her.

"Well?" she prompted, impatient.

Her voice was a rich, cultured drawl, the type Thorington had heard in the most exclusive reaches of Mayfair. And it was nothing like Callista's. But while the accent was high-flying, the tone — as though she wasn't afraid of anything or anyone — gave her away.

"Miss Octavia Briarley?" Thorington guessed.

She ignored him. "Tell me where my cousin is so I may have her head on a platter."

Ferguson stepped in front of her. "Welcome to Maidenstone Abbey, Miss Briarley."

She looked him up and down. "I believe I know where I am. May I borrow a sword?"

Ferguson laughed. "Charming. Lucretia is in the drawing room. Allow me to escort you — I would not want to miss this."

Octavia swept past Ferguson without taking the arm he offered. Her march, as she sauntered away, seemed made to conquer armies.

Thorington and Ferguson watched her for too long. Callista punched Thorington in the arm. "Take me back to the drawing room at once," she said.

He offered her his arm again, but his head was reeling.

Ferguson wouldn't give Maidenstone to Callista if she married Thorington. And this last conversation made it clear he wouldn't give it to Anthony, either — not that Anthony would follow through on Thorington's orders anyway. And Octavia's arrival only made it worse. She would have Ferguson completely won over within the day.

It suddenly seemed inevitable that Octavia would steal Maidenstone out from under them. Anthony could still find another heiress, if they hurried to do it before Thorington's financial ruin became well known. But Callista would be left with nothing. He couldn't let that happen to her, plans be damned.

If he was unsure before, the evidence before him now confirmed it — he was undoubtedly a blithering idiot.

CHAPTER NINETEEN

She was going to lose Maidenstone.

Callie scowled as she made her way through the main receiving areas to the Tudor wing beyond. Octavia had arrived barely two hours earlier, and the last Briarley cousin had already put the party completely under her spell.

Octavia likely would have won days earlier if she had arrived on time. Callie still didn't know why Octavia wanted Lucretia's head on a platter — they hadn't had the loudly public confrontation that Octavia had seemed to want when she had arrived. But Callie could guess. The blood had drained from Lucretia's face when she'd looked up to see Octavia in the room. Octavia had, in a carrying voice, apologized for not arriving earlier — it seemed that her invitation had been lost.

And then she hadn't done anything obvious to punish Lucretia. Instead, she had taken over the party, overwhelming it with perfect brazenness — and giving the guests the first new development to talk about in a week, which would make them all love her even more. Sure, several of the women cut her. And sure, several of the men looked too stunned by her to seem likely to offer for her.

But Octavia, for all her sins, knew how to command a room. Callie, for the first time, wished she'd learned those skills herself.

It was pointless to curse Tiberius for her upbringing, though. He had been an indifferent father, but until now, his lessons had served her well. And if he were alive, he would have laughed and told her she was better off making her own path.

Callie *would* make her own path.

That path now, though, seemed muddy and overgrown — something she would have to hack through, not the straight, paved road Thorington had offered her when they'd made their deal. At the time, it had seemed perfect. Marry Lord Anthony. Make him order Captain Jacobs to stop privateering and return to more legitimate shipping endeavors. Win Maidenstone and have a place that would last forever. Lead separate lives thereafter, unless mutual affection and a desire for children conspired to keep them together.

The idea should have been perfect, but brambles had sprung up on the path they'd agreed to, catching at her dress. Dark, twisted trees surrounded her, threatening to turn her well-coiffed hair back into the untamed mass she was accustomed to. If she didn't find another way forward, she'd be stuck.

Not just stuck. She'd be worse off than she was before. Captain Jacobs was beyond her reach now — either plaguing the British, rotting in prison, or lost to the waves. He had had astonishing success according to the most recent papers, but it might be months before she knew his ultimate fate. Baltimore was beyond her reach as well. Until the war was over, she wouldn't risk another voyage like the one she had taken to come to Maidenstone. And no matter how the war ended, she might not be able to go back.

She only had two choices now. Learn how to beat Octavia and win Maidenstone. Or start over and find security elsewhere.

Callie climbed the steps from the ground floor to the abandoned first floor of the Tudor wing, where the old Tudor entertaining rooms still sat unused. The steps had been worn away by centuries of her ancestors' footsteps, and she placed her feet with care. Her candle threw shadows against the walls. She took a deep breath as she reached the top of the stairs. Maidenstone Abbey wasn't what she would have chosen for herself — she'd always wanted gracious, modern rooms, ones that could be heated easily and kept free of dirt. But she should want the solidity it offered.

She couldn't lose it now. Not when she'd tried so hard to see the good in the life she might live there.

Callie turned the corner to the second, smaller flight of stairs leading up to the bedchambers. She needed to find Thorington. If anyone could help her fight her way through to a new path, it was him. Ferguson had hinted that Thorington was short of funds, which explained why he had tried so hard to win Maidenstone for his brother. She might be able to buy Thorington's help if necessary. And Thorington, with his knowledge of the ton, was the only person at the party who could teach her how to beat Octavia.

Or at least that's what she told herself. This was entirely about Maidenstone, and nothing about wanting a night out in the storm.

Nothing about wanting to see Thorington again.

But before she could fully remind herself of that, Thorington found her. The figure coming down the stairs toward her didn't carry a candle, but she instinctively knew it was him.

"Miss Briarley," he said. "You're abroad rather late. What errand lured you out of your bed?"

You.

She stopped the word before the tone of it betrayed her — and before she could consider why that was the first word that came into her head. "I seek advice from my governess. What brings you out during the witching hour?"

"I must check on my charge and make sure she is behaving herself."

She couldn't keep a silly little smile from her lips. "Have you ever known her to behave herself?"

"No, but I live in hope. Her wantonness makes my position secure, though. She's likely to need my guidance indefinitely."

He sounded like Gavin in the dark. Callie could imagine his smile, even if the shadows thrown by her candle partially masked his face.

Callie's smile grew. "Aren't you a lucky one," she said. "There aren't many wage earners who feel so confident in their employers."

"I'm no longer lucky. But I've always been confident in her," he said.

Her heart skipped. It was possible he was teasing her.

But if he was, it was the best kind of teasing.

She couldn't control her smile anymore. He had been coming to her, just as her first thought after the events of that night had been to find him. But while her heart continued its joyful drumbeat, her mind tried to rein it in, to keep focused on the task at hand. When she was with Thorington, it was too easy to forget that she wanted Maidenstone — too easy to imagine a life with him, no matter how unsuitable he was, no matter how unsteady and ramshackle her heart would be if she chose to give it to him.

She would be wise, not foolish. "Then if you are confident in me, I hope you shall accept my offer of a new commission," she said.

He examined her. When Ferguson had done it earlier, all arrogance and supercilious grace, it had irritated her. But when Thorington assessed her, she suddenly felt warm all over.

Or perhaps that was from the candle sputtering between them. She'd stopped paying attention to it, and it was in danger of expiring. Thorington took it from her, then grabbed her hand and escorted her to the base of the stairs. "Not here," he said. "We're too likely to be caught."

He led her through the door opposite the staircase. The main floor of the Tudor wing was a series of interconnected rooms, exactly as it had been built three hundred years earlier when her ancestor had melted down all the monks' treasures and turned the abbey into one of the grandest private residences in England. No one used the Tudor receiving rooms now, but unlike the room Thorington had found for them in the Gothic wing the night before, the furniture wasn't covered. Lucretia would take too much pride in these ancient rooms to strip them of their history.

It must have been one maid's entire job to keep these rooms clean. Callie couldn't see much of the intricately carved wood paneling or the massive stone fireplaces, but the rooms smelled fresh. It was a shocking waste of time for whichever maid was responsible, but at the moment Callie was grateful — these empty rooms were perfect for offering Thorington a new deal.

The room he led her to, though, wasn't what she expected.

"What's this?" she asked, stopping in the final doorway.

He held the candle high. "I give you Maidenstone's State Bedchamber. Or the Tudor one, anyway. There was one in the modern wing as well, but Lady Maidenstone told me the old earl remade it into the billiards room when he decided he'd rather shoot himself than invite Prinny for a visit."

The room was massive, yet its position at the end of the long row of rooms made it somehow feel intimate. It occupied the rear corner of the wing, with windows on two sides. But it was the bed in the center of the room that drew the eye, not the rain streaming, quieter now, down the windowpanes. The bed matched the size of the room, bigger than any she'd seen before. It had a canopy over it, with dark velvet bedcurtains hanging down over the posts. She couldn't see well, but she could just make out crowns embroidered on the pillows.

She turned to Thorington. "If you think I would be ruined on a stairway, how do you think someone will react if we're found in a bedchamber?"

Thorington ushered her into the room, closing and bolting the door behind them. He set the candle on a table and walked directly to the nearest window, where he shut the drapes. "No one will find us here," he said, moving on to the next window. "The few here who might care for Tudor history will not choose tonight to tour the rooms. And Ferguson is meddlesome, but he knows better than to invite the Prince Regent. His Royal Highness would eat through all of Maidenstone's wealth before you could find a husband. So I can assure you that the State Bedchamber will go unused another night."

"Is it only for the Prince Regent?" Callie asked as she watched Thorington make quick work of the drapes.

"Monarchs, generally, but I suppose Prinny qualifies. Most state bedchambers I've seen have never been used. Some Briarley in your past must have had delusions of grandeur to build one here."

"They've all had delusions of grandeur," Callie said.

"I shan't hold it against you. My country estate has one as well. The Dukes of Thorington were never known for their good sense."

He picked up her candle and used it to light all the other candles in the room. When he was done, he looked back to where Callie still stood by the door. "I know I'm also lacking in good sense for asking this, but tell me your commission," he said.

She swallowed. In the light, with that commanding tone and a bed behind him, he seemed like Thorington again. And confronting the duke with her plan was harder than flirting with Gavin.

When she stayed silent, he raised an eyebrow. "Or do you want me to begin? I planned to assess whether you were behaving yourself, but finding you out in the dark already gave me an answer."

The light mockery in his voice should have dug into her skin. Instead, oddly, it soothed her. She had survived him thus far. He might frighten every sane woman in England, but he didn't frighten her.

"Then if you already have your answer, I shall begin," she said. First, though, she walked to the sitting area next to the cold fireplace.

The chair she chose didn't have arms, but it was reassuringly solid despite its age. With her back to the bed, she could almost forget how strange this conversation was — and how dangerous it might prove to be.

She waited until he joined her. Then, with all the courage her Briarley heart could muster — the only benefit it had given her in days — she met his gaze.

"It's clear, now, that Lord Anthony and I won't suit each other. Truth be told, it has been clear all along. But Octavia is a threat I can't ignore. Ferguson will be completely charmed by her, if he isn't already."

"She is a challenge," Thorington said. "But you and Anthony can overcome her."

"You know that plan won't succeed."

It might have been her imagination, but she thought he hesitated for a moment before saying, "I'll talk to Anthony again in the morning. As for Ferguson, I can handle him."

She took another breath, holding it until her lungs burned. Suddenly, she didn't want to say what she'd come here to say.

Or rather, her heart didn't want her to say it. Her head, which had kept her safe for so long, would keep her safe again. She would move forward with her new plan.

Even if her heart hoped for an outcome that her head was sure Thorington couldn't give her.

Callie exhaled. "Let's cut bait, Thorington. Anthony is never going to offer for me. And even if he did, Ferguson likely won't let him win Maidenstone. But if you help me find a husband who *will* win, I'll pay you handsomely for it."

CHAPTER TWENTY

"I beg your pardon?" Thorington said.

It was all he could think to say. He hadn't expected such an abrupt change of direction from her. Their conversation, before that moment, had been threaded through with magic. He'd felt a smile tugging at his lips, a bit of light touching his heart. In the Tudor wing, with rain falling gently outside, they were removed from the world — held out of time, for a moment, so they could enjoy each other's company.

But it shouldn't have surprised him that Callista was thinking of business when all he wanted, oddly, was pleasure.

"I need a new match," she said. "One who can win Maidenstone Abbey."

She sounded so earnest.

And while he couldn't blame her for being mercenary — wasn't that what he was, every day of his life? — he felt the first flicker of anger.

"I see," he said. He leaned back in his chair, steepling his fingers under his chin. "And what, pray, is to be my payment for helping you?"

"You're my governess. Don't you wish to help me?"

Thorington laughed even as the magic disappeared. "That won't fly, my dear. As your governess, I would rather lock you up than allow you to set your cap for unsuitable men."

Callista's bright smile brought the magic back. He'd watched her enough, these last few days, to know she never looked at another like that.

She still hadn't realized the danger she was in with him.

"I don't want unsuitable men. I want someone who can impress Ferguson. You know the other attendees well enough to tell me with whom I should try to make a match."

"None of them deserve you," he said flatly.

That tone, when he used it with anyone else, was warning enough. But Callista — bold, reckless Callista — had long since stopped heeding his warnings. "I don't presume that I shall make a love match," she said, as flippantly as she might say she didn't care that her tea was cold. "But there must be someone here who would suit. And I'll give you a healthy sum if you help me to find him. Would two thousand pounds be of assistance to you?"

Darkness expanded around his heart, driving away every last bit of magic. Her offer of money tweaked his pride. But it wasn't her reference to his impending poverty that dimmed the candlelight and turned the quiet rainfall into a dull roar.

Callista would marry another. Callista *should* marry another. There was nothing he could give her, no future in which he deserved her.

But she deserved more than she asked for.

"Is Maidenstone Abbey all you want?" he asked.

"That's what we both came here to win, isn't it?"

A question met with a question. It was a familiar tactic. "Is Maidenstone still what you want to win?"

She hesitated. And the darkness relented a little as he felt something so unfamiliar that he couldn't name it at first.

Hope. His face stayed impassive. But his heart, caged and left for dead, fluttered back to life.

She looked up into his eyes. She might have been safe if she hadn't — he might have been able to stay in control if he hadn't seen the emotions lurking there, mirroring his own.

But her words, cool and indifferent, brought the darkness raging back. "I need something permanent. Something safe. Surely you understand that."

Thorington understood. He wanted the same for his siblings. It was what dynastic families always wanted — land, money, and security, the more the better. Love and other frivolities were best ignored.

As a Briarley, and the last of her family, it was proper for her to consider security over all else. But Callista wasn't made for safe. She was made for rough seas and strong winds. She was made for passion — for all the joy and longing he saw in her smile. She was made to rule her own life, not to follow in someone's shadow.

"Do you think it wise to ask me for help?" he said.

"Everyone else would have me believe it's unwise."

"And do you believe them?"

That damned smile was back. "No."

She wasn't made for safe. She was made for *him*.

The thought, the one he'd had for days now, could no longer be avoided. He didn't deserve her. He couldn't have her. But she was perfectly, unalterably his. And his rotten luck had left him just at the moment when she had come into his life.

That, more than the loss of his fortune or the danger to his siblings, was the cruelest blow he could have suffered.

He sat for another minute, caught between harsh reality and the magic of what could have been. The rain drummed down outside. Everything else was silent, as though they were miles or decades away from anyone who could catch them.

Thorington knew he should pack her off to her rooms. She would come to her senses in the morning. There was something in her eyes, even now, that was too bright for what she was asking for — as though she'd come looking for adventure, not for a business deal. She was still innocent, and he would ruin that if he touched her.

But she deserved adventure. If she married anyone else she might find at the party, she'd never have it.

It was all a lie he told himself to justify what he was about to do. The part of him that still had a conscience knew it.

But the part of him that knew what it had cost him to suffer loneliness in the name of security demanded that he show her what she would miss if she did the same. And, selfish bastard that he was, he wanted one night of magic before he lost her.

Finally, her smile dimmed. "Are you attempting to scare me, sirrah?"

"Give me your hand," he said as he stood up.

"Why?"

"You need a lesson, my dear."

He held out his hand, waiting for hers. She eyed it suspiciously. "Do you truly mean to rap my knuckles?"

Thorington laughed. "I'm a devil, not a beast. My punishments are far more subtle."

Any other woman would have run from him at a statement like that. But Callista — beautiful, irreverent Callista — laughed and gave him her hand.

His caged, forgotten heart beat harder.

He pulled her up into his arms and brushed a kiss over her knuckles. "You think you want a man who can win Maidenstone. But everything has its price. And I'm going to show you that the cost of what you're asking for is more than you'll want to pay."

*   *   *

His lips were smooth against her knuckles, but the sharp pain they caused her heart was very nearly the punishment he'd promised her. Her head had grossly miscalculated, thinking she could approach Thorington as though he was a business partner rather than a dark, enticing devil.

But her Briarley heart seized the moment.

"What is the cost?" she asked.

He pulled her closer, kissing her forehead with the same gentle grace he'd used on her hand. "I won't take your money. And if you still want to find a husband among the suitors here, solely for the sake of winning Maidenstone, I will help you. But if you choose Maidenstone over everything else that matters to you, it will cost you everything in the end."

He sounded so dark, so sure. She wanted his laughter back. "You aren't a very good governess, are you?" she said.

One of his hands curled over her shoulder. His thumb grazed her collarbone, rolling the chain of her necklace across her skin. "No. Whoever hired me should be horsewhipped."

Callie laughed. But it was weak and breathy as his thumb lazily traced over her skin again. "Then if you aren't a good governess, what are your intentions?"

Thorington's other hand caressed over her back, down to the curve of her waist. "I intend to show you what you will lose if you marry for Maidenstone instead of your own heart. Take it from one with vastly more experience in these matters than you — you aren't meant for this kind of life."

This was entirely, completely unexpected. She tried to take a step back, but his arms held her still.

"Then you shall have to help me find someone who might love me," she said, trying to keep her tone light. "I shall double your salary if you succeed."

His fingers gripped her waist, very nearly hostile. She ached —
not from his touch, but from the sudden, sharp hope for something
she still couldn't voice.

She wanted it to be him.

Even thinking it was too much to bear. It wouldn't be him.
Perhaps, if he were Gavin, she might have won him. But Thorington,
with his hand on her hip and his mouth twisting into something cold,
wasn't something she could win.

And the cost of trying to win him might be even higher than the
cost of settling for someone she could never love.

The hand that still toyed with her necklace moved to her jaw and
tilted her chin up. He forced her to look at him as he said, "This lesson
is free, Callista."

She loved how he said her name.

She was a fool for even thinking it. A fool for letting him touch
her. A fool for coming to him, when she had known that asking for his
help on this matter was akin to poking a bear.

She drew a sharp, shuddering breath. "Do you intend to
compromise me, sirrah?"

He didn't laugh. "Only if you let me. But you'll let me, won't you?
You've dreamed of this..."

His mouth dipped down before she could respond. He kissed her
with complete confidence, complete conviction.

"You've dreamed of this," he murmured against her lips. "You've
dreamed of my hands on you. You've dreamed of wrapping your legs
around me. You've dreamed of raking your nails down my back."

He was trying to shock her. Callie wanted everything he described
— wanted it with sudden, excruciating need. But she wouldn't say it.
"I've dreamed of putting your mouth to better purpose," she said.

He laughed.

Just like that, he was Gavin again. She sensed the change in him as his lips claimed hers again. He was sweeter as he kissed her this time, but there was still an intensity there that should have scared her.

But she wasn't scared. He held her as though trying not to break her, as though she was something infinitely precious. There was something vaguely terrifying about the way his fingers touched her cheek, about the way he leashed his strength as he kissed her.

It wasn't his touch that terrified her, though. It was her melting heart. It was how her hand, unbidden, slid up his chest and fisted his cravat to pull him closer. It was how his low groan, as he bent his head to kiss her more deeply, was something she never expected to hear from him — the first hint of control slipping beyond his reach.

He was like the sea, she realized, as he invaded her mouth. Dark one moment, like a wave crashing over her; light the next, smooth and unreadable.

Fool that she was, she preferred the waves.

He shifted, still kissing her, and she was too dazed for a moment to realize his intent. But then she felt his hands on her back — felt his fingers making quick, clever work of the buttons on her dress.

She should have stopped him then. But he was the first and only man she'd ever dreamed of. She knew this was a seduction aimed at teaching her a lesson — although *why* he wanted to teach her a lesson was still unclear to her. Her mind was too distracted to guess his reasons, and her heart wanted pleasure more than it wanted answers.

So she didn't stop him. She arched her back instead, using her grip on his cravat to keep him close. He groaned again.

The last button slid free. His hands returned to her shoulders, shoving the tiny sleeves down her arms. She had to give up her stake on his cravat then, but her recompense was immediate — as her dress slipped to the floor, he drew a tortured breath and traced a finger over the necklace she still wore, following the chain down to the sapphire nestled between her breasts.

"Callista, you'll be the death of me."

The yearning in his voice was the sound of starvation. It didn't fit all his wealth and influence.

It was loneliness. Pleasure so long denied that it had turned to ash.

"Gavin," she whispered.

She closed her eyes against his face — the harsh lines of his jaw seemed forged by pain, and it was more than she could bear. She felt his hands abandon her necklace and slide to her breasts. Her chemise still covered her, but the fabric didn't diminish the demand of his touch. He rolled his thumbs over her nipples, again, and again, until her greedy heart forgot his unhappiness and started chanting *more*.

More of his hands, big enough to cover her fully, clever enough to reduce her whole body to those points where he'd aroused an aching, shuddering need. More of his mouth as he kissed her again. More of the sharp newness of this — of not quite knowing what he would do next, and yet knowing, instinctively, what she wanted.

This time, she wasn't surprised when his hands abandoned her.

She wasn't surprised when her stays fell to the floor.

But she was very surprised when he left her chemise untouched. And she was surprised enough to open her eyes when, instead of kissing her, he scooped her up in his arms and carried her to the bed.

He tossed her onto it like a warrior dealing with a captive maiden. Perhaps it was the room that gave her that fantasy — three hundred years earlier, such brutality would have been unremarkable.

Or perhaps it was the way he looked at her, his eyes roving where his hands had so recently touched her. "You are magnificent, Callista," he said, his voice rough. "Never forget that."

He loosened his cravat. That gesture alone was enough to make her heart speed up. There was something dangerous in the strong column of his throat, in the way his fingers moved, perfectly assured. He cast the cravat aside and shrugged out of his jacket.

When she dragged her gaze away from his chest, she found that his eyes had never left her face. "I should ask again what your intentions are," she said.

"I should think you can guess," he replied.

He tugged his shirttails from his breeches and pulled his shirt over his head.

Callie swallowed. "This is all very enlightening, of course. But you can't mean to ruin me."

He dropped the shirt to the floor, then smoothed a hand over his ruffled hair. The attempt to make himself presentable, when he was entirely disreputable, was somehow adorable.

"Would you feel ruined, my dear? If I kissed you again?"

"No," she whispered.

He took a step toward her. "What if I touched you again? Do you already feel ruined by my touch?"

She shook her head.

He took another step. "And when I strip you out of that chemise — will you feel ruined then?"

She couldn't respond anymore.

He took the last step, nudging her legs apart to stand between them, a conqueror poised to claim her. "You deserve passion, Callista. And you don't owe anything to any man until you make a vow on your wedding day. It's not ruin unless you think it is."

Her heart had answered his previous questions, but Callie was still herself. And the part of her that had successfully run a shipping company knew when a potential partner was making false promises.

She leaned up on her elbows. "I won't feel ruined. But if anyone catches us, it won't matter how I feel. I'll be ruined anyway."

"No one will catch us," he said.

She frowned. "Why are you so intent on doing this? And don't say it's because you're my governess, or I'll knee you in the groin."

He put a hand on her knee as though to protect himself, but he smiled as he did so. "You should have been an Amazon, darling. The reason is simple, really. You want an adventure. And I want to give it to you."

She wished he'd changed the order of that — wished he'd said that he wanted her, not made it seem like he wanted to help her. But her resolve was faltering. And she couldn't deny that she had purposefully sought him out rather than staying safely in her room.

When she didn't respond, Thorington's smile said he knew he'd won. "No one will catch us," he repeated. "Let me give you this. And then you'll know whether Maidenstone is worth the price of a business arrangement instead of a love match."

He grabbed her ankle and pulled her closer. Her chemise shifted under her, and his hands skimmed under her derriere to grasp the hem and pull it up over her waist. She tensed a little as he did this — and he seemed to sense her hesitation, because he left the chemise where it was, leaned down, and kissed her again. Harder, this time — he knew he would win in the end. But his lips were somehow reassuring.

Callie didn't stop him. His views on chastity were shocking — or they were thoroughly debauched, said just to make her spread her legs for him.

But ultimately it didn't matter. Her Briarley heart wanted this, more than it had ever wanted anything.

And so she gave in to the temptation of his lovely male chest and the coarse hair curling over it. She stroked her hands over his shoulders, then down, in an echo of how he'd touched her before. He still kissed her, but as she found his small, flat nipples, he groaned again.

"Yes," he murmured, nipping at her lips with his teeth. "Touch me."

She couldn't have stopped even if he'd asked the opposite.

Her hands grew more confident as she explored his chest, then the planes of his belly, then the broad expanse of his shoulders and the lean sinews of his arms. He had braced himself against the bed with a hand on either side of her, not touching her beyond the kisses demanded by his devouring mouth.

And so she learned her first lesson of the night — she could grow aroused just by touching him, even if he didn't touch her at all.

Finally, one of his hands came to her shoulder and slid the sleeve of her chemise down to her elbow. He did the same to the other, effectively pinning her arms at her sides.

This time she didn't grow tense, and he didn't hesitate. He bent down and caught one of her nipples between his teeth.

She'd thought she wanted him before. But this, suddenly, was a different level of need. His questing mouth had taken her by surprise, and she was entirely at his mercy. He bit, lightly, then soothed the fleeting pain with the warmth of his mouth and a soft caress of tongue. Meanwhile, he stroked her other breast, teasing it, denying it.

Within minutes, as he alternated between her breasts, she was struggling against her chemise, trying to free her arms. He finally took pity on her, pulling it over her head and throwing it aside to join the pile of clothes they'd left behind. "Do you feel ruined now?" he asked.

She felt too glorious to be ruined. "You will have to do better than that, sirrah."

"My saucy colonial," he murmured. "I don't think you've learned your lesson yet."

Then he drew his fingers over her belly. She guessed his destination, and she suddenly felt shy — not ruined, not by him, but still a little uncertain. She started to cover herself, but he grabbed her wrist and pinned it over her head.

That gesture never should have seemed reassuring. But he twined his fingers in hers as though he would hold onto them forever.

Her stupid Briarley heart skipped a beat.

His other hand, though, showed no mercy. He buried his fingers in her curls, stroking, seeking. He found his target immediately, drawing his middle finger over the most sensitive bit of flesh.

She gasped. "Is this the lesson?"

He stroked her again, and again, his touch firm and confident. "Part of it. Now pay attention or you won't pass your exams at the end of it."

He didn't have to order her to pay attention. She couldn't think of anything beyond how his hand pressed against her. He teased her with feathery touches one moment, then drove her mad with demanding strokes the next. Occasionally his fingers slipped lower, parting her slick folds to slide briefly into her core.

It was maddening. And it was entirely beyond her capacity to deny him. She arched her back, wanting more. His other hand still held hers. She squeezed his fingers, trying to urge him on. Her free hand came up to his arm, digging into his flesh, wanting him to stop the torment...

Suddenly, he stopped.

And she realized that wasn't what she'd wanted at all.

"Please," she whispered.

He shook his head. "I cannot do this under false pretenses."

He dropped her hand. She leaned up on her elbows. "What are you saying?"

Then she realized he was unbuttoning his trousers.

Her heart skipped another beat.

"I should tell you this isn't just about teaching you a lesson," he said.

"No?"

"No." He kicked off his shoes as his fingers still worked his buttons. "I intend to take my pleasure, too."

His voice alone could arouse her. She didn't even need to touch him. Something ached in her belly as she watched him finish with the fastenings. But he didn't cast his trousers aside yet.

Instead, he held her gaze. "Will you feel ruined if we continue?"

She shook her head.

"Think about it," he said.

His voice was as neutral as she guessed he was capable of at the moment — as though he really did want her to make the choice that was right for her.

"I want you, Gavin," she said.

He grinned, more from pleasure than victory. "Indeed you do."

She laughed. "My saucy duke. Does etiquette say I should send you an invitation now? A calling card?"

"I've received your message," he said drily.

He dropped his trousers.

And then there were no more words.

He moved over her again, shifting them both more fully onto the bed. His fingers came back to torment her. It felt like only moments before she was back to the precipice he'd driven her to before…and yet the wait for the torment to end seemed endless.

But it couldn't have been endless. It must have been only minutes that she writhed beneath him, fisting the coverlet in her hands as she arched against him — gasping his name when he brought his mouth back to her aching breasts.

Finally, something in the way he held her changed. The rain had slowed outside, but inside, it felt like a new storm was gathering. He nudged her thighs apart. She opened for him willingly — she would have done anything for him, if it meant he would finish what he had started.

She knew what should come next. But he didn't move toward her. Instead, he leaned back on his heels, kneeling between her splayed legs, keeping her from closing them. She still wore her stockings and slippers, and the sight of pale, soft silk against his sinewy thighs sent another jolt of lust through her belly.

She should have been fascinated by his member, or concerned about the pain Mrs. Jennings had warned her about. But at the moment, she was more mesmerized by his eyes. They roved over every inch of her, from the most innocent to the most intimate, as though he wanted to commit her to memory.

"Magnificent," he whispered.

She reached her hand up and brushed it over his heart. "Perfect," she whispered back.

It was the only word she had for that moment. But it seemed to cause him pain. He didn't give her one of his smooth, cutting retorts — but he didn't smile. He stared at her for another endless minute.

Then he leaned over her. "Promise me, Callista. Promise you won't give yourself to anyone who cannot give you this."

She couldn't look away. And she was afraid, then, that her eyes had given too much away — that her voice had betrayed her, that her body had abandoned her, that her soul had ruined her.

She wanted *him*, not someone else.

But that wasn't what he offered.

"I promise," she said.

He kissed her. This time his mouth ravaged hers. If he wasn't careful, she would be bruised in the morning. His fingers sought out her core again, testing her. The head of his cock replaced his fingers, and she felt a moment of panic — but it was the panic of the unknown, not true fear.

She could never have him, but she would never fear him.

She squeezed her eyes shut against that thought, spread her legs more fully to welcome him even as her soul began its premature mourning. And then slowly — more slowly than she thought him capable of — he moved forward an inch, then another, until he was seated to the hilt.

"Am I hurting you?"

Yes. But it wasn't the sharp, almost nauseating pain of his entry that made her gasp. That had already begun to subside, especially as his fingers returned to their clever work.

It was the knowledge that she would never have him again. How could her mind choose this moment — this perfect moment of connection — to remind her of that? If she wanted to have him again, she would have to give up everything for him — her freedom, her fortune, her claim to Maidenstone.

He'd made no hint that he would give her anything in return.

She shook her head. "It only hurts a little bit. It already feels better."

He brushed his lips over her forehead. "We were made for this, my dear."

He could have been talking about humans generally — or he could have meant it about the two of them, and this moment that they seemed destined for. But she didn't ask.

He withdrew, slowly, and pressed forward, even more slowly. But as she began to move underneath him — wrapping her legs around his hips, urging him on — his pace quickened. And then he finally, roughly, stroked that hidden nub with renewed intent, thrusting into her at the same time, rocking her back against the bed.

"Gavin," she gasped.

"Give in," he said, with another thrust. "Come for me."

She wasn't the obedient sort, but she couldn't resist — he was too overwhelming, and her body refused to fight. She hung suspended for a moment longer, until another thrust pushed her over the edge. Her whole body shuddered; her head flung itself back as she choked on something that might have been a scream. Her nails dug into his back, just as he'd said they would.

The intensity of it was too much. He was the sea breaking over her, drowning her. He thrust into her again. She felt him pulsing within her, and his low groan matched the scream she'd done her best to dampen.

He collapsed on top of her. This, perhaps even more than the physical act they had shared, was too sharp in its wonder. She felt safe, secure — not just sated from lovemaking, but completely connected to him in a way she'd never felt before.

In a way she would never feel again.

She turned her face away from him, staring sightlessly at the grand, velvet-hung headboard. He rolled off of her eventually, onto his side next to her, pulling her into his arms so that her back was pressed against his chest. He kissed her hair, but he made no move to touch her inappropriately — instead, he curled his hand over hers, holding it against her heart.

They stayed there for minutes, or hours — Callie couldn't tell the time, preoccupied as she was with how her heart was slowly breaking like an infinite number of cracks spreading across a frozen pond. It was long enough for their breaths to return to normal. Long enough that she thought she could trust her voice when it was time to speak.

Finally, she could take no more. She left the bed and found her chemise, slipping it over her head. Thorington must have fallen asleep, because it took him longer than she expected to sit up and look at her.

"Thank you for the lesson," she said brightly.

He frowned. "Are you feeling well? Did I hurt you?"

"No, you were splendid."

She was overdoing it. She fastened her stays. Thorington's frown deepened. "You are remarkably calm."

Callie shrugged. "As you said, I wasn't ruined. And you were good. More than good. Quite satisfactory. But I should go to bed before I'm caught with you. Wouldn't want to have to explain this, would we?"

She was babbling. He stood up and pulled on his trousers, but he didn't bother with the buttons. He grabbed her shoulders instead, stopping her before she could put on her dress. "Callista. What's wrong?"

She waved a hand. "Oh, nothing at all. I see your concern about business arrangements and love matches now — truly, I do. But I must sleep if I'm to find a new match in the morning. Shall we discuss the possibilities during the day, when we're both less overwrought?"

"*Overwrought?*" he repeated. He stared at her as though she had sprouted another head. "Are you upset because I haven't offered to marry you?"

Trust Thorington to cut to the heart. He was definitely Thorington again — ready to assess and conquer.

She laughed, even though it cost her everything. "Don't trouble yourself over marriage. I didn't let you seduce me because I planned to trap you at the end of it. This was just a bit of fun between two adults. Wasn't it?"

The question hung in the air — flippantly given, but demanding a real answer, one that would determine both their lives.

He weighed the options in silence. But she knew him well enough now to know that his head would always overrule his heart.

"It was fun, wasn't it?" he said coolly, as she knew he would.

She patted him on the chest, over his heart — the heart she could never win, because he could never give it. If she'd thought she could win it, perhaps she would have acted differently.

But she had traveled half the world while her mother had tried, and failed, to change Tiberius. Thorington would never change unless Thorington wanted to change. And there was no sense in dashing her own life upon the rocks in an effort to save him from himself.

"Thank you," she said, stroking over his heart one last time.

If Gavin was trapped inside somewhere, he didn't acknowledge her.

CHAPTER TWENTY-ONE

She had made it back to her room the night before without being caught. She'd slept a bit, still wearing her evening dress — Thorington had done up her buttons to make her look presentable before she'd left the Tudor wing, and she couldn't unbutton them again without summoning Mrs. Jennings. Her maid would have guessed immediately what she had done.

But Mrs. Jennings had probably guessed anyway. She didn't lecture. She merely sighed, then brought Callie a compress for her tired eyes and strong coffee instead of her usual tea.

She had thought of telling Mrs. Jennings everything. But for all that they'd shared over the last two decades, Mrs. Jennings was her servant, not her confidante. Callie wasn't accustomed to sharing everything with her, just as she knew nothing about Mrs. Jennings' private thoughts.

For perhaps the first time in her life, she wished she had someone she could confide in. Her heart, after spending the small hours of the night trying to cope alone, felt like it would burst if she didn't scream out how she felt.

But there was no one to tell. The only person at Maidenstone she trusted was Thorington — the architect of her heartbreak.

And she couldn't tell him that she'd made the mistake of falling in love with him.

So when a footman arrived with a summons to join Lucretia after breakfast, Callie had accepted. Not that talking to Lucretia was a desirable task, but it was better than staring at the walls and remembering every excruciating detail of the night before.

She made her way to Lucretia's private sitting room — a small, secluded sanctuary attached to Lucretia's bedchamber. She was surprised to have been invited there. Lucretia had barely spoken to her after Callie had spurned Lucretia's offer to give up her chance at the inheritance. This was far more intimate than Callie would have guessed.

But Callie wasn't the only person invited to this little *tête-à-tête*. Octavia stood by the window, looking out over the lawns. And Lady Maidenstone sat next to a tea service, preparing to pour.

"Thank you for attending to us, Miss Briarley," Lucretia said stiffly.

Callie started to respond, but she was interrupted by Octavia, who laughed a little without turning away from the window. "Still so formal, Lucy?"

"Miss Briarley hasn't given me leave to call her by her Christian name," Lucretia said. "One of us must observe proprieties if the rest of you won't."

"When has propriety ever served you?" Octavia asked.

"When has scandal ever served you?" Lucretia shot back.

There was a vast gulf of hatred between them that Callie didn't understand and couldn't navigate. She sat, rather gingerly, next to Lady Maidenstone. "Are they always like this?" she whispered.

Lady Maidenstone smiled grimly as she poured Callie's tea and offered her a cake. "No. Usually they don't speak to each other at all."

Octavia came over to Callie and offered her hand. "It's a pleasure to meet you, cousin," she said, with a smile that very nearly seemed genuine. "I am sorry I wasn't more attentive when we met in the hall last night, but I was preoccupied with thoughts of murder."

Callie grinned as she shook Octavia's hand. "*Briarley contra mundum*, cousin. I've thought of murdering Lucretia myself."

Octavia's smile grew. "Then we shall get along famously. At least until we must turn our wrath on each other. But until then, you must call me Ava."

Ava was a softer name than Octavia. If they had always been Ava, Lucy, and Callie, rather than names meant for empresses and goddesses, would they have been softer women?

It didn't matter. They still would have been Briarleys. And Briarleys weren't made for soft, simple lives.

"Then until we destroy each other, you must call me Callie," she said.

"There," Octavia said, turning to Lucretia. "I can call her Callie. If you ask nicely, perhaps she'll let you call her that as well."

Lucretia looked entirely chagrined by how quickly Octavia and Callie had aligned with each other. "I'm sure that's not necessary."

But there was something about her voice that sounded unhappy rather than officious. She'd drawn away from them slightly, as though this was a scene she'd played before — and played with a result that hadn't brought her any happiness.

"I don't see why we shouldn't be informal with each other," Callie said carefully. "We are the last of the Briarleys, after all. And I should like to know you better."

Lucretia sniffed. "You are remarkably forward."

Octavia dropped into a chair. "Live dangerously, Lucy."

Lucretia shot her a look brimming with hate.

Callie tried to redirect the conversation. "Please, call me Callie. And if I may ask, was there something you invited us here to discuss? We may do so more comfortably if we focus on the task at hand rather than whatever happened in the past."

It wasn't the most elegant attempt at peacemaking. But Lucretia sighed. "Call me Lucy," she said, sounding more surly than such an offer should have warranted. "And I didn't invite you. That was our grandmother's doing."

Lady Maidenstone snorted as she handed Octavia a cup of tea. "I thank you for the insult, Lucy."

"Step-grandmother," Octavia clarified cheerfully.

Callie turned to Lady Maidenstone. "Then shall I ask you what you meant by the invitation, my lady?"

"All of you Briarleys are the same," she said, sounding philosophical as she poured Lucretia's tea. "So determined to follow through with your plans, however dark and convoluted, that you can't see the easier path ahead of you."

Lucretia frowned. "What are you going on about, Emma?"

"Maidenstone Abbey is big enough to house an army of Briarleys," Lady Maidenstone said. "Particularly now that there's no one left to fight over the title."

If Lady Maidenstone had given Lord Maidenstone a son, he would have inherited it all, down to the final shilling and the last blade of grass. Instead, she'd failed to produce and had been left with the merest pittance. But her countenance was entirely serene as she poured her tea and contemplated the fate of an estate she might have won for her own bloodline.

Octavia leaned forward as though she'd heard the most delicious bit of gossip. "Emma, are you suggesting that we *share?*"

Lady Maidenstone nodded. "I know that word isn't in the Briarley vocabulary. But it's a thought, isn't it?"

Lucretia set aside her tea without taking a single sip. "Out of the question. Grandfather clearly intended for one of us to be the sole inheritor."

"Your grandfather was many things. Some of them were even

wonderful. But he was not the sanest man in Devon, was he?"

Lady Maidenstone sounded cheerful as she said this. More cheerful than Callie would have been if she'd been seventeen when she was sold into marriage to an octogenarian. But Lucretia stared at her as though she'd committed the basest blasphemy. "Maidenstone has always gone to the strongest Briarley of the generation. It has never been shared."

Octavia was looking at Lucretia, not Lady Maidenstone. "You should consider it, Lucy. This competition is a farce. And you're not likely to win it."

"Because you think I'm incapable of finding a match?" Lucretia's voice rose on the words, and Callie heard pain caused by the prodding of an old, badly-healed wound. "This isn't our debut season, you know. And I have proven competent at managing houses and hosting parties."

"From what I've heard of Ferguson, he's too eccentric to give Maidenstone to the least eccentric of the three of us. Competence doesn't interest him. You were bound to lose before the party even started."

It was a frank assessment, bordering on unkind. Lucretia flushed. "The contest hasn't been decided yet, Ava. And if you convince anyone other than the basest villain to marry you after you ruined yourself, I'll expire from shock."

Silence reigned. Octavia looked down into her teacup. Lucretia's flush deepened. Lady Maidenstone fidgeted, crumbling her cake into dust.

Finally, Callie couldn't tolerate the silence any longer. "I would be willing to share if you were," she said.

She knew enough of business to know she shouldn't have offered such a large concession at the beginning of a negotiation. It put her at an immediate disadvantage — an unusual position for her, since she was accustomed to seeking every bit of advantage over her foes.

But she suddenly found it sad that *Briarley contra mundum* still applied to them, generations after the first Briarley had killed another for his own gain. It should have been Briarley against the world — but it was every Briarley against all the others, destroying each other over the centuries.

And Lady Maidenstone was right — there was enough of Maidenstone Abbey to sustain all three of them, if they agreed to share it.

Lucretia and Octavia, though, had been raised by fathers who never escaped Maidenstone's poisonous air. They shook their heads at the same time.

"I will never share a house with Lucretia again," Octavia said.

"I would rather die than see Octavia inherit," Lucretia said.

Callie frowned. "But both your chances of winning are one in three. Shouldn't you take the security of inheriting a third of the estate?"

Lucretia shook her head. "Neither of you deserve it. As I said, I would rather die than spend my life watching either of you destroy this place."

"I wouldn't destroy Maidenstone if I won it," Callie said.

It was a small lie, since Callie had already redone the entire house in her head to better fit the modern conveniences. But Lucretia was concerned about more than just the kitchens. "You've no interest at all in the concerns of a landowner. And you don't know the first thing about hosting the local gentry. The first time a harvest fails and you're expected to do something about it, you'll run away just like Uncle Tiberius did."

Callie frowned. "I can learn how to host. And I know how to run businesses to make a profit. Maidenstone might benefit more from my stewardship than it would from yours."

"And how do your businesses make those profits?" Lucretia asked.

"I beg your pardon?"

Lady Maidenstone leaned over and nudged Lucretia's cup toward her. "Calm yourself, Lucy," she said gently. "It isn't your business what Callie does."

The woman was younger than the rest of them, barely twenty, and completely out of place with her blonde hair and wistful blue eyes. But Lucretia took a breath as though she was used to Lady Maidenstone giving her guidance. "It is, though. No one else seems to care at all about our legacy. Ava destroyed as much of it as she could. And Callista is entirely too American. She's almost a traitor, in my mind."

If they were men, Callie would have called her out for that. She flushed as something unpleasant unfurled in her stomach. "I'm not a traitor. I'm a merchant."

"A merchant making the best profit no matter which side you are supporting?" Lucretia snorted. "Briarleys have always stood for something. If you had stayed in America to support their ill-conceived cause, I would have understood. Or if you had come here to throw your ships behind the British, so much the better. But you came here seeking profit, didn't you?"

Octavia had stayed mostly silent — she hadn't even taken exception to Lucretia's comment that she'd destroyed Maidenstone's legacy, whatever that meant. But here, she interrupted. "Lucy, you'd be better served trying to win for yourself than convincing either of us to abandon the hunt. After you intercepted all of my invitations, did you really think I would give up once I learned of it?"

That explained why Octavia had been so angry the night before. Lucretia shrugged. "I'll do what I have to to save this place. Emma, thank you for the tea, but sharing Maidenstone is an impossibility."

Lucretia stood. It was a clear signal that the conversation was over, particularly since it was her sitting room. But Lady Maidenstone didn't stand — she sighed instead. "Lucy, dear, I only wanted to help.

We've tried your ways already — perhaps it's time to try mine."

Lucretia's mouth twisted. "It's too late. Ava said it already — I can't win, can I? Unless my cousins remove themselves from the competition. And it wouldn't be too hard to ruin either of them."

That was a turn Callie didn't expect. She had managed not to think of Thorington for at least five minutes. But the word *ruin* reminded her, immediately, intimately, of what they had done.

She didn't feel ruined.

She felt glorious. Confused, hurt, heartbroken — but glorious.

Still, had a servant found evidence of their presence? Had they somehow guessed who had made illicit, comprehensive use of the State Bedchamber? And would Lucretia be bold enough to announce it?

"What are you planning?" she asked Lucretia, trying to sound as innocent as possible.

Lucretia walked over to her writing desk and picked up a broadsheet. "The papers are all screaming for American blood. It seems several Baltimore shipping companies have turned into pirates. It wouldn't be too difficult to whisper a few words about your investments, would it? No one would care whether it was true — the story would be too good for anyone to ignore."

She tossed the paper onto Callie's lap. It was the *Gazette* from Saturday, delivered that morning. Callie hadn't seen it yet. But the front page included a headline that she couldn't miss.

AMERICAN PRIVATEERS MUST BE DESTROYED, SAYS ADMIRALTY.

It was such a relief to switch from her private scandal to the activities of the privateers that she very nearly didn't read the rest of the paper. She knew what invective the paper would fling at the Americans, and she didn't need to read more of it. But as her mind slowly abandoned Thorington to think of her shipping company, she grew curious. She scanned the following paragraphs — the usual mix of inflammatory anti-American sentiment, with cries for justice from ship owners whose cargos had been taken by privateers. Baltimore was mentioned several times as a city that must be punished for its contribution to Britain's woes. She'd read it all before...

Until she saw mention of *Nero*.

The newspaper had somehow gotten more information of Captain Jacobs' antics than Callie had — rumor traveled faster than writing, and it was possible that any communications from her captain had been lost. It listed at least sixteen ships he had taken or sunk in his latest cruise. They had even published a bitter, petulant letter from Captain Hallett, the man who had lost *Adamant* to them and was now based at the harbor in Dartmouth. He had responded to their earlier story about his disgrace, giving more details about Captain Jacobs and the cruise that had destroyed Hallett's career.

The *Gazette* called Jacobs the Scourge of the Caribbean — a name that would please Jacobs so greatly that he would probably engrave it on his calling cards if he survived the war.

She might have been thrilled to hear it. But the ships also listed their owners.

And the three richest ships he'd taken, including *Crescendo*, belonged to a company that was owned by the Duke of Thorington.

A laugh bubbled up before she could stop it. She dropped the paper, trying to pretend that it was all a grand jest — that she laughed with humor, not with an onslaught of sudden panic. "Come after me with a sword if you must," she said to Lucretia. "But I thought Briarleys fought direct battles, not with rumor and innuendo like cowards in the shadows."

Octavia grinned. "She has you there, Lucy. Will you act dishonorably to preserve our honor?"

Lucretia looked at all of them as though she hated them. "I've nothing further to say to either of you. If you will excuse me, I must consult with the housekeeper about the plans for tonight's ball."

She left as soon as she finished her speech, not waiting to escort them out. Was she going to start the rumor about Callie's ships immediately? Or could she simply no longer bear to be in their company?

Emma sighed as she left. "Briarleys," she muttered. "It's a wonder you all survived this long."

Callie stayed another few minutes, finishing her tea, attempting to look calm and unaffected by Lucretia's threats. But inside, her heart raced.

Would Thorington have come to Maidenstone looking for an heiress for his brother if he had still had his ships? The cargo on *Crescendo* had been very wealthy, and the news reports indicated that the other two ships were even richer. They also tittered that Thorington hadn't bothered to insure them. Callie didn't know whether Ferguson's hints about Thorington's financial ruin were true — but the value of his lost cargoes would have swayed even a grand fortune from security to bankruptcy.

Now she had it all, if Jacobs hadn't been captured before selling it at the prize courts.

And while Thorington may have been wholly unaware that he had broken her heart, he also didn't know she'd played a role in his ruin.

CHAPTER TWENTY-TWO

The annual Maidenstone ball that night swelled the ranks of the assorted houseguests, bringing in every member of the landed gentry who could be assembled from within a few hours' drive of Maidenstone. London accents, drawling with boredom, blended into the softer tones of Devon, creating an endless buzz in the vast, soaring ballroom.

Maidenstone Abbey was at her best. The ballroom, situated in the Georgian wing, was grand enough to cast all other ballrooms into shade. If the Prince Regent had attended, he would have left foaming with jealousy, bound to beg another allowance from Parliament to add a grander ballroom to Carlton House. But even without Prinny's dubiously august presence, Maidenstone was capable of overwhelming.

Thorington, from his shadowed position along the wall, cast a critical eye over the gathered throngs. Some wore silk; others muslin. While there were still more men than women, the balance between the sexes was much improved compared to the days when only fortune-hunters filled Maidenstone's halls. The local girls couldn't compete with the London set, of course, but at least there were more skirts swirling among the suits. Portia and Serena wouldn't lack for attention, but they wouldn't be mobbed quite so badly.

His sisters weren't his concern tonight, though.

He shifted against the wall, searching for a better angle with a clear view of the door. The more curious guests — country-raised lordlings with no knowledge of the ton — looked at him as though he was a circus offering. The more savvy guests ignored him, which was how he preferred it.

Rafe, though, couldn't leave well enough alone. "How go your schemes?" he asked, settling in beside Thorington with a lean that made a mockery of Thorington's negligent pose.

"I do not scheme," Thorington said.

"Of course you don't," Rafe said. "How go your attempts to arrange all our lives?"

Thorington didn't look away from the door. "They would go better if you all cooperated."

Rafe laughed. "Is there something I can help with, or are you still intent on saving us all by yourself?"

"Unless you want to marry a Briarley, no."

"Do you include Callista in that offer?" Rafe asked.

His neck prickled. He saw the trap Rafe had set for him, but he didn't react. "Callista, Lucretia, Octavia — it makes no difference to me."

"I never wanted children with Roman names," Rafe said, sounding like he was seriously mulling over the possibility. "But Callista is good breeding stock."

Thorington slanted him a sideways glance. Trap or no, he couldn't ignore it. "Miss Briarley deserves more respect than that."

Rafe's face was the picture of innocence. "Meant it as a compliment, Gav. Don't say you have an interest there?"

Thorington resolutely returned to his watch.

And then she walked through the door.

He had avoided her all day. It was the coward's way out, and he was ashamed of himself for it. He had spent the day with his ledgers and his correspondence, wishing, again, that the numbers would change before his eyes. But they didn't. The only image before his eyes was Callista, and how beautiful she looked in bed. She'd looked even more beautiful after, even as she'd driven a knife into his heart by pretending it all meant nothing to her.

He never should have come down from his room. He never should have taken her the night before. He couldn't have her, after all. She had made it clear — more than clear — that she still wanted to win Maidenstone. If he married her against Ferguson's wishes, all her chances would be destroyed. The house loomed over them now, as though it waited for Callista to win — as though the beat of the dancers' feet was the steady, eager heartbeat of the house itself.

Maidenstone seemed happy, for once. The dancing covered all the past sins perpetrated there. It was just a house, for the moment, not a monument to the Briarleys' centuries of folly.

This was Callista's destiny. Not the unhappy, poverty-stricken life he could give her.

Still, he watched her. Her steps, solid and confident and made for the sea, were bolder than anything the local gentry would have seen before. Her dress must have started its life for Portia, but now it could only belong to her — a watered cerulean silk that swirled around her legs like she'd just stepped from the ocean and brought a wave with her. Her sapphire pendant, appropriate for once, winked at him from between her breasts.

His Callista could conquer the world. He would pay dearly to see it happen.

But her smile gave him pause. It was too tight — as though she expected pain, not a party. He'd never seen it that way before. It was the opposite of the fey light he'd seen in her eyes the night before, when she'd been so casual at the end of their lovemaking. Last night, she had very nearly made him believe that she didn't care at all.

Tonight, it looked like she cared too much.

He could go to her. He could pull her into his arms. He could say something that would make her laugh. He could spirit her out into the garden, where she would lose herself to the moonlight, where he would kiss her again, where he would skim his hands over that silk and find out where it stopped and where all her soft curves began. He would...

He couldn't. He hardened his heart. Let her think he was a cad. He had to think of more than just the pleasure of bedding her. She deserved more than him, even if she wanted him.

"You are a fool," Rafe said.

"You should form a society with Serena and Portia to discuss my inadequacies," Thorington said.

"Charge a membership fee to all the interested parties here and we might raise enough to solve your current difficulties."

"I'll solve them on my own."

"Is your luck turning?"

The news seemed to be slowing, but his estate managers still sent the occasional frantic missive about burned crops, broken watermills, and other calamities. "No. But I'll find a way to keep you in whisky."

Rafe didn't take offense. He sighed instead. "None of us are children anymore, Gav. The younger ones won't starve if you fail them. We can provide for ourselves."

Thorington looked out over the crowd. Portia held court with a group of young officers from the garrison at Dartmoor. Their scarlet uniforms, trapping her white muslin, looked vaguely sinister — but Portia usually knew what she was about, and her smile was happy enough. Serena, less dramatic than her sister, had snared a sober-looking young man and was carrying on a more serious — but doubtlessly still flirtatious — conversation.

And Callista was drinking lemonade with some man Thorington

didn't recognize. He looked nervous. Callista looked bored. Ennui was accepted in the ton — respected, even.

But she was made for fireworks. For midnight rides on stolen horses. For laughing until she couldn't breathe.

For coming apart in his arms. For raking her nails down his back.

He closed his eyes. He couldn't watch her without going to her. He couldn't go to her without touching her. He couldn't touch her without needing her, desperately.

He couldn't have her. And if she chose boredom, that was her problem, not his.

A footman interrupted them. When Thorington opened his eyes, the servant bowed deeply, as though he wasn't sure whether Thorington would tip him or hit him for the message. "Your grace, begging your pardon, your servant has returned from London and would like a word, if it doesn't trouble you."

He'd sent the man to London the day after he'd met Callista — partially to hire a modiste for her, but mostly to find out why she cared so much about her ships. The knot in his stomach coiled tighter upon itself. He nodded at Rafe. "Practice providing for yourself while I attend to business," he said.

Rafe saluted, but there was no humor in his eyes.

Thorington's business, as it happened, was quick. He met the servant — his most trusted messenger — in one of the sitting rooms. The man was covered in dust from the London road and looked to be badly in need of a bed, but he still bowed smartly when Thorington entered.

"What is your report?" Thorington asked.

"The modiste you requested is in the village, your grace. She will attend to Miss Briarley in the morning."

Thorington waved a hand, impatient. "And the rest?"

The man handed him a packet of papers, wrapped in a cover sheet and sealed with red wax. "There is no definitive proof of what you asked for, your grace. Tiberius Shipping has several ships, all based in Baltimore. There have been no recent voyages to London listed at Lloyd's, but that's to be expected given the war."

"Did they have a list of ships?"

The servant nodded at the papers. "The Briarley habit of choosing Roman names has carried over to their ships."

Thorington had seen the latest *Gazette* to arrive at Maidenstone. He couldn't help but be interested in the fantastical story of the Scourge of the Caribbean, especially when the man had taken three of his ships. His eyes narrowed. "Do they have a ship named *Nero*?"

"They did when the war started. Its current status is unknown."

A neutral answer, but it didn't give Thorington hope. "What else did you learn?"

"I spoke to a contact at the Admiralty, your grace. If the *Gazette* from Saturday reached you ahead of me, you'll have seen that they are posting a large bounty for *Nero*. The Admiralty wants to see it captured, and badly."

"Still no proof of which *Nero* we are discussing."

"No. But they interviewed Captain Hallett, who helmed the British frigate that was captured at the same time as *Crescendo*. He claims there was a woman aboard *Nero* when he was captured. Young, brown hair. He assumed she was the American captain's mistress. They were standing together after the battle. But now he speculates she must have been more important than that."

"Why would he think that?"

"Hallett was confined to his cabin on *Adamant* rather than being taken prisoner on *Nero*. Poor tactic, since he might have led a mutiny there, and *Nero*'s captain hasn't made any similar mistakes. He told the Admiralty that *Nero*'s captain must have wanted to keep something aboard *Nero* away from him. And his best guess was the woman."

Thorington's heart beat faster. "Do they believe him?"

His servant shrugged. "The truth is that it was as much his fault that he lost the battle as it was *Nero's*. I believe the Admiralty would have cast him out already if his father wasn't in Parliament. They've ordered Hallett to serve on one of the sentry ships in Dartmouth while they decide what to do with him. I would guess that they hope he'll resign over the insult."

Dartmouth was only twenty miles or so from Maidenstone. The servant was right; guarding the Channel rather than fighting either Napoleon or the Americans would be a bitter blow. "Has Hallett left London yet?"

"Two weeks ago, according to my contact. His father is not pleased. But he knows they could have done worse by the man."

"And does the Admiralty plan to investigate who was aboard *Nero?*"

"I doubt it. They care more about stopping the Scourge of the Caribbean. Whoever the man's mistress is, she doesn't concern them. But I'm sure Hallett would like to know who she is. He'll want a bigger scandal to make people stop talking about his own failings."

So Callista was safe from the Admiralty, for now — at least until *Nero* was captured. But the naval captain could prove problematic.

Thorington frowned. "Any word on my ships?"

His servant looked away. "You've lost all of your Caribbean vessels. *Crescendo* was scuttled. *Nero* towed it for a few days, but without a mast it was dead weight, and the Americans couldn't risk slowing down. They took the cargo. The crew is awaiting ransom in Havana. The others were safely sailed to the prize courts in Havana and have likely been sold by now."

"And the Asian fleet?" Thorington asked.

"No word, your grace," the messenger said, still looking at the floor. "They are now three months overdue."

At least the Caribbean crews had survived. He hoped he would hear the same of the men who were returning from the Orient, but he doubted it. Thorington wasn't surprised that the ships were gone. It fit his luck. If he'd insured them, it might have all come out differently — but when the curse had managed his fortune for him, insurance was unnecessary.

He turned his attention to the packet of papers, sliding a finger under the sealing wax and flicking the covering aside. The first page was a list of Callista's ships, with *Nero* at the top. The remaining sheets were the manifests for his captured ships. He thumbed through the pages until he found *Crescendo*'s manifest. The ship had carried cargo bound for Jamaica, mostly textiles and fine goods.

He found what he was looking for on the fourth page. A sapphire pendant, ordered from Rundell and Bridge, to be delivered to one of the richest planters in Jamaica.

"Damn it all to bloody hell," he said.

His servant knew better than to react.

It was only a matter of time before *Nero* was captured. Better for Callista if it sunk instead — better for all her men to die than for them to be captured and for her to be implicated. But even if it sunk, chances were there would be survivors. And those survivors would, inevitably, talk.

And then, at best, she would be ruined for her association with the American captain — traveling without a proper escort, even on a ship she owned, while engaging in a sea battle went beyond the pale of what most members of society would accept. At worst, she'd be hung for privateering. Thorington neither knew nor cared about naval law, but she was a British citizen — and owning a fleet of privateers operating against the British Navy seemed dangerously close to treason.

He shoved the papers into the messenger's hands. "Take these to my room and hide them under the mattress. And sleep well tonight.

You'll need to return to London in the morning."

The man didn't make any sign of protest, beyond an infinitesimal sigh that Thorington didn't begrudge.

Thorington strode from the room. With each step, he revised his plan.

The ballroom, when he found it, no longer looked impressive. He saw bloodthirsty jackals instead of cavalry officers, cruel harpies instead of innocuous ladies. Smiling strangers could turn to lynch mobs in a heartbeat. The fact that they wore jewels instead of homespun made them no less vicious.

And then, off to the side, he saw her again. She sipped her lemonade, seeming to give only half an ear to her would-be suitor.

Already she was fading. Callista, with the name of a nymph and the heart of an empress, never should have worn that despondent look.

His hand clenched at his side. He should stay true to his original plan. He had nothing to offer her — no money, no heart, no happiness. All he could give her was the power of his title.

As his duchess, no one would dare bring treason charges against her. No one would dare to whisper that his wife had been compromised. If it was clear he had her well in hand, he could save her.

The ballroom slipped away. In his mind he stood on the steps of Thorington House, nineteen again, with Anthony crying in his arms. Portia and Serena, still unsteady on their little feet, clung to his legs, wide-eyed and silent. Rafe was away at school and Cynthia and Pamela were visiting the shops with their governess — a fact all three would come to bitterly regret.

Their mother wore unrelenting black, with heavy veils swathing her face. The bruises underneath would be unrelenting, too. His father, the Duke of Thorington, was red with fury, his anger overlaying his usually florid complexion to turn him into something that might have been a caricature.

Gavin squeezed Anthony, jostling him to stop the crying.

"I won't accept the next one," his father vowed. "The girls were one thing, but if this poet's whelp inherits I'll never forgive you. If you get a bastard in Italy, you can keep him."

His mother's back was stiff. The pleading, which Gavin had heard from his shameful eavesdropping, had stopped an hour ago. Now she vibrated with the same rage that fueled his father. "The way you keep your bastards? All those Johns and Marys are bleeding us dry."

It was the first Gavin had heard of them — but not the last, since he would go on to pay their allowances forever.

His father didn't deny it. But he looked confused, as though he had never considered them relevant. "I never dishonored you."

She laughed. The bitterness settled over Gavin like cloud of dust, one he wouldn't be able to wash away later. "If you had ever loved me, you wouldn't have left me to find my own happiness."

"If I ever loved you?" The duke's fist clenched. "I loved you more than you ever accepted. But you were always too enamored with others to see it. Now get in the carriage."

Gavin didn't think, at first, that she would do it. In his earliest memories, his parents had fought. They always raged at each other — sometimes for minutes, sometimes for days. Then his father would stay at his club for awhile, or his mother would take them all to the country.

But they always came back together. And those times, whether they lasted hours or weeks, were always perfect.

"Come give Mama a kiss, children," she said.

Gavin wasn't a child anymore. But he offered Anthony up to her. He heard something that sounded like it might have been a sob, but she brushed her veiled lips over Anthony's forehead. Then she knelt to kiss Portia and Serena. Portia was too young to understand, but Serena had seen her mother leave before. She flung herself into the duchess's arms, sobbing when the duke inevitably pried her away.

And then their mother turned to Gavin. "Promise me you will protect them," she said.

He nodded automatically, not knowing what it meant — not realizing, at the time, that it was a vow for life.

He thought she would be back within a month. "Safe travels, Mother."

She squeezed his hand. "Be a good man, Gavin. I hope you will be."

But she failed to extract a promise from him on that score.

The carriage door closed behind her. The girls couldn't see her, but Gavin was tall enough to see her slump against the seat. He realized, then, that this time might be different — that this time she might not come back.

That realization left him stunned. When his voice came back, it was too late to say anything. The carriage had disappeared around the corner, carrying her away.

He couldn't save her. And when he inherited five years later, it was too late. She was on her deathbed from consumption in some squalid village in France. All he could do was bring back her corpse.

But he could save Callista.

He unclenched his fist. He took a breath, becoming the duke again. He locked his heart away. This was about protection, not emotion. The vow he'd made to protect her, not something so frivolous as how she felt in his arms.

Love couldn't save her. But power could.

And Thorington would be damned before he saw her ruined by anyone but him.

CHAPTER TWENTY-THREE

Her latest suitor — she didn't remember his name — brought her yet another lemonade.

She would rather have whisky.

She drank it anyway. She couldn't lure one of these proper gentlemen into marriage if she drank whisky in public.

"How are you finding Devon, Miss Briarley?" he asked.

It was the question they all asked. "Overcrowded at the moment," she said.

His laugh sounded startled. He didn't seem to know how to respond, so he sipped his lemonade instead.

Her annoyance grew. It wasn't his fault that she was annoyed. He hadn't done anything wrong, save for standing in her vicinity when she wanted complete solitude.

Thorington hadn't come to her. He had avoided her all day. Even when she could force her mind to forget him — talking to Madeleine and Prudence, walking with Serena and Portia, dressing for the ball — her body, with its odd aches and subtle bruises, would remind her of him.

But he didn't seem to remember her at all. She'd spotted him immediately when she'd entered the ballroom. He had ignored her, though. And then he had left within minutes, as though he couldn't even breathe the same air as her.

It was for the best. She shouldn't want to see him. He would only break her heart. And she'd stolen his ships, after all.

The longer he ignored her, the happier that knowledge made her.

She eyed the other dancers. It was easy enough to find her friends in the crowd. A waltz was about to begin, and Prudence and Madeleine were pairing off with their husbands. Serena had abandoned the young man Callie had seen her with earlier and was deep in conversation with Rafe. But Rafe didn't look at her as she spoke — his gaze wandered over the crowd until it settled on someone else.

Callie looked in the direction that he did. Octavia was standing off to the side, shockingly arrayed in purple silk that displayed every curve. And she was similarly ignoring Portia, who had left her group of cavalry officers to talk to Octavia.

Callie didn't have time to consider whether it was coincidence or coordination. Her gaze had skipped over Lucretia, but some niggling observation brought her back. Lucretia stood amongst the dancers with a man in the blue coat of the British Navy. He looked oddly familiar, but Callie didn't think she'd met him before. Was Lucretia making good on her threat to cause trouble?

That concern was forgotten when a shadow fell over her. She looked up and found Thorington standing before her.

His coat was an inky midnight blue, cut so perfectly that any observer could see that his broad shoulders owed nothing to a tailor's skill. His hair fell over his brow more artfully than usual — more like fingers had recently run through it than anything his valet might have encouraged. He smiled at her, and she returned it instinctively — but when she looked into his eyes she saw nothing but shadows.

"Miss Briarley," he murmured.

"Sirrah," she said coolly.

Next to her, her nameless companion gasped. She ignored him.

Thorington took her lemonade and shoved it into the man's hand. "I believe I have this dance," he said.

"Actually," the man started to say.

Thorington looked at him.

He backed away with a bow. "Of course, your grace."

"And if I don't wish to dance with you?" she said.

His teeth flashed. "I've come to dance with you, not murder you. Will you give me the honor of a waltz?"

She considered him. There was something she didn't trust in his eyes — something hard. Commanding. No sign of anything they had shared over the past week. No sign that he even remembered the night before.

But she was so very bored. She gave him her hand. For a moment, as their fingers touched, he looked vulnerable. She thought he might apologize...

Instead, he bowed. "Your willingness humbles me."

"Do not make me regret it," she said.

He pulled her into the dance. The musicians were quite talented, making it even easier to sink into his embrace. His hand settled on her waist, pulling her so close that she couldn't tell where protectiveness ended and possessiveness began. They must have made a charming picture — navy and cerulean matched against each other, their gazes locked.

"You look lovely tonight, Miss Briarley," he said.

After the day he'd spent ignoring her, the compliment was nearly as infuriating as it was exciting. "Are you surprised?"

"No. Although I look forward to seeing you in dresses made for you. Your London modiste has arrived in the village. She will call on you in the morning."

Callie frowned. "You have a strange way of showing your regard, sirrah. I've heard nothing from you since our...last lesson."

She shouldn't have said it. She'd made such an attempt the previous night to pretend she didn't care at all. A statement like that would give her away. But her skin felt prickly, and she ached to hurt him.

She shouldn't love him — but she was proud enough that she couldn't bear to be ignored.

Those shadows were back in his eyes. "Busy, you know. But your duchess lessons will start again tomorrow."

She wished she had kept her lemonade. She wanted something to throw in his face. But she smiled as though it was all a grand jest. "Of course. We can also discuss who I might look to marry, since your family has failed me."

He sighed. "Shall we enjoy our dance before discussing business? If I recall, we are quite well matched for that, at least."

She recalled it, too. It made her want to leave him on the floor. But that would start gossip she wasn't sure she could live down.

So she gave herself up to the dance. They swirled around the room. She slowly forgot that this was Thorington — that this was a business relationship, not a courtship. As the music continued, Maidenstone became a fantasy around them. She could pretend that she was mistress of it, that she could command the musicians to play all night, that she could dance with Thorington — Gavin — as her only consort.

That fantasy was more real for her than the reality. She didn't want to consider losing Maidenstone. She also didn't want to consider winning it with some nameless fool at her side.

But when the music stopped, she had to wake up.

Gavin looked down at her with an odd, sad smile. "Thank you, Miss Briarley."

It sounded like he was saying goodbye to her.

"Was there business you wished to discuss?" she asked. She didn't want to, but it was better than letting him walk away.

His smile disappeared. He hesitated, long enough that she guessed he wanted to say something momentous.

"Will you do me the honor of becoming my bride?"

Her mouth opened.

"Say yes," he ordered, when she still couldn't speak. "It will make everything easier."

Nothing in his tone said anything of love. She was stupid enough to be disappointed. She took a breath. She was dealing with Thorington, not Gavin. And she had to have all her wits about her.

"Will it be easier for you? Or me?" she asked.

"Both." He pulled her out of the way of the cotillion beginning to form, brushing aside a man who tried to ask her to dance. When they had some semblance of privacy again, he said, "You need me more than you need Anthony. And I have reconsidered my decision to sell him to you."

Still a business arrangement. She shook her head. "We've already established that Anthony won't have me. And you'll never let me have my way. Why would I take that bargain instead of finding an easier match?"

"You deserve an equal, not a lapdog."

For just a moment, his façade cracked. What he wasn't saying spilled through the chinks in his armor — some conviction about what they could be together.

And she wanted to believe it. But if this was a business match, she needed to let her head rule. Unlike her Briarley heart, which knew the answer, her head needed time.

"I must weigh whether what you offer is worth the risk," she said. "Can I have a week to consider?"

His jaw firmed. "You should be accustomed to risk," he said. Here his voice turned silky, almost menacing. "After all, you stole *Crescendo*, did you not?"

That was more of a shock than his marriage proposal. "I beg your pardon?"

"*Crescendo*. It's a ship. Formerly mine, currently the ocean's, if reports of its scuttling are correct."

He sounded remarkably calm. She felt like fainting. "I need to sit down."

He held her still. "Should I take that as a yes?"

"No."

"Then I should take it as a no?"

She really was going to be ill. She tried to pull away from him, but his grip was too strong and her stomach too weak for a fight.

"No." She swallowed the bile that rose in her throat. "Why do you think I have something to do with it?"

He ran a finger, shockingly, over the pendant nestled between her breasts. "Some planter's wife in Jamaica would be in vapors if she knew a pirate dared to wear her jewels."

Callie closed her eyes. "I'm not a pirate."

"Near enough."

"I don't think..."

"No, you don't," he agreed, cutting her off. "But I do."

Her temper flared up. She opened her eyes, too angry to hide from him. Her fingers gripped his as though she could force her way through skin and bone to reach that cold, mocking part of him she wanted to hurt. "You won't tell anyone, will you?"

He laughed. There was no mirth in it. Those green eyes didn't hold the secret light she loved to see. He was the duke, not Gavin. The plotter, not the seducer.

The man he had warned her about, not the man she knew he could be.

"I won't tell. I won't see you hang for piracy."

"I won't hang," she said contemptuously. "I have a letter of marque. Even your government recognizes the legality of that."

He put a finger to her lips, looking around to see if anyone had heard. Luckily, most gave Thorington a wide berth — but anyone who looked was sure to notice his proprietary touch.

She tried to pull away again. He didn't let her go. "You may not swing from the neck, but your reputation will," he said. "You need a powerful ally if you're going to weather this. Someone more powerful than my brother."

She finally realized that he was worried for her. It would have been sweet if he hadn't been so domineering.

If she could calm him, it might be sweet after all. She loosened her grip on his fingers, caressing his thumb with hers in a secret movement that only the closest watcher would see. "It will come out all right, your grace."

Her voice had softened on the words, giving him the address he'd wanted, for days, to hear from her again. He flinched as though she'd whipped him.

"I vowed to keep you safe," he said. "Do you trust me?"

This was odd. Too odd. She frowned. "What are you going on about?"

"I keep my vows. Forgive me, Callista."

His voice dropped on those words. She opened her mouth, ready to protest, ready to tell him that he was being needlessly dramatic. Ready to rouse him out of whatever dark daydream he had about her safety.

And then he kissed her.

It wasn't romantic. It wasn't sweet.

It was sudden. Irrevocable.

Unforgivable.

The branding heat of his lips marked her as his, just as the gasps of the assembled company would see her married to or ruined by him.

Callie started to pull back, but his hand on her head kept her pressed against him — kept him in control, unless she wanted to cause a bigger scene by forcing her way out of his grasp.

And so she didn't struggle. But her eyes burned as despair, unexpected and unwelcome, welled up to form a sob she forced herself to smother.

He was exactly the man he had warned her about. And as he kissed her — demanding and without desire — she lost the man he might have been.

CHAPTER TWENTY-FOUR

He had meant to save her. But the look in her eyes when he stopped kissing her said he'd lost her instead.

He couldn't explain himself, though. The ballroom had gone silent. Anything he said would be heard by everyone. And if he turned away from his goal now, took the time to explain, she'd be utterly ruined.

There was only one choice left. He trapped her hand in his and turned. They faced the crowd, appearing united. "Miss Briarley and I shall be married as soon as we have a license," he said.

He didn't raise his voice, but he didn't have to. Those who heard him would tell those who hadn't.

And the only person whose thoughts mattered already knew what he'd done.

Callista didn't say a word to him. She surveyed the crowd with a cold hauteur that would do her well as a duchess. But she ignored Thorington completely.

He wanted her to fight, he realized. Or at least to say something.

"It was the only way, Callista," he whispered when the crowd began to talk again.

"Before you make excuses for something you fully intended to do, know that I do not care whether you are sorry or not," she shot back.

It was an echo of what he'd said to her in the music room, before a waltz that had turned everything to magic between them. He felt the first stirrings of remorse.

When had he ever felt remorse over saving someone?

Ferguson strode up, too annoyed for his usual strolling gait. "Callie, I should wish you very happy, but I doubt this blackguard is capable of making you so. Did he force you?"

She was silent for the longest time. He knew she was weighing the thought of destroying him against the cost to her reputation if she declined him.

"Did he force you?" Ferguson repeated.

Finally, Callista shook her head. "I wanted to marry him, cousin."

Thorington noticed the past tense of her statement. The part of him that cared more for her feelings than her safety wanted to smash something.

But it was enough to appease Ferguson. "The heart is a mystery, isn't it? If you ever need protection from him, Madeleine and I will gladly take you in."

"I would never hurt her," Thorington said.

It was as mild a statement as he could make without ripping Ferguson's throat out. But Ferguson just looked at him with something suspiciously like pity. "You don't have to beat her to make her miserable. But you've both made your bed. My offer to negotiate your marriage contract still stands."

Callista shrugged. "As you said, I've made my bed. I can make my own arrangements for the future."

Her tone said she already had a deal in mind — and Thorington wouldn't like it.

Lucretia pushed her way through the crowd. Her escort, a man in naval dress, barely kept pace behind her. "Are you really to be married?" she asked.

She was slightly breathless, as though she'd sacrificed perfection in her rush to reach them. Thorington nodded. "Miss Briarley hasn't been in residence long enough to get a marriage license from the local diocese, so I'll send my man to London for one. We'll be married as soon as he returns."

Callista smiled up at him. "How charming, your grace."

He wondered how she would make him pay.

"I see," Lucretia said. "My felicitations, cousin."

She sounded devastated. But there was no surprise in her voice. She had already resigned herself to this outcome.

Ferguson, ever helpful, tried to improve her mood. "Don't fret, Lucretia. I've no intention of giving Maidenstone to Thorington, if that's what has spoiled your evening."

That single sentence was enough to change Lucretia's entire demeanor. "Truly?"

Ferguson nodded.

She smiled. "Then I must congratulate you again, Callie. You have made an excellent choice."

"How like a Briarley of you to gloat over my downfall," Callista said.

Lucretia shrugged. "I told you I'd do anything to keep you from winning. But it seems my actions weren't necessary after all. Captain Hallett, shall we proceed to supper?"

She turned to her escort. That name was like a spark to a fuse.

The moment hung, frozen. Thorington's eyes narrowed. All his senses focused on the captain who stood before them — a threat Thorington hadn't noticed until Lucretia had said his name.

Callista's hand tightened on his arm. But she laughed a little as though she hadn't been disturbed at all. "Courting a naval man, Lucy? I would have thought you'd want someone who knew how to manage Maidenstone."

Lucretia shrugged. "I can manage Maidenstone myself. Captain Hallett is an old acquaintance from London. It's convenient that he's based in Dartmouth now. When I saw the papers, I thought he might appreciate a day or two of amusement."

Hallett stared at Callista. Thorington wrapped his arm around her shoulders. "The more who are here to celebrate our nuptials, the better," Thorington said, as smoothly as he was capable of when all his instincts screamed to take Callista away. "I'm sure your captain is welcome here."

Hallett wasn't diverted. "Miss Callista Briarley? The Baltimore cousin?"

"Soon to be my duchess," Thorington said. "And you haven't been introduced."

If Hallett heard the warning, he didn't have enough sense to leave. "I had the misfortune to meet a Baltimore ship on my last cruise. But you've heard that, haven't you? All of England has heard, it seems."

Callista, ever reckless, had the audacity to laugh. "No one from Britain would want to meet the Scourge of the Caribbean."

For the first time, Thorington wished she'd aimed for safety. Hallett's face turned red. Even Ferguson, who couldn't have known what was happening, took a step forward. "Supper is an excellent recommendation, Lucretia," he said. "Shall I escort you both?"

Hallett evaded Ferguson's attempt to steer him. "You," he said, looking at Callista. "It was you on the *Nero*."

His voice rose as he said it. Thorington stepped between them. "You should go to supper, Captain Hallett," he said. "Enjoy the hospitality while you can."

The man laughed, but it was cold and bitter. "Hospitality? Or charity? The *Gazette* has made me into a laughingstock because of *her*."

Even Lucretia blanched at his tone. "Arthur, it isn't so bad," she said.

"I'll never have a command again, they said. I'll be confined to calmer waters. And all because of this traitor," he said, gesturing to Callista.

His voice was still low enough that they could contain the scandal — but only barely. Thorington refrained from grabbing him by the collar, but it was a near thing. Instead, he leaned in, using menace rather than his usual coldness. "You will not make such an accusation against my duchess. Now, go to supper and keep your mouth shut, or leave Maidenstone. You have ten seconds to decide before I toss you out myself. And if you were embarrassed before, you have no idea how badly I can destroy you."

Hallett opened his mouth as though he wanted to argue. But Thorington's stare changed his mind. "I will leave," he said, holding up his hands. "But if I cannot have my revenge against Captain Jacobs directly, I know where to look."

Hallett left before Thorington could decide how to dismember him. It was for the best — Thorington couldn't kill the man in a ballroom. And so far, Hallett had done nothing but make idle threats.

But the look in his eyes wasn't idle. And Callista wouldn't be safe until she was married to Thorington.

Callista, though, didn't care for her own safety. She was still too angry. At least now she had another target for her rage. "You arranged for this, didn't you?" she said to Lucretia.

Lucretia's eyes flickered. "I didn't know you were a privateer."

"But you showed me the *Gazette* this morning. You must have invited Hallett on purpose."

"I knew him during my debut year. It was polite to invite him when I invited the rest of the neighborhood."

Callista snorted. "Dartmouth is more than twenty miles from here."

"Close enough," Lucretia said defensively. "Maidenstone is still my home, even if I haven't won it. I shall invite whomever I wish."

Ferguson turned to Thorington as the women continued to argue. "Did you know about my cousin's shipping endeavors?"

Thorington nodded.

"Even her illicit shipping endeavors?"

"Especially her illicit shipping endeavors," Thorington said.

Ferguson looked him over. "As the Duchess of Thorington, she will be very difficult to ruin."

Thorington nodded again.

Ferguson heaved a sigh. "You were supposed to be an out-and-out villain," he complained. "Must I reconsider my opinion of your character?"

"I have bigger concerns at the moment than your opinion."

He was watching Callista, not Ferguson. Ferguson's laughter said he knew it. "If I forced Madeleine to do anything, she would make sure it was the last thing I did. I would wish you luck with Callie if I thought you deserved it."

She was still arguing with Lucretia, but she overheard the comment. "He doesn't deserve it, and it wouldn't help him anyway," she said to Ferguson.

At least there was fire in her voice. But she still refused to look at him.

Before Thorington could drag her away and explain himself, Madeleine and Prudence descended. They took her to the supper room, making it clear he wasn't welcome to join them.

And for once in his life, Thorington realized he was without a plan. He knew how to protect her. But gaining her forgiveness, when she would never forgive him for ruining her chances at winning Maidenstone?

All of that was beyond his skill. He had no idea where to start.

And they would both pay the price when he failed.

CHAPTER TWENTY-FIVE

He was going to die.

Callie knew it would be more expedient to kill him after the wedding. She would be a duchess for her pains. But that meant actually going through with the wedding — saying vows to him. Taking his name. Becoming his.

She would have to murder him before, then.

She had sent Mrs. Jennings to bed without letting her maid undress her. It was after three in the morning and the house had finally gone silent, but the press of exhaustion against her eyelids couldn't compete with the anger still rushing through her.

She walked the now-familiar halls to the Tudor wing, through stillness and shadow, letting her outrage carry her forward. She would have to settle with Lucretia as well — her cousin deserved retaliation for bringing Captain Hallett to the ball. But Callie's battle tonight wasn't with a Briarley...

Unless she counted her own heart. That wretched traitor remembered the Gavin she'd met over whisky, not the duke who had forced her into an engagement. Even now it hummed with happiness that she would have him, not someone else, as her partner.

She wouldn't have Gavin, though. She would have Thorington. And that was an entirely different proposition.

Most of the doors in the Tudor wing were closed, but the last two rooms before Thorington's were open and empty. It was unlikely anyone would hear anything. She turned the handle and pushed his door open.

Her candlelight connected with his. Thorington reclined on the bed, propped up by pillows. The candle illuminated the book in his hand. It was an incongruous picture. Her gaze flickered over the rest of him — no cravat or jacket, no boots, but still wearing a shirt and trousers. The shirt gaped open at the neck, giving her just a glimpse of his chest.

He looked like a warrior at rest.

When she looked back up to his face, he was watching her with those hooded, inscrutable eyes. He clapped his book shut in one hand, snapping it like a trap. Then he swung his feet down and sat on the edge of the bed.

He didn't stand for her like a gentleman would. But then, a lady wouldn't have come to him.

"You shouldn't be here," he said.

She looked down. Her nerves, unexpectedly, felt like giving out. What had she hoped to accomplish by coming here? She couldn't murder him. She couldn't even escape him. He was one of the most powerful men in England. If she jilted him after he'd kissed her publicly, it would be the end of her. The infamy would follow her anywhere she went — and Callie wasn't popular enough anywhere to weather it. She'd have to give up the Briarley name, find some other home.

But she couldn't let him win. She couldn't let him steal her fortune when she would rather share her heart.

"You shouldn't have kissed me," she said.

She finally looked up and met his gaze. In the shadows, she saw something that looked like misery.

But he was the man he had warned her about. And that man was incapable of misery.

She sensed the moment when he became the duke again, when that twist came back to his mouth and his eyes turned mocking. He leaned against the wall with his hands behind his head as though she'd come to entertain him. "You weren't upset when I kissed you last night."

He was going to die.

She walked across the room and set her candle next to his. She let her skirts brush against his knee as she passed him, but she made no further move to touch him. Then she sat in the room's only chair. Or slouched, more like — she crossed her arms over her breasts and stretched her legs out before her in a position that was wholly negligent.

She wanted to look like she didn't care. "I was willing to practice with you," she said, when her voice was capable of selling a lie. "But I didn't wish to be saddled with you."

"Saddled with me?" He stayed still, but his eyes narrowed.

"Yes, saddled with you. At least when I had a horse named Duke, I could sell him when he no longer fit my purposes. You won't be gotten rid of so easily, will you?"

"No."

Stark and final.

"Then I have come to arrange terms," she said.

He paused. She didn't try to fill the silence. Anything she could say, when her heart and mind were warring over what to do, would only harm her negotiation. But his words, when they finally came, surprised her.

"Will you give me the opportunity to explain myself?"

She doubted that he had ever asked such a question before. If he had, he was sorely out of practice. He sounded stiff and slightly angry, not remorseful.

She shook her head. "There is nothing to explain. You saw what you wanted and took it."

"As you took my ships?"

That wasn't anything like what she wanted to hear. "Is that why you want to marry me? To get your ships back?"

He leaned forward, all pretense of calm gone. "I'm not marrying you to regain my fortune. I'm saving you from Captain Hallett."

"Hallett hadn't even made a threat before you kissed me," Callie said.

"It was only a matter of time, my dear. You should have changed the name of your ships before you took up privateering. My messenger to London took less than a day to unearth your secret. If I could discover your activities, anyone could. Someone else would ruin you if Hallett didn't."

"You investigated my shipping concerns?"

"Of course," he said. "You were a potential investment for Anthony when I sent my man to London. Wouldn't you have done the same?"

She thought of the hours she'd spent reading the society papers, searching for clues to who Thorington really was. When she stayed silent, he laughed, not entirely unkindly. "Of course you would have. I didn't expect to discover that you were a privateer. But once I knew, I couldn't ignore the ruin you're destined for."

"My ruin is my problem, not yours."

She knew she sounded sulky, but her pride was tweaked and her heart was bruised. Thorington didn't give her any mercy. "I made a vow to protect you. I won't let anyone harm you."

Callie was having trouble slouching. She wanted to lean forward and shake him.

She stayed still. "I suppose I should thank you, although I don't feel grateful at the moment."

"I would save you whether you felt grateful or not," he said.

There was so much good in him. Callie saw it, even though he wasn't saying it — even though he didn't seem to believe it himself. The cool, rational part of her knew that he did what he thought was best for her. That this marriage was intended for her benefit, not his.

But her heart wanted more than a vow of protection. And her head didn't believe Thorington was capable of giving it.

She drew a breath and ordered herself to stay the course, like a soldier standing still during an enemy assault. "You must agree to my terms before I marry you."

"If it's ships you want, you can have them," Thorington said. "As I said, I'm not marrying you for your business."

"That's part of it," Callie said.

"And the other part?"

She wasn't sure she could say it, now that the moment had arrived. She had practiced the words in her room while she'd waited for the house to go to sleep. But her request was so…heartless.

Heartless like Thorington, not Gavin.

But if she was to marry Thorington, not Gavin, her heart couldn't bear it. She would slowly, inevitably fall even more in love with him than she already was. And she would never win Thorington's heart to replace the one she'd given him.

So she had to start as she meant to go on. And that meant protecting herself from anything she could trick herself into believing was a love match.

"I want a marriage of convenience," she said.

He leaned back as though he'd expected those words. "You want to share my house but not my bed?" He smiled grimly. "I have practice there."

Callie shook her head. "The opposite, actually."

He ran a hand through his hair. "You want to share my bed but not my house?"

"I cannot live with you, Thorington. Not if I want to retain my freedom. You'll make every choice, won't you? If you decided I had to marry you for my own good, even though it would cost me Maidenstone — even though I never said I wanted to marry you — what's to stop you from deciding I cannot run a shipping company?"

"You are far more capable at shipping than I am," he said. "I won't take it away from you. I vow it."

She heard the weight in his voice. Thorington kept his vows. Her heart tried to leap, but her head punched it back down.

"Perhaps you won't take it away outright. But you've spent the entire party giving me lessons in how to be someone I'm not. If I live with you, where will those lessons end? When I look like all the other women in London? When I can host a party without saying anything at all?"

Thorington shoved his hand into his hair again. "Callista...Callie. It's not like that. I wouldn't want that."

Callie waited. Her shorter name sounded sweet on his lips, and she almost melted when she heard it. But even though his face was etched with misery, he didn't say anything else.

And he still hadn't apologized for forcing her to marry him.

Her patience snapped. "Enough. I can see the value in producing children with you to continue our lines. And if I must be married, I would very much like to have a family of my own. But that's all I need from you. Everything else I can provide for myself."

"All you want from me is children?"

She nodded.

"You'd keep me like your stallion? Use me for breeding, then put me out to pasture?"

He said it so coldly. Callie swallowed. "You can see the children, of course. If they interest you."

"Legally they would be mine. I could take them from you and

never allow you to see them again." His voice dropped as he spoke, taking the temperature of the room with it. "You could ask my mother how that felt, but she is no longer able to give advice."

She hadn't realized until it was far too late that she'd touched a wound. Not just touched it — poured acid into it.

"Shall we start tonight?" he continued. His voice turned savage. His hand dropped to his trousers, unfastening the first button. "A demonstration of my skills before you buy me?"

She swallowed again. "I have already seen your skills. I shall return to my room, I think."

She stood. But she was too close to him, and he grabbed her wrist before she could escape. "You can have your ships. And you can have my seed. But don't allow yourself to think you can use me."

"I will never believe that," she whispered.

She looked down into his eyes as she said it. They were finally close enough that even in the darkness she could see the expression there — desperation and regret mingled together, with enough anger and self-loathing to feed the harshest words.

"Will you not?" he whispered back. The savage tone was gone, replaced by despair. "I've known you less than a week, and I would enslave myself to touch you again."

His words shook her. But she couldn't forget what he had done. "You'll be sated soon enough," she said. "When you are, you'll turn your attention to my business. I won't have any power at all to stop you. Now, let me go."

She tried to shake him off. His grip tightened. "You haven't heard my counter-offer."

"What is it?"

"Not that it matters — if you don't marry me, you will be so ruined that not even Ferguson and Madeleine will receive you publicly. But I'll grant you your ships. We will set aside your dowry in a trust for our children."

"That isn't a counter-offer," she said.

His other hand returned to his trousers, undoing the remaining buttons. "I'm merely adding a codicil. I'll father your children. But I will be the only one who touches you. And you won't deny me anything when I come to your bed."

*   *   *

He had expected her to demand a marriage of convenience. But he hadn't expected this.

It was the only reason he could find for why he was so angry. Surely it was merely that she had offered him something he hadn't planned for.

Surely it wasn't that he was hurt.

He'd shocked her into silence. Her wrist felt so fragile in his hand, but he wouldn't let her go. No matter what she said, no matter how she said it. She was *his*. His to protect, his to touch, his to love.

That word was too dangerous. He pulled her into his lap and kissed her, hard.

She made a surprised sound in her throat, but she didn't push him away. She opened her mouth instead, inviting him in. He took what she offered, wanting to touch every bit of her, to taste every part of her soul.

There was salt at the corner of her mouth. He grazed his thumb over her cheek and felt moisture there.

"Callie," he whispered.

It was the only word he could say. He wanted her to hear what was behind it — sadness, regret, certainty. He couldn't be the man she deserved. And he was the very devil for stealing her.

But it never could have ended differently.

She grabbed his hand and pulled it away, not letting him trace her tears. "Business," she said. "This is a business arrangement. You can't take more than what we agreed to."

He wasn't sure whether she was reminding him, or herself. But it made him angry again. "Do we have an agreement?"

"I keep my ships, you give me children, and we live in separate houses? I accept if you do."

He wanted more than that. He wanted so much more. There was nothing in that agreement that promised laughter. Or sweetness. Or any of the hundred new and varied emotions he felt when he saw her. It was as bloodless as the original agreement they'd made in the same room a week earlier — as though nothing had happened between them that merited something more.

Something better.

But he had never deserved her.

"I accept," he said.

He wanted her to hear what he couldn't say. Any words he tried would be the wrong ones. He kissed her instead, branding her with his mouth. He let go of her wrist so his hands could rove over her, seeking the delicious boundary between silk and skin. The dress was beautiful, but he didn't need silk to find her appealing. He would have been happier to see her in her divided skirt, standing in the mud, teasing him.

He wanted her to know that. He attacked her hair, not stopping the kiss as he scattered pins on the floor. He hadn't seen her hair framing her face since she'd asked a real lady's maid for help with her hair. He had been a fool to say she should.

Her hair fell around them, slowly, a veil dropping and yet revealing what he sought. He found the final pins to set her free, then ran his fingers through the winding strands. She arched her neck, letting her head fall back into his hands. He moved lower, kissing the pulse point above her collarbone, making her gasp.

"Callie," he whispered over her skin. "I accept."

But he didn't just accept. He worshipped. He skimmed his lips over her collarbone as his fingers dropped through the waterfall of her hair to find the buttons of her dress. He yanked harder than he should have. Some of them fell to the floor to join the hairpins, but he was beyond caring. She never should have been in that dress. She should have been in something stronger, something made for the sea.

He shoved her sleeves over her shoulders and down her arms. The silk slipped over her chemise, and he shoved that down as well. Her stays were still fastened, pushing up her breasts, offering them to him.

Only to him. He cupped them in his hands as her nipples hardened and the arch of her back gave him the response her voice denied him. She filled his palms perfectly, and he reveled in how they fit each other.

But his dreams of her couldn't be fulfilled by breasts alone. He unfastened her stays and threw them aside, then moved her off his lap and onto the bed.

She had dreams of her own, though. It was clear in how she sat up and put a hand against his chest. "I want to see you," she said.

He arched a brow.

"Your grace," she added.

His heart broke on the words. He wanted her to tease him, call him 'sirrah' again.

But this was business. He pulled his shirt over his head.

Her smile was reward enough for now. She trailed a single finger down his breastbone, through the hair scattered across his chest. Then lower, to his stomach, which flattened under her as he sucked in a breath. Then lower still, to his unbuttoned trousers and the aching need waiting for her.

Even through his trousers, it was torture. He should have kept everything slow; she was still all but an innocent.

She was also more daring than anyone he knew. And the slow grin she gave him as his shaft hardened beneath her fingers fueled his deepest longings.

He flipped her onto her stomach, shocking a laugh out of her. He needed that laugh, needed to hear something lighter when all he'd brought her was darkness. He skimmed his hands down to her ankles, pushing her slippers off her feet. Then he moved higher, gathering her skirt as he went, revealing endless legs. When he found the edges of her stockings, at another perfect boundary between silk and skin, he paused.

When the silence grew too thick, she looked back over her shoulder. "I accept," she said.

There were so many other words he wanted to hear from her. So many other words he wanted to say to her. He looked into the fathomless depths of her eyes and saw everything he wanted there, waiting for him.

But, fool that he was, he didn't know how to dive for it.

He moved his hands higher, over the last torturous inches of her thighs to the sweet curve of her derriere. He shoved her skirts over her waist, pooling them around her. And he kissed the base of her spine, right where all her backbone gave way to softness.

"I accept," he whispered against her skin, so softly that she wouldn't hear him.

His thumb trailed over her cleft. His fingers curled under her and parted her folds. She gasped as he stroked her, gasped again when he slid a finger inside her. She was already wet for him.

He leaned over her, trailing kisses through her hair as his fingers increased their tempo. "I accept," he murmured into her hair, hoping it would keep his secret.

Her hands clawed into the blankets as he, relentless, pushed her harder. Endless minutes of it, until she writhed underneath him. He bit her shoulder, lightly, then kissed the pain away. "I accept," he said, in the softest voice he was capable of.

She cried out then, convulsing, shaking against his hand. He didn't wait for her to settle; he couldn't, not anymore. He freed himself from his trousers, slid an arm under her, pulled her up onto her knees, and drove into her.

For Callie, this was something she hadn't dreamed of. His arms, his legs, his cock — she was surrounded, filled. Utterly at his mercy.

Thorington didn't have mercy. But Gavin did. He whispered something as he rocked into her. She couldn't hear the words, but the tone was a promise. His rhythm was devious, relentless. Her need built again.

She should have been shocked. She was enthralled instead. His fingers twined in her hair, pressed against her neck. It could have been business. He could have been using her...

Or it could have been love. He could have been serving her.

He slammed into her again.

"I accept," she sobbed into the pillow. "Gavin, I accept."

She wanted to say something else. But those were the only words they had, the only words for the contract they'd offered each other.

She came on his final thrust, as he emptied his seed into her.

He'd given her what he'd agreed to give her. It didn't feel like business, though. As he collapsed, as he pulled her into his embrace on the narrow bed, as they splayed around each other, as they twisted in their half-removed clothes, all she felt was love.

She loved him. She loved him, and he could destroy her with it.

She couldn't think about it. She ran her fingers over his chest. It heaved beneath her as he fought to catch his breath.

"God, Callie," he said. "You are magnificent."

Her heart bloomed. Her head couldn't stop it.

But reason still ruled her tongue. She couldn't bring herself to lie

— couldn't bring herself to say the words that would tear the moment apart, to hurt him before he could hurt her.

She could stay silent, though. She pressed a kiss against his heart, letting her lips give him the words her voice wasn't allowed to say.

They stayed there for endless minutes. It must have been hours; the room turned grey instead of black as the candles guttered and made way for dawn. She should have gone back to her own bed, but it was beyond her power to leave.

He hadn't made that choice for her. She had trapped herself more effectively than he ever could have.

Finally, as the grey slowly turned to gold, Callie sat up. Putting herself back together wasn't a task either of them were equipped for, but she pulled her chemise and dress up and shoved her hair into a messy knot.

He watched her as she did so, trailing his fingers down her back over the row of buttons he'd destroyed. He did up the ones that remained, pressing kisses in the gaps. She shivered.

She felt like crying.

She stood and shook out her skirts. He stood behind her, smoothing his hands over her hips.

"I will do my best by you," he said. "I vow it."

She bowed her head, let him kiss the back of her neck. "I know it."

But even though he escorted her back to her room, even though he held her hand as though they were sweethearts, even though he'd made a vow he wouldn't break…Callie didn't know if Gavin's best was enough to make up for Thorington's worst.

CHAPTER TWENTY-SIX

Callie had never had much patience for dressmakers. She had even less patience for this one.

"Please, hold yourself as still as possible," the modiste said the next morning as she draped Callie in yellow silk. "If I do not cut this properly, it will be ruined."

"I have been standing still for hours," Callie said.

"It has only been twenty minutes," Mrs. Jennings said, not looking up as she perused a pattern book.

"It feels like hours," Callie said.

Her maid sighed. "You haven't had a new dress made in over a year. You might enjoy it if you let it happen."

Callie stood still. But it all felt too sudden. She'd had only a few hours of sleep after Thorington had escorted her back to her room, but it wasn't fatigue that made it difficult to concentrate.

It was the question of what to do about Thorington. She was already tired of thinking about it. Would she drive herself mad thinking about him between now and their wedding?

Already she realized she had made a mistake the night before. She knew better than to negotiate anything in anger. It was one of the earliest lessons she'd learned when she had taken over her company, and she had never made that mistake again. But she hadn't been able to stop herself.

The memory of Thorington's lovemaking, though, gave her endless opportunity for regret. She finally understood the lesson he'd wanted to teach her during their first night together. They weren't meant for a business arrangement. Her heart couldn't bear the thought of spending her life with anything less than all of him.

But could she accept the risk? She'd known him for a week. She never would have bought a ship after so little research. In their marriage, he would have all the power and all the authority. No matter what happened, there was no escaping him until one of them died. She couldn't win a divorce from a duke. And if he took his marriage vows as seriously as he took all his others, he'd never let her go.

You don't want him to let you go, her heart whispered.

She tried to put him out of her mind. But it was impossible — especially when a steady stream of visitors wanted to talk of nothing but him.

The first, surprisingly, was Octavia. When she knocked, Callie shook her head at Mrs. Jennings. "I do not wish to receive any callers," she said to her maid.

Mrs. Jennings, for once, overruled her. "She is your family. It would do you well to have more family after all this time."

Her maid opened the door before Callie could stop her. If Octavia had heard their conversation, she made no sign of it. "I wanted to congratulate you last night," Octavia said as she strode into the sitting room Callie had commandeered for the fitting. "But so many others were offering their best wishes that I thought it better to call on you this morning."

"Thank you," Callie said.

Octavia was sharp enough to notice Callie's reticence. "You aren't blushing as I expected a newly betrothed woman to be. Is something amiss?"

"Of course not. I merely failed to sleep enough last night."

Octavia looked Callie up and down. Callie twitched, earning another reproof from the modiste.

"Are you not happy? I'll grant that Thorington isn't the one of those brothers I'd have picked, but he is a fine enough match. If you like dukes, of course."

"Do you not like dukes?"

"I find there are far too many of them at the moment," Octavia said. "Two at one party isn't just unusual — it's unwelcome. They make all other men shabby by comparison."

Callie remembered the night before, when she'd caught Rafe watching Octavia. Octavia's earlier comment suddenly struck a different chord. "How do you feel about brothers of dukes?" she asked.

Octavia tsked. "You will have to be more subtle than that, cousin. I'm not fresh from the schoolroom."

Callie held up her hands.

The modiste yelped. "Do not move again, Miss Briarley, I beg you."

"I apologize," Callie said to the modiste. To Octavia, she said, "I'll say nothing further on the matter. But I wish you luck finding a match. Ferguson won't let me win with Thorington as my husband, and I can't bear to see Lucretia get her way."

"Nor can I," Octavia said. The steel in her voice was perceptible even under her drawl. "Especially not after she brought Captain Hallett here to trouble you."

Callie cast a sideways glance at the modiste and her assistant, gauging what she could safely say. But there was no way to ask Octavia how she'd heard of Hallett — whether she had merely observed the name in the *Gazette*, or whether she had guessed Callie's business. She moved the conversation to safer waters. "Did Lucretia really steal all of your invitations? How did she manage that?"

Octavia nodded as she took one of the pattern books from the pile in front of Mrs. Jennings. "I live at my brother's former hunting box. It's in the farthest corner of the Maidenstone estate, removed enough that I can go for weeks without ever crossing Lucy's path. I'll have to fire all the servants. She must have paid them a small fortune not to tell me about the party."

She said it casually, as though they'd fought similar battles before. But there was an underlying note that Callie was too familiar with. "Were you lonely there, all by yourself?"

"I find ways to amuse myself." Octavia flipped through the pattern book. "When you are done with your modiste, I would like to order a few dresses. I haven't seen a modiste in far too long."

Callie let Octavia change the subject. They talked of dresses for several minutes, as the modiste finished with the yellow silk and moved on to green. But the peace between them was soon disturbed by another arrival. Lucretia walked through the door. She stopped, startled, when she saw Octavia. "I didn't expect to see you here," she said.

"Callie and I are becoming fast friends," Octavia said. "Perhaps I'll share Maidenstone with her when I win it."

The look on Lucretia's face was something between annoyance and jealousy. "I shall return later," she said, backing out of the room.

Callie waved her in. The modiste sighed and reset the pin she'd just placed. "Please," Callie said. "I want to talk to you."

She knew her voice didn't sound like an invitation — she couldn't keep the warning out of it. But Lucretia surprised her by coming in anyway. "I owe you an apology," Lucretia said.

"Is this like your last apology?" Callie asked.

Lucretia looked confused. "Which apology?"

"The one in which you apologized for how rudely you greeted me, then vowed to keep me from winning Maidenstone."

Octavia laughed. "That's one of Lucy's favorite apologies."

Lucretia frowned. "I am still sorry for my rudeness. And I am sorry for bringing Captain Hallett here. I can be sorry and still be determined."

"You haven't learned anything about staying out of others' lives, have you?" Octavia said.

There was no humor left in Octavia's voice. It was strange how quickly she could turn dark — as though there was a vast well of danger beneath a bright, brittle façade. Lucretia flinched.

That flinch was so fast, so instinctual, that Callie wondered again what had come between them. Callie had no love for Lucretia. On the surface, Octavia was a far more entertaining companion. But Octavia had hidden depths that Callie couldn't begin to guess. And Lucretia flinched as though Octavia had hurt her before — as though Octavia could only hurt her again.

They'd played princesses in Maidenstone Wood. But which of them was the princess, and which was the villain?

It wasn't a question she could answer then. Stepping into their drama might provide a welcome relief from her swirling thoughts of Thorington, but she didn't have the capacity to think of their problems while trying to solve her own.

"I will accept your apology," she said to Lucretia. "But only if you can assure me that Captain Hallett won't cause any further trouble."

The way Lucretia avoided her gaze said everything.

"I am sorry," Lucretia said again. "I invited him without thinking fully about the consequences."

"Did he leave last night as he promised?"

"He didn't stay at Maidenstone. But I do not know with certainty that he left the neighborhood."

Callie frowned. "Thorington won't like this."

"No, he won't," Octavia said. "It's for the best that you're marrying him quickly, and not just because it might improve my chances of winning Maidenstone. Men like Hallett would think twice before disgracing Thorington's wife."

Her statement brought back a memory from the night before, when Prudence and Madeleine had taken Callie away from Thorington and escorted her to supper. She'd been far too angry to pay more than half a mind to their words — she had still been in that red haze, where comprehension and thought were impossible. But Prudence had laughed when Callie had said that Thorington was sending to the Archbishop of Canterbury for a special license.

"He must be desperate to marry you, then," Prudence had said. "When Thorington tried to force me, he insisted on planning a wedding at St. George's in London."

Callie tried not to be jealous, but it was a hard fight. "I'm sure he wouldn't waste such extravagance on me," she muttered.

"It wasn't extravagance. His mother is buried there. Marrying there, even though I'm sure he didn't care for me at all, seemed important to him. He must care for you if he's putting you above that."

Callie stabbed blindly at some bit of food on her plate. "He isn't accommodating me. He's forcing me."

Prudence sipped her champagne. "I don't know Thorington well. We had barely spoken before he decided to use me to take revenge against Alex for something in their past. But I feel confident saying that if Thorington were marrying you only for his benefit, you would know it."

Callie had awoken that morning, after her fitful nap, with the feel of Thorington's hands still on her hips — and Prudence's words in her mind. She thought of them again now, as Hallett's name hung in the room like an omen.

"Would you marry Thorington?" she asked Octavia and Lucretia. "If you had the choice?"

Octavia frowned.

Lucretia looked vaguely ill.

"Well?" Callie said. "Let's even say he offered for you properly, in private, rather than kissing you in public."

Octavia shook her head slowly. "I want peace. Thorington may not know the word."

"He would never ask me," Lucretia said.

She sounded bruised. Callie remembered, belatedly, that Thorington had told her of Lucretia's offer to him. She softened her voice. "Do you wish he would have?"

Lucretia eventually shook her head. "He would have run me over within a week."

They both spoke as though Thorington was unmarriageable. As though Thorington's skill for surprising her was a bad thing. As though sparring with him was unwelcome.

He had promised her dragons, not treasure. She should have run from such an offer.

Instead, she didn't want anything else.

Callie realized then that she was doomed.

*   *   *

"I trust you've guessed why I have assembled you here," Thorington said to his siblings.

They were in one of the receiving rooms in the Tudor wing's State Apartments, as far into the row of rooms as one could progress before reaching the bedchamber Thorington and Callie had made use of two nights earlier. Thorington had oddly begun to feel like the wing belonged to him. The heavy wood paneling and well-worn stone suited him, perhaps more than the elegant trimmings of wealth he'd amassed and lost over the last few years.

His siblings, though, belonged in the modern era. Portia and
Serena sat in chairs facing him, separated from him by the table he
had taken as his makeshift desk. Anthony stood behind Portia's chair,
leaning on it with studied nonchalance. Rafe's nonchalance wasn't
studied — he lounged on a couch at the side of the room, resting his
head on one arm and his booted feet on the other.

"Are we here to congratulate you on your marriage, brother?"
Portia asked.

Serena made a shushing gesture at Portia, but Thorington cut her
off. "If you wish," he said.

Portia's jaw dropped open.

Anthony's face matched hers. "Do you truly mean to discuss it?
With us?"

"I would rather not," Thorington said. "But I should explain why
I've condemned you all to poverty."

From the couch, Rafe snickered. "No Italian shepherdesses in
your future, Gav?"

Thorington cast him a dark look.

Serena waved an impatient hand, mirroring one of his usual
gestures. "I'll find a husband if I have to, but that's neither here nor
there," she said. "Are you happy?"

No one had ever asked him that. And it wasn't a question he had
an easy answer for.

Could 'happy' describe how he had felt the previous night — that
odd, desperate mix of need and want? He had been so determined to
save Callie from harm, so victorious when he'd done it — then so sure
he'd somehow ruined everything with his best-laid plans.

But she had sought him out after. Sure, what she offered was the
opposite of what he wanted from her. He couldn't imagine a future
in which he shared her bed but couldn't talk to her — a future in
which he took everything from her body while she gave her laughter

to someone else.

Memories of the last week washed over him whenever he closed his eyes. Callie in the clearing, staring him down as though she could conquer anything. Callie in her divided skirt, asking for her pistol. Callie with the sea behind her, offering him sympathy. Callie waltzing in his arms, dazzling him. Callie drinking whisky and asking for a kiss. Callie in the shadows of the Tudor wing, giving herself to him, but taking just as much in return.

Callie. It was always Callie.

It would always be Callie.

Thorington wasn't what she deserved. But he could try to be.

And if he made her happy, he'd be the happiest man alive.

At the moment, though, he had to lock questions of the heart away until he knew she was safe. "I will be happier if my bride survives unscathed until our wedding day," he said.

"Surely you're the only threat to Miss Briarley's safety," Anthony said.

His tone was acid, but his smile was lighter than any Thorington had seen from him since entering Maidenstone a week earlier. "I am the only threat to *your* safety. But Callie has other enemies."

"So it's Callie now?" Portia teased. "What happened to your propriety?"

"Propriety is for the middle classes," Thorington said. "Now, will you entertain my request for help, or should I dismiss you all?"

As a request for a favor, it was poorly done. Thorington was mostly out of patience and entirely out of practice. But, rare as it was for him to ask for help instead of giving orders, even a badly-phrased statement such as that one resulted in stunned silence.

"I beg your pardon?" Anthony finally said.

Thorington had to unclench his jaw before he could respond. "I need your help."

The silence was heavy enough to match the furnishings. Thorington glanced at Rafe. Rafe had swung his legs off the couch and sat up when Thorington mentioned Callie's safety. But even he, the sibling who knew Thorington best, seemed unable to form a sentence.

"If you don't wish to help your future sister, I shall find another option," Thorington said after a few moments. "You are all dismissed."

Serena finally found her voice. "Of course we want to help her. I think I speak for all of us when I say we're pleased you've chosen Callie."

They all nodded in unison as Serena continued. "It's just so... unusual for you to ask us for anything."

"It's *impossible* that you asked," Portia clarified.

Thorington drummed his fingers on the table. He didn't quite understand why his temper was rising. His siblings always tested him, but at the moment he wanted to shake all of them. "I thought you would be willing to help after all I've done for you."

Anthony sighed, as dramatic as the poet who'd sired him. "Is this a request or an order? I would help with anything you need, regardless of what you've done for us, if you ever asked."

Rafe had watched Thorington closely throughout this conversation. "Gav *is* asking," he said softly. "Never thought I'd see the day."

Those words were like a final tumbler slipping into a lock — subtle, barely perceptible, and yet crucially important. Thorington had never asked for help because he had never believed that anyone could help. Nor did he believe that anyone else could relieve him of his responsibilities. He was the duke, after all — anything within his domain was, ultimately, his responsibility.

But as his siblings gaped at him, he realized that refusing their help hadn't just made his own life harder — it had cheated them as well. They had never taken care of themselves, not because they couldn't, but because he hadn't allowed it.

"Have I really been such an ogre?" he asked.

Portia nodded. Serena kicked her ankle.

"Not an ogre," Rafe said. "An insufferable autocrat, perhaps."

"You aren't that badly behaved," Anthony said. "At least, you weren't before you tried to force me to marry."

Thorington sighed. "It's too late for that. My financial losses will be known before you can sign a marriage contract. But I couldn't see Callie ruined."

"But you were the one who ruined her," Serena said, confused.

He explained Callie's connection to the infamous Scourge of the Caribbean, and the risk Captain Hallett posed to her reputation. His siblings didn't react as they should have.

They all laughed.

"This is *famous*," Portia said. "I'd far rather have a pirate for a sister than another one like Ariana."

Serena kicked her ankle again. Portia kicked her back. "Serena would too," Portia declared.

Serena scowled at her sister. But then she nodded. "It's true, although I'm sure I'm too well-mannered to say such a thing."

Portia snorted.

Anthony's grin was broader than anything he'd given Thorington in ages — almost as light as when he was younger, before he'd begun to chafe against Thorington's rules. "I told you Miss Briarley would never get vouchers at Almack's. Better you than me, brother — I still like society, and it still likes me."

Brother. Anthony hadn't called him that in years.

Thorington tried to ignore how the sound of that word, and all their good-natured laughter, was like balm to his heart. But he couldn't quite make the walls around his heart close anymore. He'd always been able, before, to put their safety above any other considerations.

But maybe, like Callie, they weren't made for safety. Maybe they were made for something far more dangerous.

Something like the love he felt for them, when he let himself put a word to the sharp pain in his chest.

Once that word was in his mind, he couldn't shut it out.

"I will love her even if no one accepts her," Thorington said.

Another shocked silence.

Rafe cleared his throat. "Have you told your duchess this?" he asked.

Trust Rafe to ask the question. Thorington scowled. "I was rather too busy trying to save her from Captain Hallett."

Rafe rolled his eyes. "Shame we're cursed with Father's soul, isn't it? Our siblings are capable of voicing their love, I'm sure."

"Glad my baseborn blood is good for something," Anthony said with a laugh.

"This is all very entertaining," Thorington said drily. He couldn't quite get the tone right — for all his practice over the years, he found it difficult to find just the right coolness when his heart was suddenly overheating. But he pressed on. "However, I didn't summon you to ask for lessons in how to whisper sweet nothings."

"It's rather easy, actually," Anthony said.

Rafe was the one who sighed this time. "Gav is being remarkably patient. We should listen to him now."

"If *you* need the lesson, Rafe…" Serena said.

This time, Portia kicked her.

Thorington exchanged a quick, suffering glance with his brother before continuing. "I am going to track down Hallett and make sure he never threatens any of us again. And I need all of you to watch after Callie while I pursue him."

CHAPTER TWENTY-SEVEN

Callie awoke three days later, on what was to be her wedding day, and realized she was going to go mad before she ever met Thorington at the altar.

She couldn't blame him for it. He'd held precisely to the letter of their agreement. Other than a brief interlude on that first day, when he'd given the modiste vapors by interrupting the fitting to give Callie a single, silent, utterly seductive kiss, she'd only seen him in bed.

But that kiss still haunted her. He'd come into the sitting room, strode over to her like he owned her — and then kissed her like he worshipped her.

"What was that for?" she had asked, dazed, when he finished.

He paused for the longest time, as though the words he wanted to say were in a language he couldn't speak. Finally, he said, "I accept, Callie. I accept."

She heard something else behind those words. She might have even responded, if he'd given her time. But as her jaw dropped open, he continued. "I'm going after Hallett. Stay safe, my dear."

He'd left before she could say anything at all. His sisters had taken his place. And Callie couldn't recall more than five minutes in the last three days when she'd been left alone again.

It hadn't been obvious at first. But on the second day, when the same people arrived, at approximately the same times, and kept her from leaving them, she suspected that she was being guarded.

On the third day, she knew it.

Serena and Portia occupied her afternoons. They had become friends with Ferguson's twin sisters, Lady Catherine and Lady Maria, and the four of them had insisted, daily, that Callie spend her afternoon hours with them. Callie had mostly ignored Ferguson's sisters throughout the party. But the four girls shared a wicked sense of humor and knew more gossip than anyone of their tender years should.

So that was all lovely — or at least it was on the first day. By the third day, Callie would have happily sacrificed an arm to spar with Thorington instead of listening to another story about scandalous people she didn't know.

Anthony had taken up the commission of guarding her evenings. He didn't reference their would-be engagement, other than to give her an exuberant hug and welcome her to their family. The change in him, when he knew he would be her brother instead of her husband, was remarkable. He and his friends — a circle of men her own age, all with dashing wardrobes and impeccable manners — were most attentive in bringing her refreshments and attempting to entertain her.

But Callie would have rather read the papers with Thorington than danced with any number of stylish Corinthians.

Madeleine and Prudence must have agreed to chaperone her during the mornings. The duchess and the countess would insist that she join them for tea after breakfast. They wouldn't release her until Serena and Portia claimed her.

Yesterday, she had finally asked them if Thorington had arranged this. Prudence had smiled mysteriously, which was answer enough. Madeleine had said, "Ferguson doesn't like being wrong about people. But I find it pleasant to have proof that my husband isn't always right."

They all laughed at that. Callie liked Prudence and Madeleine. They were kind, sincere, and seemed to enjoy her company as much as she enjoyed theirs. And she felt an odd little flutter when she realized she seemed to have made friends with them.

But as nice as it was to have friends, she would rather ask Thorington for a lesson in comportment — and hope that the lesson became one in debauchery.

When her interminable days were over, Anthony always escorted her back to her room. And when she pushed the door closed and turned to face the bed, Thorington always waited there for her.

She turned onto her side, facing the indentation where Thorington had slept beside her during the night. The twisted sheets were cool again. He'd left hours earlier, in darkness, responding to a knock on the door. Perhaps Callie should have been worried for him. Each night, either before or after their lovemaking, he'd told her he still hadn't found Hallett. He'd even gone all the way to Dartmouth and back, but Hallett wasn't at his post.

She hadn't worried when he'd left, though. She'd fallen asleep again, too sated and safe to resist.

She traced her fingers over his pillow. It had regained its shape, as though he'd never been there — as though he was something she'd dreamed up to comfort herself with.

But he wasn't a dream. And he had kept precisely to the arrangement they had agreed to.

She could have stayed cold and pretended this was business. But all her doubts about their future together fell away when he touched her. She couldn't remember to be afraid when Gavin smiled. Even though she spent her days worrying over the possible loss of her freedom like a dog might gnaw on a bone, all of it melted away when he said something sardonic and made her laugh.

Wasn't she happier with him than she had ever been alone?

She rolled out of bed and tugged the bell pull, hard enough to risk jerking the cord from the wall. It was only seven in the morning, but she would go mad if she spent any more time in bed. By the time Mrs. Jennings arrived, Callie had already scrubbed her face until it was pink and brushed her hair until it crackled.

"Shall I dress you for your wedding, miss?" Mrs. Jennings asked. "Or do you want to wear another dress at the moment?"

Callie sucked in a breath. "Have you seen Thorington?"

Her maid shook her head. "The rumor in the servants' hall is that he went into the village with Lord Salford and the Duke of Rothwell."

Either he had a lead on Hallett, or Ferguson was planning to kill him before the wedding — Callie couldn't think of another reason why either Thorington or Ferguson would willingly spend time together. "Another dress, then," Callie said. "It might be hours before the wedding."

His messenger was due back with the special license sometime that day, and Thorington had insisted they would marry as soon as the paper was in his hand. Their wedding would be the first time she'd seen him during daylight hours since he had kissed her in front of the modiste.

Would it be the last time? Would he hold her to their agreement — an agreement she was no longer sure she wanted? Would he only come to her at night, like a forbidden lover stealing pleasure in the dark?

Thorington kept his vows. He would keep this one, even if neither of them wanted it, unless she released him from it.

Callie took another breath. Her thoughts were running away from her.

She suddenly felt like she might be sick.

Mrs. Jennings brought a simple walking dress and undergarments from Callie's dressing room and laid them out on the counterpane.

But when she looked up and saw Callie's face, she frowned. "Are you feeling well?"

Callie nodded.

"Sit," Mrs. Jennings ordered. "Would some of Captain Jacobs' cognac help?"

Callie laughed, but even to her ears it sounded shaky. "That dreadful man. I never should have taken his advice about privateering."

"You don't mean that," Mrs. Jennings said as she disappeared into the dressing room.

Her maid was right. Callie had finally had a letter from him the previous day — hastily scrawled and sent from Havana two months earlier. The note was circumspect and unsigned, which would save her if it was intercepted. But he said that her 'investment' had earned eighty thousand pounds as her share, which she could claim in Havana or have remitted to London as time and war permitted.

Eighty thousand pounds. It was nearly enough to make her think privateering wasn't so bad after all.

She found, though, that she didn't care as much as she had before about whether Jacobs listened to her, or whether she could regain control of her company.

Mrs. Jennings returned with a flask. "I hid some cognac in your trunks. Never know when you'll need it."

She handed it to Callie, then sat beside her as Callie took a tentative sip.

"I hate cognac," Callie said, after she finished coughing.

"It does settle the nerves, though. Lord Tiberius always insisted we have some on hand for your mother."

Callie took another sip. She didn't cough this time. "My father excelled at giving Mother nerves."

"He did." Mrs. Jennings' sigh was almost wistful. "It's good that you're settling down, though. You'll have fewer nerves if you're not involved in sea battles."

"Thorington isn't exactly safe," Callie said.

"No, he's not."

Her maid's tone sounded suspiciously cheerful for such a pronouncement. "Do you think this match is a good one?" Callie asked.

"What would you like me to say, Miss Briarley?" she responded.

"The truth," Callie said. "You've known me for twenty years. You must have some opinion on whether the duke is suitable."

"Of course I do," Mrs. Jennings said. She took the flask from Callie's hand and made sure the cap was tight. "But it isn't my place to say. And in any event, you know the answer."

Callie knew what she wanted to hear, at least. She wanted someone to tell her that it would all come out right in the end. She wanted someone to say she was making the right decision if she stayed with him.

Maybe it was the cognac, or maybe it was the memories that haunted Maidenstone's air. But suddenly, strangely, she thought of her parents. She'd heard a few of their arguments, particularly when fleeing from debts or evading revolutions. Some of those trips had required them to be cooped up together in a single coach for most of the journey, rather than arranging a coach for Callie and her mother and a separate horse for her father.

She still remembered the longing in her mother's voice during their flight from Paris in '03. The Peace of Amiens had failed, Napoleon's officers were combing the roads for British men to arrest in retaliation, and they had only escaped because Tiberius — who was always at his best when unexpected danger arose — had convincingly dressed as a woman on the road to Calais.

It was odd that she remembered that now, of all times. But she'd never really forgotten it. She'd slept in the carriage; at twelve, she'd known they were in danger, but she was also innocent enough to trust that Tiberius would save them. But when she awoke, she heard her parents whispering.

"Isn't it time we were back in England?" her mother said.

Callie pretended she was still asleep. She heard the rustle of her father's skirts as he shifted on the bench across from her. "I will never go back to Maidenstone."

"You don't have to go back to Maidenstone. We could have a townhouse in London…"

"You know how I feel about London. It's suffocating."

Her mother sighed. "The coast, then. Brighton is both fashionable and far from your father."

"Brighton is a backwater, and the Prince of Wales is a fool," Tiberius said, still amiable. "I'll hang myself before I bow and scrape at his feet there."

"But Callista is going to be grown soon. What kind of match will she find if she doesn't acquire polish?"

Callie hated when her mother said that. Tiberius just laughed. "There's time enough for that, if she wants it. But I think Callie would be better served by seeing the world."

"She's not your son, you know. She's your daughter."

Callie hated when her mother said that, too.

"I know," Tiberius said. His voice was becoming impatient — the argument must have started before Callie awoke, since it took ages for him to lose his temper. "But she would rather go fishing with me than go to the shops with you. And I'm not going back to London just to indulge your belief that she would do well on the marriage mart."

"She'll hate you for it someday, you know," her mother whispered. The sound was almost vicious. "Adventures are all well and good, but how will she feel when you get yourself killed? And she's left alone to fend for herself?"

"I haven't been killed yet," he said drily. His skirts shifted again, and Callie could picture him swishing them to annoy her mother. "And Callie can take care of herself."

It was odd that he had said it, since she was only twelve — there was no proof that she would be able to take care of herself. At the time, though, she'd been filled with pride that he thought so highly of her. But what he had predicted had come true. Her mother had died in Jamaica less than two years later, and he'd followed her to the grave a few years after that.

And Callie had taken care of herself, as her father had expected her to.

But now, thinking of Thorington and what their marriage might be, that memory hurt all over again. Callie knew how to fish. She knew how to run a shipping company. She could probably escape from any lynch mob or revolution.

But she didn't know the first thing about how to settle down — how to be with someone who wanted to take care of her, rather than expecting her to take care of herself.

As her mother had predicted, she hated Tiberius in that moment.

Callie waited for Mrs. Jennings to say something else, but her maid wasn't going to tell her how to live her life. Callie was on her own.

But she didn't have to be on her own anymore.

A knock sounded on the door. Her heart leapt, hoping.

It was only Portia and Serena. "You're early," Callie said, her voice frigid in her disappointment.

"We have a summons for you," Serena said.

Her voice was as bright and sun-filled as her hair. She handed Callie a note. Callie slid her finger under the seal and unfolded the paper.

Your grace - Maidenstone clearing, as soon as you are able. Wear your riding skirt. - Thorington

A preemptory demand — the kind she should have feared.

She didn't fear, though. A slow smile dawned, one that had Serena and Portia looking at each other slyly.

Her Briarley heart knew the answer to the question she'd asked Mrs. Jennings. Her head, for once, lost its hold on the reins.

"Bring me my riding skirt," she said to Mrs. Jennings. "I need to visit the Maidenstone."

CHAPTER TWENTY-EIGHT

When Thorington had answered the knock on Callie's door at five in the morning, he had expected his messenger.

What he got was infinitely less desirable.

"Thorington," Ferguson said. "A word?"

He stepped into the hall and shut the door behind him — not because he intended to entertain Ferguson's demand, but to avoid waking Callie. Then he crossed his arms. "Never thought you'd spend the wee hours of the morning guarding women's virtue."

Ferguson examined his nails — a fine trick when it was nearly dark in the hallway. "I am surprised by it myself. But I'm sure you'd do the same if Lady Serena or Lady Portia were threatened."

Thorington stilled. He thought of Portia's easy smile and Serena's eager heart. He was sure they knew what they were about, and equally sure they wouldn't welcome his interference after all the dancing masters and cavalry officers he'd scared away. But still...

"Are they in trouble?" he asked.

Ferguson shrugged. "Not that I know of. But they've become friends with my sisters. We will have our hands full when they return to London, unless we find a convent for them."

Odd that Ferguson thought they might have some shared future beyond this party. But Thorington had more pressing concerns. "You didn't interrupt both our nights to discuss them, though."

"No." Ferguson looked up from his cuticles. "I have some intelligence that might interest you."

Thorington waited.

"You would be more fun if you played along," Ferguson complained.

Thorington laughed. "If you find me more fun, you might wish to continue our acquaintance. We can't have that."

"You're stuck with me," Ferguson said. "I've taken an interest in Callie's future, which means I've taken an interest in you. You and Salford can commiserate, if you are friends again. He doesn't appreciate my interest either."

"With such a bleak future ahead of me, I'm not sure I care to hear your intelligence," Thorington said.

"It is a shame you're not the blackguard I thought you were. If you were, I wouldn't care to tell you that Captain Hallett took a room at the nearest inn last night."

"He's in Salcombe?" Thorington said. "You waited until now to tell me this?"

"I only heard it a few minutes ago myself."

Since Ferguson looked as well-dressed as he always did, Thorington suspected it had been more than a few minutes. But however the man had come by his intelligence, Thorington wasn't going to waste it. "If you'll excuse me, I must go."

He stepped around Ferguson, headed for the Tudor wing so he could put on something other than the previous evening's clothes. But Ferguson's voice followed him.

"Meet in the entry in twenty minutes. Salford is coming with us."

Thorington turned. "I wasn't aware I had asked for company."

"An oversight on your part, I'm sure," Ferguson said.

Thorington sighed. But wasting time trying to evade Ferguson might cost him his only chance of finding Hallett before the wedding.

"Very well. Try not to undermine my threats with your poorly-timed humor."

Ferguson smiled. "If you give me the chance to interrupt, that's your own doing."

Thorington gave him a rude gesture before walking away. As he returned to his room and dressed, he should have focused on Hallett and how he would handle the man. But his thoughts returned, as they always did, to Callie.

He'd left her sleeping, curled up in the bed he already thought of as theirs. He was awake when Ferguson had knocked, facing her, content to breathe the same air as her. The pain of sleeping next to her, when he knew he couldn't have her during their days, was sharply sweet.

If he couldn't talk to her during the day, he was determined to have as much of her as he could at night. And she, true to their agreement, had given him everything he asked for. It had left him exhausted, exhilarated, as he'd searched for Hallett. He'd barely slept when he was with her, either from lovemaking or from the whispered conversations she wouldn't grant him during daylight.

The sky outside his window lightened as he dressed. After only three days, sunshine felt cruel. His old, familiar loneliness was somehow harsher when illuminated. All the miles he'd covered between Maidenstone and Dartmouth, all the inns and taverns he'd visited, all the neighbors he'd called upon in his search for Hallett — they were important, but they were merely a distraction.

He couldn't bear the thought that his days would always be like this, when his nights were the opposite. The heart Callie had rescued couldn't survive starving during the day and gorging itself at night.

He had agreed to the deal she had demanded. Already, though, it wasn't enough.

And as soon as he eliminated Hallett from their lives, he was going to renegotiate.

* * *

They reached Salcombe as the sun broke over the horizon. Thorington dismounted before the other two caught up to him. "Ferguson, take the horses to the stables and watch the back of the inn while Salford and I go in," he said.

It was wishful thinking to hope that Ferguson would obey him. Ferguson's laugh confirmed it. "I shall bribe the stable hand to do it. I won't miss this interview."

Salford slid off this horse. "Accustom yourself to his help, Thorington. Hard as it is to believe, Ferguson has his uses."

They found a stable boy and left their horses and the back entrance under his watch. Then they went into the inn and gave the innkeeper a guinea to arrange the private parlor to their liking. Thorington had originally planned to roll Hallett out of bed so there was no chance he could escape. But on the ride to Salcombe, Salford had urged a different approach.

"If you awaken him and try to have this conversation while the man is still in his nightshirt, he will be even more defensive than he's already likely to be," Salford said. "A cornered animal will bite. Unless you intend to kill him, you'd be better served by inviting him to join you in a private parlor."

Thorington had thought of killing him. It was the only way to guarantee that he couldn't spread rumors about Callie, and it was cheaper than buying him off. But Hallett's father was in Parliament and would likely raise an outcry. Even if Thorington didn't swing from the neck for it, Callie wouldn't be happy with him for disgracing them both.

So he took Salford's advice and sent a message up to Hallett. When the man arrived twenty minutes later, his expression was an odd mixture of smugness and fear.

"Have you come to apologize for your threats, your grace?" Hallett said.

Thorington sat, entirely at ease, behind the table he'd used as his desk when he and his siblings had stayed at the inn before. Salford and Ferguson sat on either side of him, giving the room the air of a tribunal. There was a single, armless chair directly in front of the desk. Thorington gestured toward it. "Sit," he commanded.

Hallett's jaw tightened. "I don't take orders from you."

Thorington shrugged. "As you wish. Why are you in the neighborhood again?"

"I heard there was to be a party at Maidenstone today. I thought I might attend."

If someone like Thorington or the men of his acquaintance had said that, it would have sounded like a dire threat. But there was something too indecisive about Hallett's eyes, too weak about his voice. He had already proven that he was the type who would hesitate over firing his guns until all was lost — or fire too soon and miss his chance.

So Thorington went in for the kill. "I shall be brief. You will leave the neighborhood immediately. You will never speak to Miss Briarley again. And if you speak of her to anyone, I shall destroy you."

He'd kept his voice cool, almost pleasant. Next to him, Ferguson silently applauded.

Hallett clenched his hands on the back of the chair he'd refused. "She ruined me. She owes me what she cost me. I want revenge against Jacobs so that the Navy will take me back."

"I doubt it," Thorington said, tapping his fingers on the table. "I think you'd far rather have a soft life on land, if you had the money for it. And anyway, I heard it was your incompetence that cost you your ship. If you'd been as good at sailing as you are at writing letters to the *Gazette*, you might have stopped the Scourge of the Caribbean before he captured anything."

"Did that bitch say it was my fault?" Hallett said.

Thorington started to stand. Salford put a hand on his shoulder. "Manners, Captain Hallett," Salford chided as Thorington sat again. "If we allow Thorington to kill you, as he so wants to do, Ferguson and I will have to support him at the inquest. None of us want that, do we?"

Hallett paled. The implication was obvious — if he was killed, there was a chance that two dukes and an earl could bury the crime before his body was even cold. But he was still too angry about his disgrace to behave rationally. "Did your *fiancée* say it was my fault?" he spat out.

"She knows her business on the sea," Thorington said. "If she told me you were incompetent, I would believe it."

She hadn't told him that — he'd heard it when he'd received news of *Crescendo's* loss, and had it confirmed by his messenger. But there was a part of him that wanted Hallett to attack. The idea of planting his fist in Hallett's face was appealing.

Hallett dropped his hands from the back of the chair, then clenched them again. "I won't have a traitor telling tales about me," he said. "Better for me if everyone hears my side of the story before she says anything."

"Better for you to keep your mouth shut," Thorington said. "My wife will not stoop to speak of you at all."

"But I'm *ruined*," Hallett whined. "I will never have another ship. My brother will inherit my father's estate. I've got nothing."

Ferguson yawned. "This is tiresome. Pay him off, Thorington, so we may go back to our beds."

Thorington didn't have the money to pay Hallett off, and Ferguson knew it.

But Hallett's eyes lit up. He was willing to strike a deal. "Twenty thousand pounds and you'll never hear from me again."

It was an exorbitant sum. In the past, when he could afford to be careless, Thorington would have given it to him without blinking just to rid himself of the annoyance.

Today, though, when he most needed the money to save Callie's future, he couldn't do it.

He rolled his eyes, hoping Hallett didn't sense his hesitation. "I'll see it done for cheaper. Twenty thousand pounds would be better spent bribing your father to look the other way while I kill you."

"And how would your father feel if he knew that his son wanted to marry a pirate? What if your firstborn isn't yours, but belongs to the Scourge…"

He cut himself off when Thorington surged to his feet. Salford didn't stop him this time, but Thorington stayed behind the desk, still marginally in control of his temper. "Ten thousand pounds, and you can be grateful that I haven't rearranged your face," he said. "And if you break our agreement and talk to the press, I will win a libel judgment against you so large that you'll be transported for your debts."

"Ten thousand pounds and Lucretia Briarley," Hallett said, all bravado. "And her share of Maidenstone."

"That's not a deal I can make," Thorington said.

Ferguson examined his cuffs. "I can't abide the thought of being related to you, Hallett. Nor can Lucretia, I would guess, since she told me you were here."

Hallett deflated. "Briarleys," he muttered, disgusted. "Faithless creatures."

Thorington leaned over the desk. "I tire of you, Hallett. Take the promise of ten thousand pounds and leave now. Or you can stay and let me practice my boxing. Your choice."

He knew when the man was defeated. Hallett's eyes flickered over the three of them, looking for any support at all, but Salford and Ferguson wouldn't abandon Thorington's cause. Hallett's shoulders slumped.

"Ten thousand pounds," he said. "I need it immediately."

Thorington's mouth soured. He knew what he would have to do. But he nodded. "Give me your bank's direction and I will transfer the funds."

"I would wish you happy, but I don't mean it and you won't be anyway," Hallett said, his voice small and nasty in his defeat.

Thorington pointed at the door. "The feeling is mutual. Go before I change my mind."

He waited until Hallett was gone, then turned to Salford. "Does your offer of a loan still stand?"

Salford exhaled. "Well done with Hallett. I shall loan you the money for as long as you need it."

"It may take a few years to pay you back," Thorington said slowly. He didn't want to say it aloud because it would make it real, but he was honor-bound to tell the truth about this. "I plan to rebuild my fortunes, but it will take time. It may not even be possible now, with my luck."

"You'll have your ships back when you marry Callie," Ferguson said.

"Those are hers," he said. "And they shall remain hers."

"I was entirely misled about your character," Ferguson complained again.

Salford contemplated him soberly. "Your luck may surprise you."

"I doubt it," Thorington said with a short, bitter laugh.

"Do you have a pair of scales at home?" Salford asked.

"Of course."

"And when you put all the weight in one pan, what happens when you remove it suddenly?"

Thorington pictured the wild swing as the scales rebalanced. "What are you saying?"

"We have no way of knowing, of course," Salford said. "I don't think anyone has been in precisely our situation before. But your current luck may be an overcorrection of your previous luck. When it evens out, I suspect you'll be back to the same luck as everyone else."

It was an interesting theory. Plausible, even. And he hoped Salford was right.

Ultimately, though, it didn't matter. All that mattered was whether he could give Callie the life she deserved.

His doubts suddenly fell away. He knew the answer to that question. It had nothing to do with his fortune, and everything to do with the heart she'd rescued.

He just had to convince her of it.

He opened one of the drawers, digging out ink and paper. Then he scrawled a note, sealed it, and handed it to Salford. "Do me another favor, if you will, and make sure Callie gets this. Ask one of my sisters to deliver it — she's more likely to trust them than either of you."

"Where are you going?" Salford asked.

Thorington smiled. "I'm going to make my own luck."

CHAPTER TWENTY-NINE

Callie stopped on the very edge of the circle around the Maidenstone. She left her horse where it was, knowing there was no point in trying to coax it out of the trees. Thorington wasn't in sight, but she trusted he would find her there.

For the moment, the circle was hers and hers alone. She looked down at her toes. Her boots just barely touched the manicured grass. Had it only been a week since she'd been here for the first time?

It felt like a month. She stepped into the circle.

The grass, the sun, and the stone were the same as before. The Maidenstone clearing was completely at peace — an ancient sort of peace, unconcerned with whatever momentary problems Callie struggled with. The stone had seen any number of Briarleys come there, either for guidance or penance.

No one would carry the Briarley name after her generation. All lines ended, eventually, and the Briarleys had survived longer than they might have. Did the Maidenstone sense that she was one of the last?

She scoffed at her own superstition, but her scoffing was half-hearted. She walked to the stone and traced her hand over the family motto again.

Briarley contra mundum. It felt like those words had been engraved on her heart at birth. Tiberius had whispered them to her often enough.

But maybe she didn't want the motto of her ancestors to control her future.

She wished, almost bitterly, that everything had been different. That she had met Thorington somewhere else — somewhere bright and cheerful, where the weight of history didn't press down upon them. That she hadn't been an heiress, and he hadn't been a duke.

It wouldn't have mattered. No matter where she'd met him, or how, she would have fallen in love with him.

If things had been different, though, perhaps she would have known how to survive the fall.

Something cracked in the undergrowth. She smiled — the same sudden, unbidden smile that his note had drawn from her. The stone was just a stone again. The Briarley motto was a legend, not her fate.

And her heart knew what it wanted.

She turned. Thorington leaned against a tree, watching her.

"Impressive, isn't it?" he said.

They were the same words he'd spoken to her when they'd first met in the clearing. Her smile widened. "You startled me, sirrah."

He unfolded himself from his position. This time, he didn't stay on the edge of the clearing. He walked directly into the sunlight. She enjoyed watching him — took pleasure from the curve of his lips, the angle of his jaw, the perfect control of his stride.

He reached her before she'd looked her fill. Her breath caught in her throat as he kissed her hand. The sunlight turned his green eyes into something almost eerie.

"I have better manners than to converse with a stranger in the woods," she whispered, giving him the line she had used before.

But this time, he deviated from their original path. He smiled tentatively. "You may call me Gavin, if you like."

"Gavin," she said. Her smile widened. "My name is Callie."

"Callie," he repeated. He kissed her knuckles again. "An infinite pleasure to meet you."

Her Briarley heart burst.

"You aren't a fortune-hunter, are you?" she teased. "I've heard Maidenstone Abbey is rotten with them."

He laughed. "No. Although I should be. I must warn you, Callie — I am not as rich as I once was."

"I am richer than I've ever been," she said. "You may find a way to reclaim your lost fortune in these woods."

She meant it — she meant all of it. But his grip tightened and a bit of shadow returned to his eyes. "I am not marrying you to get my ships back from you. You know that, don't you?"

Callie sighed. "Please don't talk about ships. Can you be Gavin for another moment?"

The shadows deepened. He took a breath.

"Callie," he said. "You must know — I don't accept anymore."

There was a roaring in her ears as her smile fell away. "What?"

"I don't accept what you offered. I don't accept a marriage of convenience."

He took another breath, one that cut into her stomach and twisted against her spine.

Then he dropped to his knees.

She stared down at him, uncomprehending. "Do you...do you not want me?" she whispered.

"You know better," he said. "Surely you know." His voice was strong, resolute — there was no hesitation in him, but no shadows either. "I love you, Callie. I don't think I knew what that word meant until I met you. And, selfish bastard that I am, I want more. I want everything. I want all of you. I want to grow old with you — *you*, Callie, not the vessel who bears my children or the woman who feels she must live without me. I want to give you everything you deserve.

I want your soul and mine to be so bound to each other that we'll stay together through any eternity after."

He still held her hand, but his touch turned reverential. "Release me from my vow. Please. I cannot accept what you offered when you — and I — deserve all of this."

His face blurred in front of her before she realized her eyes were filling with tears. She dashed them away with her free hand, but they kept coming. She laughed, suddenly — a fey, wild laugh, as though the devil had caught her in the clearing and proven he was an angel instead.

"I release you," she said.

Gavin smiled. "You don't have to release me for long. Will you do me the incredible honor of marrying me?"

She dashed the tears aside again. "I accept," she said. "Gavin, I accept."

He pulled her down into his arms. She laughed as she fell — laughed again as she realized she would survive the fall, and anything else, as long as he was with her.

He kissed her, slow and sweet. Kissing led to more — scandalously more, but she thought the Maidenstone might enjoy witnessing love instead of bloodshed. He was slow, and patient, and completely ruthless in his attempt to wring every last bit of pleasure from her.

After, when she had recovered her breath, she tilted her head to smile at him. He lay beside her, so close that his face was only inches from hers. Under the sun, nourished by their love, her heart took root in his.

"I love you," she whispered. "More than I ever dreamed."

"I love you," he said. "Beyond any wish I ever had."

There would be days when he was a duke. There would be days when she was a privateer. There would be days when they argued, when the household went sideways, when the children misbehaved and supper was burned and her nerves were frayed and his temper was lost.

But beneath it all, they were Callie and Gavin. And they were better together than they would ever be apart.

*   *   *

The messenger returned with the marriage license just as they reached Maidenstone Abbey. He also returned with something entirely unexpected.

"Your grace," he said. "Your business manager in London sent an urgent message."

Thorington took the license and shoved the other letter back into the messenger's hands. "Leave it in my room. I don't want another tale of woe today."

The messenger shoved it back. He flushed as Thorington raised an eyebrow, but he held his ground. "Your grace. Read it, if you please."

Thorington opened the note. Callie watched as his eyebrows rose again — this time involuntarily. "It can't be," he said.

His servant nodded, too excited to observe propriety. "The news is all over London, your grace."

"What is it?" Callie asked.

"My Asian fleet," Thorington said. "It arrived safely in London with full cargoes."

He sounded dazed. Callie, emboldened, touched his back. "Your luck isn't so bad after all."

He laughed, still sounding disbelieving. "It is bad. But I'll take this as a good sign."

Then he grabbed her and kissed her again.

He repeated that kiss two hours later, when they said their vows in Maidenstone's chapel. She had thought that saying vows would make her feel trapped. But these vows, and the light in Gavin's eyes, made her feel safe — a foundation upon which they could build anything together.

After, they accepted congratulations from the other houseguests. Thorington's siblings were united in their pleasure. "We are delighted, Callie," Portia effused. "*Delighted*."

"Thorington needed someone to bring him to his knees," Serena said cheerfully.

Anthony embraced her, then Thorington, as though they'd captained a winning scull at Eton rather than making wedding vows. "If Thorington needs training in how to whisper sweet nothings to you, send him to me."

Thorington scowled, but Callie laughed. "I shall take my chances with him as he is."

That earned her another quick kiss. "I do not know that I will survive through dinner without forcing you to come away with me," Thorington murmured.

"I promise not to scream if you steal me — until you make me, that is."

"My saucy colonial," he said, trailing his fingers lower over her back, then grazing inappropriately over her derriere.

She suddenly, desperately, wanted him to take her away.

But there were more well-wishers to accept greetings from. Rafe, more circumspect than his siblings, merely kissed her hand and clapped Thorington on the back. He left, abruptly, as Octavia joined them.

"Felicitations again, cousin," Ava said as she kissed Callie's cheeks. "You may not have won Maidenstone Abbey, but Lucretia will be dismayed when she sees you've made a love match."

It wasn't charitable of Ava to say that. And Callie remembered it when Lucretia came to congratulate her after Octavia melted into the crowd.

"I wish you very happy," Lucretia said stiffly, encompassing both Callie and Thorington in her statement. "And I hope you shall forgive me for inviting Captain Hallett to the ball."

Thorington nodded. "I thank you for telling Ferguson of his whereabouts."

Thorington had told Callie of the deal he'd made with Hallett as they were riding back to the abbey. Callie smiled at her cousin. She still felt tentative, but her heart was so open and eager with Thorington's love that she, like an addict, wanted to seek the same goodwill from others. "All is forgiven. I would have lost Maidenstone even if you hadn't brought Hallett here, thanks to Thorington."

Lucy's smile was equally tentative, but it seemed real enough. "Thank you for that. If you must know, I think you made the better bargain."

Callie thought again of princesses and villains as Lucretia walked away. "Which of them do you think will win Maidenstone?"

Thorington shrugged. "Doesn't matter to me. Do you regret that Ferguson won't give it to you? I know how much winning Maidenstone meant to you."

She heard that tentative note in his voice again, the one she thought had died forever in the Maidenstone clearing. She turned to him, meeting his gaze. "I believed I wanted the house. But what I really wanted was a place to call my own."

"I have any number of houses you can call your own," he said. "You might even like my country estate better than Maidenstone. And my house in London will be far more convenient for you to conduct business from."

Callie shrugged. "The houses don't matter, as long as you come with them."

Thorington looked down at her. She was as beautiful as ever, with her hair caught up in an intricate knot and woven through with orange blossoms. But it was the mischievous spark in her eyes that made his heart beat faster.

"When I steal you, I don't intend to let you out of my bed for at least a fortnight," he murmured in her ear.

"Perhaps I shall steal you instead," she mused. "It's possible to smuggle a man anywhere for a price."

God, she was magnificent. He laughed, and the happy thrum in his voice didn't feel so foreign anymore. "Do your worst, my love. I vow it will be the best."

She leaned up and kissed him, soft and full of promise. "I vow it, too. Now, your grace, will you play the blackguard and kidnap me before anyone else interrupts us?"

With an invitation like that, he couldn't resist.

THE END

Books by Sara Ramsey

The Heiress Games

Duke of Thorns

Muses of Mayfair

Heiress Without a Cause
Scotsmen Prefer Blondes
The Marquess Who Loved Me
The Earl Who Played With Fire

Thank you!

Thank you so much for reading Callie and Thorington's story! If you enjoyed it, you'll be happy to hear that there's more to come in the Heiress Games. Octavia's story is up next — she finds unexpected love and redemption with Rafe in *Lord of Deceit*, which will come out in 2015.

If you missed my previous series, Ferguson, Madeleine, Prudence, and Alex were all introduced in earlier books. You can catch up with them in the Muses of Mayfair series:

- It all starts with *Heiress Without a Cause*, in which Madeleine and Ferguson engage in a madcap courtship.
- Amelia and Malcolm steal sheep and hearts in *Scotsmen Prefer Blondes*.
- Ellie and Nick find love instead of revenge in *The Marquess Who Loved Me*.
- Prudence and Alex go from friends to lovers in *The Earl Who Played With Fire*.

You can buy all four books at your favorite bookseller.

To hear about future books, please make sure to sign up for

my newsletter at www.sararamsey.com. I only send emails when I have a new release or major announcement. If you want behind-the-scenes peeks into my writing life (warning: they usually involve Champagne and historical facts), or if you just want to connect, you can also friend me on Twitter (@ sara_ramsey) or Facebook (www.facebook.com/sara.ramsey).

Finally, if you enjoyed this book, please tell a friend — the best compliment you can give is to pass the book along to someone else. If you didn't enjoy it, you can recommend it to an enemy — I won't tell. And if you really want to spread the word, rating the book or writing an honest review is always very much appreciated. Thanks again for your support, and happy reading!

About the author

Sara Ramsey writes fun, feisty Regency historical romances. She won the prestigious 2009 Romance Writers of America® Golden Heart® award with her second book, *Scotsmen Prefer Blondes*. Her first book, *Heiress Without A Cause*, was a 2011 Golden Heart finalist.

Hopelessly uncool as a child, Sara Ramsey has over-compensated by becoming obsessed with fashion, shoes, and #regencyworldproblems. She has great taste in Champagne, bad taste in movies, and a penchant for tiaras. She also believes in taking naps, wearing sunglasses at night, and using Oxford commas. Sara currently lives in San Francisco, California, where she can be found drinking overly-artistic lattes and working on her next Regency historical romance. Read all about her Regency obsessions and upcoming works at www.sararamsey.com.

17570380R00188

Printed in Great Britain
by Amazon